Protecting Kate

Amy J. Hawthorn

Dedication

With great thanks to our National Guard for sacrificing infinitely more than "one weekend a month."

And to everyone who has helped me with this book. Whether it's been encouragement or advice, your gifts mean the world to me.
Maya, Jayne, Lexi, Shayla, Dee, Virginia and as always, Jilly and Inez. I'd be lost without you!

Dark horse – a racehorse, competitor, etc., about whom little is known or who unexpectedly wins.
Source – Dictionary.com

Work. Even now, the word leaves an odd taste in my mouth. But what's a worthless rich boy supposed to do when he's already seen and done all there is to do? Do whatever it takes to help those he cares about stay safe. And if someone wants to call protecting your friends work, well then, so be it.
– Rick Evans

Welcome to the origin of Dark Horse, Inc.

Prologue

Electric and vicious anger mixed with disbelief, fueling Kate's purpose as she stormed over the heated slate floor. The moment she heard the garage door closing, something inside her snapped into place.

At the open, cherry-wood pantry door, she crouched. She forced the tremor from her voice and concentrated on the dark, terrified eyes glimmering in the farthest corner. "Come here, sweetheart. It's okay. He's gone. Come here, baby girl." Keeping her voice low and gentle, she coaxed the small, tangled mess. The little dog ran into the pantry, terrified, after her husband kicked out at it.

She hoped he only scared the poor thing, but she couldn't be certain until she looked the stray over. "Come here, pretty girl." Low whimpers greeted her, but the dog refused to budge.

Kate headed to the marble counter beside the stove to pull off a sliver of roasted chicken from the breast. Blowing on it, she tossed it from hand to hand. She'd spent half the day cooking Preston's favorite meal. He'd promised to make time for dinner at home before yet another business trip. Instead, he'd taken one look at the dog and exploded into his biggest rage to date. On most days, she'd capitulate and do whatever necessary to keep the peace, but today she refused to back down. For some reason, it became more important than ever to take a stand.

She would not "toss the mangy mutt back outside" as he'd ordered. For one, the temperature dropped twenty degrees when the storm rolled in, leaving the animal soaked and shaking. Secondly, the scrawny pup needed so much more than one good meal.

So Preston grabbed his already packed bags and stormed out. If he wouldn't be home to eat dinner yet again, she'd make better use out of it. Right that moment, she couldn't make herself care if he ever ate again.

He'd been remote, bordering on callous over the past few months, and he'd never allowed pets in their home, but she never would have expected him to kick a dog. She thought over the changes in him recently as she stooped down and then crawled on her belly toward the pup. Well, in truth? She'd have to admit he'd been an ass toward her a few times.

Her designer sweater would be ruined by the slate tile. She'd have to hide it from Preston, but she didn't care. Memories of him blowing up at her for the simplest things emerged from the dark corners of her mind. Once, he'd grabbed her arm and shook her because she'd picked the wrong dress to wear to a dinner party. He insisted she should wear a dress in a size too small cut in a deep V past her breasts, which seemed inappropriate for the somber occasion.

She'd worn it and smiled, uncomfortable for three hours to make him happy. Afterward, she'd hidden the bruises on her arm from him for a week out of fear they might bring on another rage.

Even though he'd put them there.

Granted, she didn't think when she'd brought the stray pup inside. At the entrance to their driveway, it'd darted across the road in front of Kate's car. She slammed on her brakes to avoid hitting the poor thing. Her heart melted with one look into its big, sad eyes.

She knew about his allergy to pet dander, but he refused to let her explain. The little Schnauzer shouldn't bother his allergies and, for heaven's sakes, they had an enormous house. She could find room for one small dog. If nothing else, she could house it for the night and take it to the vet in the morning. The vet could look it over and put her in contact with a rescue.

But, just like everything else in her life, he took control, made the decisions, and her opinion didn't matter. She'd given up on voicing it years ago, because she'd wearied of his constant disapproval. More than once, he'd given her the cold shoulder when he'd tired of her "theatrics."

She'd spent the past seven years of her life giving her everything to him, so did bringing home one stray dog count as "theatrics?" *No. It didn't.* The poor thing looked as if it hadn't been groomed in, well…forever. It's not like she'd picked up a neighbor's dog and claimed it as her own. It needed care.

"Are you hungry? I bet you are. Come here and eat, baby. Come here." She laid half of the chicken on the floor partway between herself and the dog. She pulled her hand back and waited. She whispered sweet nonsense and gave it all the time in the world.

Eventually, whether due to Kate's patience or her hunger, the dog stood on trembling legs and limped forward.

Oh no. It'd seemed fine when she'd brought it in the house earlier.

Tears welled as she watched it eat the first piece of chicken. She placed the second piece closer to herself. When the dog came forward, she picked it up and wriggled out of the pantry.

Not caring what Preston would say, she sat the filthy animal on the counter near the sink and looked it over. It still wouldn't put any weight on one paw. Her heart cracked in two as it looked up at her with cautious hope, its eyes darting between her and the chicken.

Afraid it would fall, she set it on the floor and pulled more chicken from the bone with her filthy hands. She didn't have a single care over their ruined dinner as she picked up her phone. Sitting on the floor to feed the pup, she dialed a number she hadn't used in over three years, but still knew by heart.

"Leigh?" She fought to keep the waver from her voice.

"Katie Marie? Kate! How the hell are you?" She smiled when heard her cousin's voice. Leigh sounded as feisty as ever. Some things never changed. Thank God, because right now she needed to draw from the never-ending well of energy of Leigh Ann MacDonald.

"Uh, well." The last dregs of her strength evaporated. She didn't have the faintest idea how to begin her story.

"Stop. What's wrong?"

"I can't do this anymore. I want to come home." Her voice cracked on the last word.

"You're not talking about a vacation, are you?" Concern filled Leigh's tone.

She couldn't help but be grateful. As always, Leigh caught on quickly. It would make things so much easier to explain.

Time to quit deluding herself. There would be nothing easy coming from her decision.

The sick churning in her gut forbade her from staying one more night in the house. Three stories, five-thousand square feet and six gorgeous bedrooms—it screamed wealth, hearth and home. She'd dreamed of filling it with love and the laughter of children.

She'd never again be able to look at it with anything other than revulsion. Every woman had her breaking point, and Preston's cold-hearted act snapped hers in two.

Time to let all the pain and heartache out. Even a farm-raised, tough as nails, Kentucky girl had her limits.

"No, no vacation. I'm moving out and filing for divorce. He won't be home from this business trip for two days, but I want to leave tonight." If she ever saw the house—cold, sterile and filled with bad memories—again, it'd be too soon.

"That bastard. I don't know what he did, but I guarantee it's every bit his damn fault. Should I bring the shovel or the rope?" Leigh's Kentucky twang grew stronger when she got emotional and, right then, she wore it loud and proud.

A single, exhausted, tear-filled laugh escaped Kate. Maybe she'd sobbed? Who knew? He'd ended their marriage with that single kick. The unconditional love and support of her cousin and best friend opened the floodgates.

"He kicked my dog. I mean, it's a stray, but…"

"What kind of man hurts a dog?" In a few simple words, Leigh cut to the heart of the matter. Her father always said a man protected and took care of the weak. Preston? His reputation and career came first. She couldn't remember the last time he'd taken care of her, even in the smallest way.

Her words filled with her newfound determination. "No real man hurts an animal. I'm done being unhappy and walking on tiptoe every day."

Bless her heart, Leigh didn't judge. "I'm sorry, Kate. I've never liked him, but I didn't know things were this bad."

"Damn, I've missed you. How about you bring a pickup? I'm leaving." A wobbly smile broke through her heartbreak like sunshine shattering its way through a long bout of clouds.

"Missed you too, Katie Marie. I'm leaving now. I'll be there in about hour. Dig out your suitcases."

She couldn't wait to get home.

Chapter One

One year later...

"Katie Marie MacDonald, how'd you end up with Pudgy?" Leigh's tone sounded like a mother faced with a guilty toddler hiding a mess.

Kate wiped sweat from her forehead with the back of her arm. Hiding her shame, she kept her head down as she cleaned red barn paint from her hands. After nearly a year of work, she couldn't say she missed the days of manicures and charity lunches. They'd also been filled with stress and lies.

Caught red-handed, she turned to look at the mutt in question rather than facing her cousin's admonishment.

Oblivious to the trouble he'd brought her, the Australian Shepherd mix sat nearby in the afternoon sun and wagged his tail. The poor dog was probably at least nine years old and his long gray and black coat missed patches of fur in places. He was anything but pudgy. It would take time to get some weight back on him, but at least she'd bathed him and gotten rid of his fleas. She wasn't sure she could do much more about the sad condition of his coat. That was going to take a little more TLC.

She laid her rag on the paint can's lid and faced Leigh, who leaned against her car and looked at her as if she'd lost her mind.

Leigh'd been born with a tall, svelte figure and a natural willowy beauty Kate had always envied. Her cousin would have been a natural on the pageant circuit, while Kate had battled every calorie and fought doggedly for every sash and crown.

Kate knew a lecture brewed behind those gorgeous green eyes, waiting for the slightest sign she paid Leigh any attention. It wasn't the first and it wouldn't be the last she'd receive. Then again, what were best friends and family for? She might as well get the confession out of the way.

"Mr. Williams is back in the hospital and said he didn't have anyone to take care of Pudgy." *Damn it.* This was her home. She could do what she liked with it. Why, after nearly a year of independence, did she continue to justify herself and her actions?

Leigh cocked her head to the side. "Mr. Williams is in his eighties, if not older. His lungs are failing and, as badly as I don't want it to happen, there is a fair possibility he may not come home. You're going to be stuck with that dog. You are allowed to tell people no, you do know that, right?"

"Yes, I know that I can tell people no." She just felt guilty when she did.

"Well, do yourself a favor and use the word once in a while. You have always been a people pleaser, and I get that it's because of that big heart of yours, but I think you need to say it once in a while. N. O."

"So what do you think? It's been a while since you've been out here." Kate pointed to the barn she'd been painting.

"Nice subject change. But it looks good. You've really turned this place around. Your dad would be so proud." She watched as Leigh took in the changes. In a little less than a year, she'd made numerous repairs to her childhood home and added a new porch. The thirty acres of gently rolling fields were green with a bright spring blanket and the storage buildings all sported fresh paint. Her favorite was the addition to Dad's old barn. She wasn't sure exactly what she would do with it, but she had no doubt it would get used.

It might not be much, but she was proud to call it hers. She hadn't been able to do all the work herself, but she'd had a hand in each chore and had the calluses and the pride to show for it.

Who would have thought it? Katie Marie MacDonald, former Miss Kentucky, had calloused and paint-stained hands. She couldn't be happier.

"So what's the pampered Mrs. Jubilee Fluffyface up to this week?" In answer to Leigh's question, Kate pulled her phone from her back pocket and showed her this week's picture of the dog she'd rescued nearly a year ago. The beloved Schnauzer had been missing for nearly a month when she'd found her. She'd taken it to the vet the morning after she'd left Preston. The vet checked it over and found that its owners had implanted her with a microchip. They'd been contacted and overjoyed to have their daughter's pet returned. In thanks, they regularly updated her with pictures of the little dog and girl in whatever trouble they got into.

The smiles were a welcome treat in a life otherwise filled with hard work and divorce turmoil.

"What's Joe doing here this time of day?" Her cousin's truck ambled up the driveway, churning up gravel dust. Leigh's brother did enjoy his toys. His latest love was a huge navy blue beast of a truck, though she'd never before seen the old horse trailer he currently pulled behind it. The filthy trailer couldn't be Joe's. He kept meticulous care of his equipment.

"You really have worked your ass off around here. Is the inside of the barn as ready as the outside?" Leigh nibbled her lip like she had when they were kids and she'd been guilty.

"The inside's in great shape. What's up?"

Joe parked and stuck his head out the window. "Is the barn ready?" He looked to Leigh and not Kate. *What have these two gotten me into?* It certainly wouldn't be the first time they'd gotten her into trouble.

Leigh merely nodded at him before she turned back to face Kate. Kate crossed her arms over her chest and tilted her head, waiting for the confession. Joe jumped out of the blue beast and headed for the back of the trailer.

"Remember how I said you needed to tell people no once in a while? Well, please, please remember you can say it. Joe's promised to help me find her a good home if you can't take her."

If the old trailer hadn't been her first clue, Leigh's words would have been. In addition to raising cattle on his small farm, Joe worked as a sheriff's deputy full time and was a single parent. She loved him to pieces, as did half the county's women. Unfortunately, he didn't have time for them in his already packed schedule.

"What did you two bring me? Does Joe need a babysitter for a hundred-year-old heifer?" It went without saying that he would never pass one of his herd off to another to care for, but she was obligated to give them both a hard time. Love and the MacDonald name demanded it. "Just spit it out before you chew your lip off."

"You can say no, remember?" Leigh's sigh expelled enough air to fill a hot air balloon. "But when I saw her, I knew she was meant for you."

Joe made a clicking noise with his mouth and came back around the trailer's end holding a lead. He clicked again and a dappled-gray foal followed him hesitantly.

Kate's heart swelled and her stomach sank all at once. Fierce protectiveness and anger tangled with instant love.

"Who does she belong to? She's too thin. The owner should be whipped." Drawn to the little foal like a moth to a flame, she slowly approached and held out her hand for it to smell. She stroked her hand down its neck and murmured sweet nothings. "She's filthy. Poor baby."

"She belongs to you, if you want her. Her mother gave everything she had, but she didn't make it. They were both neglected and badly malnourished. She needs a new momma. The county doesn't have the space for a horse at the shelter, no matter how small she is." Leigh looked down and dug the toe of her sneaker into the grass. "I told Debbie at the courthouse you were thinking of starting a rescue, so if you want to fill out the paperwork, you can adopt her. If not, I'll take her back and explain."

"I'm starting a rescue, huh? Funny, this is the first time I've heard about it. You knew that if I saw her I couldn't refuse." She crouched and it butted her with its head and nuzzled close. She melted.

"Guilty as charged. I also know that you're busy and have more than enough work on your hands already, but I knew she was meant for you. Doc Jones looked her over and said, other than being underweight, she's actually a healthy little girl. Her momma really did give her everything she had. I only wish we'd found them sooner."

Joe handed Kate the lead and adjusted his faded baseball hat. She leaned into his tall frame for their customary hug.

"I think everyone knew there was trouble out at the Caudill's, but no one knew that they had horses living behind their place. Tom has been nothing but trouble since we were in school, but he'll be in prison for a long time now. They finally caught him dealing meth, then they found a lab in his house. If he had given his animals half of the attention he'd given his drugs, they'd be in great health." Joe paused to scratch his chin thoughtfully. "He was already behind bars when we went out to his place with the search warrant. The lab was expected, but the dead mare and this foal weren't. We also took a few dogs to the county shelter. They were living in some of the worst conditions

I've ever seen, Kate. I hope to see them add animal cruelty to the charges they bring against him."

Leigh walked over to give the little girl a pet. "Doc Jones sent milk replacement pellets to get you through the first few days, and she's been nibbling on grain. Doc said to call him anytime with questions, and he'll help you. Oh. I also sweet-talked Joe into babysitting for you so you can go to the Governor's shmancy shindig next week without any worries." Leigh turned her bright smile on her brother as if she were getting away with something.

"You mean you conned me into babysitting." He gave Leigh a look that could only come from loving and irritated brother. "She'll be fine out at my place for the day. Kylie will be overjoyed to see her."

"How is my favorite little tomboy doing? I miss her." Joe's little girl was hell on wheels. She adored her young cousin, mud, frogs, action figures and all.

"In trouble, as always." Joe shook his head. "I have to figure out some sort of birthday party soon. You should come up and visit."

"I'll help with the party if you want. She and I can decorate together, and we can have a barbeque. She won't want fancy or frilly. Just let me know, and tell her I said that I miss her." Kate leaned into Joe for their customary hug.

"Will do. After I unload this little lady's supplies I gotta get back before Kylie runs the sitter off." He pinched her nose.

"Leigh, thank you. She's a bonnie little thing. I already love her." Bright emotion swelled beneath her heart.

"You've put a ton of work into this place, but the barn and stable has been your focus. I knew all along you'd eventually get yourself a horse. When I saw her I thought 'there's Kate's baby.'" Leigh met her gaze.

"How did you end up out at the Caudill's dump?"

"Someone said the there was a child living out there, so Joe called me to help. We saw evidence of at least one child living there recently, but no luck in finding them." Leigh rubbed a hand over the center of her chest, and her eyes went misty. For all her bossiness, deep down beat a marshmallow heart.

"Have you heard from Preston? He's leaving you alone now, right?" Leigh's concern touched her.

Kate couldn't hide her pride, and she grinned before she answered. "I haven't heard from him in over a month. I think he finally figured out that he has to accept that the divorce is real. I have to admit, it feels good to be single, knowing I can do whatever I wish."

"I'm so happy that part of your life is behind you. Are you ready for the charity auction? We can use it to celebrate the one year anniversary of your independence. Have you picked a dress yet? I wish I could go with you, but I truly can't." Regret laced Leigh's voice.

"If I could find a way to bow out gracefully myself, I would. If it weren't for Stephen's invitation, I wouldn't go." Kate patted Bonnie and stood.

"It's not every day that a girl gets invited to the Governor's for a barbeque." Her cousin placed her hands on her hips and narrowed her eyes.

"I knew him well before he was elected. Besides, he's not the Governor anymore." Kate made air quotes around the word governor. "He's Stephen Mitchell, former Governor, who I met at a charity marathon ten years ago, and I'd rather stay home." Kate clicked at the foal.

"You really are burnt out on glitz and glamour, aren't you?" Leigh opened the barn door wider.

"It's not the glamour so much, but all the two-faced bullshit that goes with it. Seriously, though? I think I'm finished with that part of my life and I don't miss it one bit. I just want to be me." Kate had everything she needed in life. She had her home and family. What else could there be?

Trent watched a two-year-old filly flutter her long lashes at Rick and sidle closer to the rail. *Typical.* Not many women were able to resist the playboy and that was fine by Trent, he didn't need the drama. "Did the white sands of Waikiki and hanging out with Oprah finally lose its luster? How long are you in town for?"

"I was on Maui, in Wailea, idiot. There's a difference, and no, I didn't see Oprah once. It's the wrong time of year. No, someone asked for a favor and I'm trying to decide how best to handle it." Rick scratched his head as he looked at the little bay filly.

"What kind of favor?" Trent's gaze wandered further astray, taking in the sun as it set behind acres and acres of lush green Kentucky bluegrass portioned off by pristine white fencing. Although he'd been home from the desert hell of Afghanistan for six years, the beauty of being back home still took his breath away. He'd promised himself to never again take the sight for granted.

The pretty little bay inched even closer to Rick and nodded her head, shamelessly flirting with and baffling him. He was one of the best men Trent knew, but had no clue what to do around horses. Considering the man had saved his life, he'd forgiven him the sin and more.

Rick took a step further from the fence before answering. "A distant cousin wants me to do some investigating for him. The person in question has some pretty significant political pull. Everyone else has turned a deaf ear his way, and he's out of options."

"Are you going to help?" Trent asked more out of habit than curiosity. He already knew the answer, whether or not Rick realized it yet. It might take him some time to take that final step and say yes, but

Rick would help. His unshakable core of honor wouldn't allow anything else.

"It's a sticky situation, but I'm thinking about it. He doesn't have anyone else to turn to." And that was something that both he and Rick had adjusted to when they were children. They'd come from opposite ends of the spectrum—one obscenely rich and one dirt poor. They found common ground because they were both ignored and left to raise themselves, alone far too young. "If I do, and if I run into any trouble, are you willing to lend a hand? I'll pay you generously."

He could, too, since Rick had money to burn.

Trent stifled the urge to punch his friend and settled for flipping him off. "I don't want your money. If you need help, you ask for it. Would you expect me to pay you for a favor?" Although he knew Rick had been raised in a world where everything had a price, it didn't make taking his money easier for a man who'd been raised on a horse farm in Kentucky. In Trent's world, helping a neighbor was as natural as breathing.

"Of course not. But this is different."

"How? You're helping someone who needs it, right? I don't get it."

"It's like…a job." He said the word as if it were in a foreign tongue. For Rick, maybe it was. He'd been given every luxury known to man, but it hadn't stopped him from signing up for the National Guard in a fit of rebellion at the age of nineteen—otherwise, they might not have ever met.

But Rick's act of defiance nearly cost him his life in the hellish desert.

Nearly ten years later, they both wore the scars from that time, inside and out.

"Are you going to charge him?" Trent adjusted his hat and ran a hand over his filly's muzzle, only to be ignored again.

"No, I don't need to, and he's family of a sort. But you'd be working for me, if I take it." Rick put both hands on his hips and squinted at the horse.

"If you take the job and need help, all you have to do is say so, deal? If paying me makes you feel better, do it, but I don't want or need your money." He'd put every penny he didn't need to ensure Walker Stables was a huge, profitable outfit into savings over the years. Once he'd given Rick control of his investments, they'd multiplied like rabbits in the dark. He didn't need the money either.

"Deal. Why does she keep doing that thing with her eyes? Do horses get lashes in their eyes?" Trent couldn't help but laugh at the confusion on his friend's face. When both his friend and his horse looked irritated at his amusement, it only made him laugh harder.

Chapter Two

She handed the keys to Leigh's new car over to the valet. According to Leigh, showing up at "the Governor's shmancy deal in a rusted out pickup could be the social faux pas of the century." So, because her cousin threw a fit and insisted they trade vehicles for the weekend, she'd dressed in her finest to have a good time—per Leigh's orders.

Kate really couldn't care less, but she'd learned over the years that, with Leigh, it was best to pick her battles wisely. She also understood her cousin's new four-door might be a simple American made sedan, but—as a gift her cousin had bought for herself after paying off all her student loan debt—it represented a source of pride for Leigh.

A doorman welcomed her inside the stunning mansion meets-gentlemen's-farmhouse with a sweep of his arm. "Welcome, Miss. Go on through. Everyone is gathered out back or in the ballroom."

Yep, Stephen's "farmhouse" had its own ballroom, but Leigh didn't need to know that.

No stranger to this home, Kate headed straight through to the back deck where she knew the man of the hour would be holding court. She found Stephen and his two sons manning a charcoal grill large enough to feed a football team.

Colby, the youngest, spotted her and waved her over.

"Kate! So glad you could make it. Would you like a drink?" Probably ten years younger than her, in his early twenties, he grinned sheepishly and blushed. She couldn't help but wonder what that was about. They'd known each other for years.

"No, I'm fine. How are you guys?"

"Great." Colby's brown eyes and thick brows were an identical match to his father's, but when he barely met her gaze, he confirmed that something was up. "Are you sure you don't want a drink? I'll go get you something from the bar. I'll be right back."

"Colby, stop before you scare her off." Stephen closed the lid on his section of the grill and turned to her. "Hey there, Kate." Her old friend leaned in and brushed her cheek with his. With kind blue eyes, silver hair and bright smile, he was the perfect gentleman, but she smelled a trap.

"Stephen." What else could she say?

"You need a drink. I'll be right back," Colby insisted moments before he slunk off.

Stephen rolled his eyes at his youngest son and spoke over his shoulder to his oldest who stood guard over a herd of steaks. "I'll be back in a few minutes. The chicken's almost ready."

"Kate, I need a favor. I hate to drop this on you the moment you arrive, but thanks to my son with the social graces of a doorknob, I'll have to hit you with it now."

"What's going on?" The sinking feeling only fell deeper into her belly as he cupped her elbow and pulled her into the kitchen.

"Our plans fell through for the original auction. Susie called, said she's sick and can't make it. When Senator Bailey mentioned the auction and made a fuss about needing a Miss Kentucky to Colby, he panicked and blurted out that you were going to be here, so Bailey assumed you were filling in for Susie. If you're willing, we need to auction you off tonight, dear."

Damn. Damn, damn, damn.

She hadn't wanted to come at all, and now she'd been pulled back in to the spotlight.

Shit.

"What's the charity this year?" She'd learned her lesson the hard way. Never again would she associate herself with anyone or anything blindly.

"It's Carol's year to pick, so she chose the local animal shelter. They're behind on their vet bills and in desperate need of an expansion." She could see the torment in her friend's eyes. He knew he'd put her in a tough spot, but he'd hooked her with her love of all things furry.

"Okay. Is anyone else standing on the block?" She hated the idea of being up there alone.

"If you can believe it, she's even willing to auction off an evening with Daniel." His lop-sided smile matched hers at the idea of his son being auctioned. Even though their oldest was well into his twenties, his wife, Carol, continued to dote on both her boys.

"Okay. I'll play, but I didn't dress for the part."

The corners of Stephen's mouth wrinkled with genuine warmth as he made a show of looking her up and down. He beamed at her. "Sweetheart, you are stunning exactly the way you are. I can't tell you how much Carol and I appreciate this. She'll be overjoyed." She would, Kate knew. Carol's heart was divided by her love for only two things—her family and animals.

"What time is the auction?" Already she felt like a thoroughbred on the auction block, nerves fraying one at a time.

"Eight this evening. You know how Carol likes to make sure everyone has time to eat, get seconds and have dessert. She's forever feeding anyone who comes through the door, no matter that no one in this crowd has ever missed a meal in their lives. I almost forgot—I have a surprise for you." Her wariness must have shown, since he added, "This one is a good surprise, I promise."

"Okay, hit me with it." Her evening couldn't get much worse.

"There's been a new addition to the family." He beamed with pride. "We purchased a yearling from Walker Stables. They brought her in this morning, and I know you'll love her. She's a gorgeous little girl. A couple of weeks ago, we took one look at her and fell in love. You'll have to make time to see her before you leave." Her mood lightened at the sight of his bright smile. He might as well be a proud new parent or grandparent, based on the way this chest filled with pride.

"I'd love to." The smile she wore now came easy.

"Hey, there's my beautiful wife." Stephen's smile brightened further when the petite blond came directly to his side and kissed his cheek.

"You smell like a charcoal grill." She wrapped her arm around his waist, seemingly not offended by the smell as she grinned up at her husband. "Are the meat and corn on schedule?"

"Yes, my dear. I wouldn't dare mess with the timing of your dinner party." He didn't look in the least offended by her asking.

Stephen and Carol had been married for thirty years, yet each time she walked in the room, his face lit up. Kate couldn't help but be a little envious of that kind of love.

At least until he added, "Kate, an angel as always, has saved the day. She's going to take Susie's place at the auction."

Kate tried to smile as she wiped her sweaty palms down her skirt.

Carol's enthusiasm wasn't daunted in the least by the no doubt uncomfortable expression on Kate's face. "Oh, Kate, thank you! I can't tell you how much I appreciate this. The yard is buzzing with politicians. With it being election year, they're likely eager to throw their money at any charity that might get them noticed. I plan to take full advantage of their drive."

"I'm afraid I didn't dress the part of a former Miss Kentucky, tonight, Carol. If I had known, I would have but...I'm sorry." Kate almost skipped wearing the heels that went with her simple sundress, but she knew showing up at the Mitchell's, even for a barbeque, in less than a dress and heels was not done.

"Don't you dare apologize. You're saving the day, and you look beautiful. We're close to the same size, so one of my formals will fit you just fine. Come on. Let's get you dressed up and then we'll get the introductions over with." Just like that, Carol took charge in her loving, albeit, steamrolling way.

Ten minutes later, Kate stood—stripped down to her bra and panties—as she waited for Carol to decide which dress would work best. Used to years of pageant prep, Kate should be right at home. How many times had she changed backstage in a hurry or waited for what felt like hours? *Too many to count.*

But now, in a friend's private bedroom, being fussed over as if she were royalty, she wished the floor would open up and swallow her whole. She'd already reminded herself six times that Carol's heart was as big as the ocean, and she meant well. If she had the slightest hint that Kate wasn't happy, she'd immediately stop Operation Dress Up and call a halt to the auction altogether.

While the last thing Kate wanted was stand and smile and wave at the crowd—which would end with her suffering through a date likely fraught with groping and sleazy advances—she wanted the animal shelter to get its donation more. With that in mind, Kate plastered on her brightest smile when Carol held up a lovely ivory colored sheath.

"What do you think of this one? I think it will flatter that gorgeous tan of yours and you can wear your own shoes. Try it on."

Kate accepted the offered gown and stepped into it. In moments, Carol zipped her into the satin and sparkles.

"Look at that. It's perfect. I mean, you're a little bigger up top than me, so you actually have a little cleavage. Your hips are a little narrower, but the gathers at the side take care of that. What do you think? I think it's stunning. Here, let's freshen up your makeup, and you'll knock their socks off. I dare say, we may raise more money with you taking Susie's place. She's pretty, but she's too young and a bit of an airhead, if you ask me. With your combination of beauty and class, you'll have these men throwing money at you. You look like a supermodel meets first lady. Why, I dare say Jacqueline Kennedy might have been envious."

The decision as to whether or not she would actually wear the dress had been taken out of her hands. As if she'd slipped back in time—when she'd sat or stood like a doll and done what she was told—she allowed Carol to take over. In no time, she'd been polished and fluffed to Carol's idea of perfection.

They headed down to the ballroom arm in arm. Carol beamed as she took Kate around the room, making introductions along the way. Kate smiled her best smile and played the social game, feeling more like an actor filling a role she'd outgrown than the woman she'd worked to become in the past year.

Then she heard it. "Dove?"

How could one word spoken by one particular voice instantly fill her with a sense of dread so concentrated that she shook with it? As always, a little too loud and a little too cheerful, the sound rang false. How had she lived so many years with him and not noticed how …empty his voice had been?

"I didn't know you'd be here. You look stunning as always. Farm life must be treating you well." Preston likely meant his last few words as an insult, his tone revealing clearly that farm life wasn't fit living for anyone other than the poor by his estimation.

He was the last person she'd expected or hoped to see. Though he fit right in with the crowd in his designer slacks, pale blue button up and classic blueblood looks, to her he stood out like a beacon. Just the sight of him made alarms go off in her mind.

The group of men he stood with were ones she hadn't yet been introduced to. She wished she could go back to her oblivious little bubble and forget he was there altogether.

She forced herself to smile brighter, a mask to hide her distress from the room. "It is. I haven't been this happy in a long time. If you'll excuse me?" The chatter in the room around them dimmed to near silence as everyone scented potential drama in the air.

Stephen appeared and grasped her hand gently. "Kate, if you'll come with me? We have a few things to finalize before the auction, if you'll excuse us."

"Of course." She allowed her old friend to pull her into the kitchen once more. The moment the door closed behind them, he nudged her into a barstool at the long sparkling counter.

"I'm sorry. I don't know why he's here. I—" Her words tumbled out at a rapid, jumbled pace.

"Stop right now. You do not apologize for anything to do with that man. I'll find out how he got in and make sure it never happens again. I suspect he rode in on the coattails of Phillip Bailey. They've been seen together a lot lately. Why he'd do it, I don't have a clue. You'd think that with Bailey up for reelection, he'd want to keep better company. I'm the one who should be apologizing to you. I'll make him leave."

"No. Don't make a fuss. I just need a few minutes to myself. He caught me off guard. After a few minutes of quiet, I'll be good as new."

"You're sure?" His kind eyes held a wealth of doubt.

"Absolutely. Which stable is the new girl in?" Changing the topic and her surroundings would no doubt do a world of good for her swirling and panicked thoughts.

"She's in the smaller barn, in the last stall. We've got her next to Charley."

"That makes sense. Charley's almost as big of a softie as you. Tell Carol I'm fine, and that I promise not to get her dress dirty."

To bypass the party crowd spilling off the back patio, she exited through the mudroom that led off the house's side. She found a pair of Carol's old boots near the door and swapped them out for her heels. They were a little big, but it would be far safer than walking through the fields and stables in heels or barefoot. Both options spelled disaster and, the way things were going, she didn't need to tempt fate.

The moment she stepped foot onto green grass, she breathed easier. The more distance between her and the house, the lighter she felt. She took a deep breath and focused on the gently rolling meadows lined with white fencing. The sun sat low and heavy in the evening sky, as if the long day had sapped its energy and it couldn't hold up its head any longer.

She walked to the nearest stable and into open double doors. The soft rustle of animals in their stalls greeted her. Just as Stephen promised, she fell in love with the horse on the spot.

She huddled in the back corner of her stall, but she turned her head as Kate approached.

"Hey there, gorgeous. Aren't you a pretty little thing?" She was. The chocolate brown little filly walked up, eager for affection, and eased her head over the gate. Kate offered her hand for the little girl to sniff.

Fathomless brown eyes looked back at her. With a little nod of her head, she seemed to give Kate permission to touch. *Who could resist such a sweet offer?* She reached out and ran a hand over the soft hair.

"There's my dove. I knew she'd be out here with the animals. Boots with evening wear? I don't know why I'm surprised." With her heart pounding, Kate snatched her hand back in shock. She recognized his snide tone as well as she knew her own face.

Startled, the sweet little filly backed away, returning to her corner. Kate couldn't say she blamed the animal, as she wished she could do the same thing.

Without a single hope that he'd actually listen, she turned to face Preston and found him posed in the open door with Senator Phillip Bailey. A jagged fingernail of dread scraped from her nape all the way down her spine. She'd never stood up to him before, but she could now.

She could have fought him before, too, but hated confrontations. Standing up to him was more for herself than it was to tell Preston off. When faced with old habits, she needed the reminder that she answered to no one. That was why she'd made the leap and filed for divorce. She hadn't once regretted her decision. She wouldn't start now. One of the horses behind her shook its head and the ripple of ears and mane helped ground her. She lived in her own world now, not Preston's.

"I couldn't wear heels in the grass, now could I? We don't have anything to say to each other, Preston. Please go away. Contact my attorney if you think differently." Her instincts told her to make a hasty retreat, to go back to the house, but the two men blocked the doorway.

Intentional or not, they'd trapped her.

Preston sneered as he came nearer, practically tiptoeing across the ground, minding each step. Though it'd been a couple years since they'd last met, she recognized Senator Bailey as he captured her with his piercing gaze. Somehow he looked both the same and different. He'd covered his gray hair with a milk chocolate brown shade. And…he'd had a facelift or some other type of surgery? She'd bet her farm that he had. Plastic, almost stiff features replaced his former classically handsome face. She imagined his skin would feel like rubber.

Creepy.

Preston closed in. Her confidence faltered with the shrinking distance. The scent of his signature cologne reached her, the all-too-familiar smell carrying bad memories.

Trent had left Molly for a few minutes to check on the Mitchell's stallion, housed in a separate stable. It had been over a year since he'd seen the cocky beast. He knew Caesar couldn't be in better hands than the Mitchell's, but he couldn't resist a quick visit. He'd been there the day the big chestnut entered the world then delivered him to their farm three years ago.

The conceited horse preened and greeted him as if they were old friends and, in a way, he guessed they were. He'd stayed longer than he'd planned, which meant Stephen and Carol especially would expect him to stop by and at least grab a plate of food before he left. He'd rather dodge the party altogether, but when Carol gave a man the look that said "eat, or else," a man ate.

At least a smart one did.

He'd been up since four a.m. and gone nonstop since. He wanted nothing more than a shower and his bed, but neither would do him any good until he checked on Molly one last time. When he approached the barn's corner and heard the low sound of unfamiliar voices, he stopped. These weren't his stables, but the hushed tones were all wrong nonetheless.

"Trust me, she'll be out here with the animals. She never could get of enough of them. Telling her I had an allergy was the only way I kept her from filling the house with mutts and alley cats. If you pursue her, you may want to develop the same allergy."

"I don't have time for a wild goose chase. What makes you think she'll cooperate if you haven't spoken to each other in months?"

"She's a doormat and a do-gooder down to her very core. She won't be happy about seeing me, but even if the sight of me makes her sick, she won't want to be rude to you. Politeness is in her DNA."

"I need her… cooperation. I looked over your photos. I need her. No one else will do." There was an odd, flat tone to the man's words that made Trent's senses go on alert.

"You'll have it. Remember, she's a doormat and charity is the way to her heart." Their voices dimmed and Trent guessed they'd probably entered the stable.

Assholes, the both of them. But who did they expect to find in the stable? As far as he knew, there weren't any female stable hands in the Mitchell's employ. No matter, he'd had enough. They could take their shit somewhere else.

He'd get rid of the trouble, say goodbye to Molly, then the Mitchells, grab a bite to eat and head home to end his long day. *That's it.*

He rounded the corner and stopped in the barn's open doors. Several things hit him at once.

A stunning brunette with hair halfway to her ass stood near Molly's stall in a dress that displayed a body capable of making grown men cry. The boots, though a smart choice for the barn, were the last thing he'd ever expect to see on such a beautiful woman. Her classical good looks spelled trophy wife.

The slightly taller man in a blue button-up and city shoes had moved into her personal space and, though he seemed to know her well, the look on her face made it clear she was anything but happy to see him.

The second, slightly older man stood back a bit and watched with interest. He'd honed in on the brunette, fixated to a point that left Trent doubting a bomb blast could break his focus. Like the first man, he wore expensive shoes that shouted boardroom or…*shit—politician.*

Maybe he couldn't toss the two pricks out with the trash, but he could put an end to their harassment.

"Preston, I divorced you, remember? Please leave me alone." Her voice reminded him of honeyed bourbon. The warm, smooth tones whispered through him, making every cell take notice and reach for more.

"Kate, this will only take a minute of your time. We have a proposition for you…" The first man stepped even closer before he reached out to grasp her arm. She shrank back, pressed against the stall door. When Trent saw the golden tan of her arm turn white beneath the man's brutal grip, he saw red.

She winced and tried to yank her arm free, but the man held fast. "I just need you to listen to me. Damn you, always so stubborn," the man said through gritted teeth, as if ready to lose his temper.

Trent had heard and seen enough.

"Kate? There you are. I'm sorry I was late." He slid in beside her and asshole number one immediately released her arm and stepped back. *Figured.* Trent couldn't think of much worse than a coward who'd lay a hand on a woman, but didn't have the balls to stand up to another man.

"Can I help you? I promised to introduce my…Kate… to pretty little Molly, here." Trent's smile filled with pure menace and let the men wonder about his relationship with the brunette. He turned his back to the men, dismissing them.

He glanced at her face to verify that she understood and would cooperate. Light brown eyes met his full of equal parts shock, wariness and relief. He could work with that. Once the tension in her heart-shaped face eased, her beauty jabbed him in the gut. Something deep and primal took root, an unbreakable leash holding him fast to his course.

Heaven help the man who tried to sway him.

"Where'd you find the boots? I didn't even think about your shoes when I made my offer." He clicked at Molly, and she cautiously came to stand in the middle of the stall. Another strike against the two idiots. They'd made one of his horses nervous. Molly might belong to the Mitchells, but she'd always be one of his animals.

"They're Carol's barn boots. I didn't think she'd mind." Her voice knocked him in his chest and slid down low beneath his belt.

"Smart girl. A man's gotta love a lady who knows her way around a farm." He clicked again and murmured to his girl. He loosely caged his arms around the two legged female and did his best to focus on the four legged one. "Come see Kate. You'll like her. Ignore those two suits. They're leaving." Molly came forward and allowed Kate to rub a gentle caress over her nose.

He turned his head back to the men and didn't bother to hide the fury from his expression. He hoped they understood they weren't welcome and, if not for the females, he wouldn't let them off with a verbal warning. "Gentlemen, we'll see you later, correct?"

"Kate, we really need to speak with you about a business matter." The instant her ex-husband spoke, he felt tension roll off her.

"Not now and not today you don't. She's mine for the evening. We have a date with Molly." He eased in as close as he could get without touching her expensive dress. He reached a hand out to Molly and breathed in the sweet, seductive scent of the woman before him.

Silence filled the barn for what felt like an eternity and then he heard the rustle of footsteps leaving. "They're gone now. Do you want me to back off or wait a moment in case they come back?"

The heavy silence was broken only by the sound of Kate's heavy breaths and the swish of Molly's tail. "Wait a moment, please." Not much more than a silken whisper, her words brushed over him. She'd been so quiet that he'd almost missed the waver of anxiety. They'd really rattled her.

He clenched his fists on top of the stall door. He breathed in her scent and pushed his anger down. "My pleasure." And it was. So what if the polished princess before him was the polar opposite of what he wanted in a woman? She was no hardship to look at and that voice of hers went straight to his cock. He needed to keep her talking as he fought the urge to look down her cleavage.

"How do you know Steve and Carol?" The deep voice brushed by her ear in a warm caress.

Okay, she could do this. She could make small talk with the best of them, so one farm hand shouldn't be a problem. "I met Stephen years ago at a charity function. We've been friends since then. You?"

"They're old family friends. I've known them for ages."

She concentrated on the big round eyes looking up at her with trust and resisted the need to turn and face the man behind her. She'd been too rattled by Preston's appearance for anything other than a fleeting impression to register.

One moment she'd been trapped alone and the next a tall, dark knight in faded jeans came through the doors. She hadn't known whether to feel relief or fear, but it had taken about two seconds to realize that he was no friend of Preston or the Senator.

When he'd walked over and mentioned their date, she wanted to swoon with relief. But swooning? That wasn't her.

"I think they're gone for good." His warmth left her and she turned to face him. "Wait, watch the dress." His long arm reached around to prevent her from leaning back against the stall door and his rough palm met the bared skin of her back. Shivers of pleasure cascaded through her.

"Oh no. I forgot I'm wearing Carol's dress. I've gotten used to my old tees and jeans."

Dark blond hair that fell in waves almost reached his shoulders. Jeans so faded and worn they looked thin in places covered long, muscled legs that ended in old, battered boots. A faded black T-shirt stretched across broad shoulders and storm-gray eyes looked down at her.

"What made you leave the party in a dress like that and come out to the stables?" His other hand dropped and brushed over her hair, stopping just below the first, at the small of her back. With light pressure he pushed her toward him until not much more than a breath of space separated them. The air they shared simmered, ripe with sultry intensity. His stony gray gaze held her immobile.

He stepped back, pulling her with him and away from the stall without breaking their stare. She forgot how to breathe. Luckily for her, there was no need for air in the heavy daze they'd created.

Molly rustled against the door behind her and broke the spell. She silently thanked the little filly. She dragged in a deep breath and fought for lucidity.

What did she say? She didn't want to burden him with her drama when he seemed like a decent enough guy. He reminded of her of men like her father or her cousin, Joe, steady men who worked for everything they had and took care of it because it meant something to them.

"The crowd and noise gave me a headache, and Stephen knows how much I like horses so he told me about Molly. I just wanted a few minutes of quiet."

"Are you used to being around horses then?"

"Yes. We had horses when I was little and I spent as much time as I could with them and my dad. Right now, I have an orphaned foal that's stolen my heart."

"Orphans can be tricky. Do you have help?"

"I do. The local vet has agreed to help. We'll get by all right."

"Would you like me to walk you back to the party? I was headed that way for a bite to eat. Carol will have a fit if I leave without at least taking a plate with me." A rueful smile stretched his face and softened the masculine angles.

"What time is it? Yes, I really need to get back." She couldn't be late. She'd already caused enough trouble.

He pulled a cell phone from his back pocket and checked. "It's five 'til eight."

"Shoot, I really need to hurry, I'm sorry." She'd be late to the auction.

"There's no need to apologize." Great, she'd met a seemingly nice man who didn't have money or social status on the brain and now he looked at her as if she'd grown a second head. "I'll get you there, Cinderella. My truck is right outside the barn. How about I drive you up?"

"Yes, please. I need to be there by eight. I shouldn't have come down here, but I just wanted a few minutes of peace and…it was stupid of me."

"Stop. There's nothing wrong with seeking a few minutes of quiet with the horses. If you know Stephen and Carol any at all, you'll know they don't give two shits about you spending an extra few minutes at the barn."

"I suppose you're right." She didn't know why, but she couldn't bring herself to tell him why she had to be back at eight. There was no harm in what she was doing, but she hated to think that his opinion of her would change. She knew it was ridiculous, but she couldn't shake the feeling.

He walked her to an enormous charcoal dually with a small horse trailer attached to the back. He opened the door wide, grabbed her low on her waist and plucked her up as if she weighed no more than a bale of hay.

Dizzied, she held on to his shoulders. She told herself the odd feeling had everything to do with not having been carried since she'd been a small girl and nothing to do with the feel of cut muscle beneath her hands.

He set her in, shut the door and, as good as his word, he had her up to the main house in no time at all. The clock's glow on the dash read two minutes after eight.

Shit.

The truck barely came to a stop before she opened the door and hopped out. She shouted a rushed thank you over her shoulder and ran for the mudroom. She changed shoes, hurried to the bathroom where she'd left her purse, brushed her hair, swiped on a fresh layer of lip gloss and all but sprinted to the back patio where everyone had gathered.

She stopped at the closed doors, took a deep breath and plastered on her best pageant smile. She'd rather muck stalls than stand up on the auction block, but she'd be damned if she'd hurt Carol's feelings or leave her friend in a lurch.

She opened the doors and braced herself.

"There she is. Come on up here, Kate." Stephen motioned for her to join him and Daniel up on the small stage they'd erected on the enormous patio. "Perfect timing. Carol just auctioned off a date with Daniel to Mrs. Bentley for five thousand dollars."

Good. Mrs. Bentley was in her seventies and a delightful woman who loved animals nearly as much as Carol. It would be a win-win for her friend. Her son would most likely spend the evening shouting into the older woman's ear and having his cheeks pinched. A nice, uneventful date combined with the generous donation would make everyone happy.

"Sorry, I'm late. I got swept away by that sweet little horse of yours. I couldn't tear myself away from those big brown eyes."

"No worries, dear. You're right on time. Next up for bidding is an evening with the lovely Kate MacDonald. I'll trust the winner to be a perfect gentleman. Kate is like a daughter to me, and I won't hesitate to break out some old-fashioned whoop-ass on her behalf." Stephen winked, turned on his bright trademark smile and worked the crowd like he'd been born to it. She'd always loved that it was a genuine charisma and not plastic acting.

"Since she's no less dear to our hearts than our own boys are, we'll start the bidding at five hundred dollars."

"Five hundred!" Shouted Mrs. Bentley and the crowd laughed when Daniel made a show of complaining.

"Aw. Mrs. B! Are you two-timing me?" Everyone laughed when Mrs. Bentley made a show of blowing him a kiss from the crowd.

"Six hundred!" Carol put in her bid so Kate turned, smiled and curtsied to her friend.

"Eight hundred!" A smiling, bald man in the back of the crowd put in his bid.

"One thousand dollars." The oily smooth voice of Phillip Bailey placed a bid that made her blood chill. She didn't know the man. She'd never heard a single bad word associated with his name but the knowledge that he was associated with Preston made her nauseous.

"Fifteen hundred." She recognized Harlan Walker, an old friend of the Mitchell's, and his deep, booming voice. She turned her head to see his lovely and feisty wife, slap him on the shoulder in pretended indignation.

"One thousand eight hundred!" Kate laughed when the slender Sandy Walker outbid her husband.

"Two thousand." The senator bid again and she made a mistake that would keep her awake for the rest of the night. Every time she closed her eyes she'd see the cold, calculating gaze focused on her as she'd attempted to make a quick survey of the crowd. She'd failed. When his dark stare trapped hers, the voices in the crowd faded. He'd caught her in a sinister web and though she wanted nothing more than to break free and rejoin the world around her, she couldn't.

Daniel, standing at her side, took her hand and squeezed it. He leaned in close to her ear and spoke. "You are kicking auction ass!"

She shook her head and followed the sound of a familiar voice and saw that Thomas Price, owner of a neighboring farm had his hand in the air.

"Four thousand dollars from Thomas Price. Going once." The tight ball of nausea eased a fraction. A tightness in her chest that she hadn't even known was there lightened with cautious relief as the widower beamed at her from across the crowd. He was sweet, in a bland, characterless way. She'd be bored out of her mind, but she'd tolerated much worse over the years on Preston's arm.

"Five thousand." Nausea struck, boiling and acidic, when Senator Bailey bid again.

There was no escaping him. Her fingernails dug into her palms.

"Six thousand!" Carol bid again, but her kindness wouldn't do Kate any good.

"Seven thousand." Harlan and Sandy Walker shouted at the same time, she heard the laughing smiles in their voices. Physically, they couldn't be more different. Harlan stood tall and broad with a full head of salt and pepper hair. He dwarfed his slender, auburn-haired wife. Yet, as always, the two were united and ridiculously happy in their love for each other. At one time in her life, Kate thought she'd had that kind of relationship herself, but it had been a lie.

"Eight thousand dollars." Bailey bid again and she wished Stephen would just call an end to the auction and her misery. Bailey wanted her. Why? She had no idea, but it couldn't be anything good. Nothing associated with Preston was, and he stood not more than three feet away from the senator with a knowing grin.

The crowd went quiet.

"Eight thousand dollars." Stephen paused. "Going once." He paused again as if waiting for someone, anyone to bid again. "Going twice." The crowd's silence weighed heavy, suffocating.

She smiled until her cheeks hurt.

"Ten thousand dollars." Her heart jumped to her throat and the crowd gasped. She knew that voice. The stable hand who'd driven her up to the house had just bid ten thousand dollars. He stepped out of the shadows from the back of the crowd.

"Ten thousand dollars. Going once, going twice, and she's sold. One dinner date with former Miss Kentucky, Kate MacDonald, goes to Trent Dawson for ten thousand dollars!" She'd never heard Stephen speak so fast the entire time she'd known him.

She swayed on her feet. Daniel stepped closer and cupped her elbow. He leaned in to whisper again. "Don't make me pinch you, pretty Kate. You look like you're about to faint. Dad will kick my ass if I pinch you, but he'll skin me alive if you fall."

"I'm sorry. I haven't eaten much today. I've been so busy. I know better." Daniel stayed silent, but his expression held a wealth of doubt.

She attempted to shake off the shock-induced fog and smiled weakly at Trent. He gave her a gentlemanly nod, reminding her of an old west cowboy, then he stepped back and disappeared into the shadows.

Daniel escorted her off the small stage. If she didn't know any better, she'd think someone was staring holes into her back the entire way to the kitchen.

Was it Preston or Bailey? But it didn't really matter, did it?

Chapter Three

Shit. What had he gotten himself into? How could one woman make him break not one, but two of the rules he lived by in less than an hour?

First, he'd turned his back to a possible threat. Yes, the two suits in the stable hadn't been much of a risk. He could've taken them both down without breaking a sweat, but there were reasons that a man never, ever left himself vulnerable.

Second lapse of judgment? He'd let himself be drawn in by a pretty face and a voice that had seeped into his bones with a sweet warmth that had apparently made him a complete dumbass.

After she'd run from his truck as if her heels were on fire, he'd finished parking and made his way to the house. On his way to the kitchen's back door, he'd encountered the large crowd. Preferring to avoid the party he'd planned to walk around the edges and detour around to the mudroom door. Then he caught a glimpse of Kate from the side. The night's shadows and the party's bright lights had shined in the dark chocolate and caramel of her hair. What had Carol called them? Fairy lights? The trees, patio, everywhere he looked the place twinkled and there she stood, straight and tall in the spotlight as if she were royalty.

Then he'd heard Harlan's booming voice call out a bid of fifteen hundred dollars. It was a voice he knew well and so was the next bidder, Sandy. When Kate laughed at the Walkers' antics, her face lit up and sucker punched him. She was simply the most beautiful woman he'd ever seen.

And absolutely not for the likes of him.

The Walkers' bids answered a couple of questions at once. One, why she'd had to be at the house by eight o'clock and, two, it must be some sort of charity event. Generous to a fault, the Walkers enjoyed sharing their wealth.

He'd taken another step in the shadows around the back when he'd been doomed.

An unknown male placed the next bid for Kate and, though she continued to wear that perfect smile, she somehow did the impossible and stood even straighter. If he knew one thing after years of raising horses, he knew body language. Her spine was so brittle, a stiff breeze might snap it.

He surveyed the crowd and immediately understood. In the middle of the crowd Senator Bailey stood with his hand up. Not more than a couple of feet away hovered the other man, the ex-husband who'd been in the barn with Kate.

Shit.

It didn't take rocket science to see she wanted nothing to do with her ex-husband and the senator who seemed to be using her ex to get to her.

What a mess.

After another bid, her tension appeared to ease until the senator bid again and her stiffness returned. Stephen's oldest son seemed to sense something was wrong as he glanced at Kate and, though he kept a closer eye on her, there'd be no help coming from that front. He loved the Mitchells, but politics were in their blood. They more than likely wouldn't do anything to cause a scene.

Bidding commenced and the lead switched through the crowd but, judging by her posture, Kate had come to the same conclusion as he had.

The senator wanted Kate badly and the warning in Trent's gut screamed that he shouldn't let that happen at any cost.

Bailey held the highest bid at eight thousand dollars, and it seemed no one in the crowd would be willing to top him.

Stephen had looked mildly uncomfortable as he'd readied to close the bidding.

"Eight thousand dollars. Going once. Going twice."

"Ten thousand dollars." He'd stepped out of the dark and hoped Stephen got the hint and took care of things.

"Ten thousand dollars. Going once, going twice and she's sold. One dinner date with former Miss Kentucky, Kate MacDonald, goes to Trent Dawson for ten thousand dollars!"

Former Miss Kentucky? She looked the part, but what the hell was he going to do with a ten-thousand-dollar pageant queen?

He decided against facing the crowd. The last thing he wanted to face was the curious looks of politicians who wondered what a poor stable hand was doing bidding on a beauty queen.

He headed back to his truck to pass the time, going through his email and attending to business matters on his phone.

He'd sorted through three fourths of his emails by the time the crowd dwindled down to just a few stragglers, ones probably hoping for a few minutes with the former governor's ear. By now he should be able to get in and out of the kitchen, grab a plate of leftovers and give Carol a check for her charity without too much fuss.

What had he been thinking?

Had he really bid ten grand on a beauty queen? He wouldn't consider the money a waste, because Carol knew her charities and it would be put to good use, but he'd never done anything so reckless.

He opened the door and instantly remembered why.

"Carol, I'll get the money somehow. The charity needs it, and it's not fair that they'll be shortchanged. I have some savings. I can—"

"You absolutely will not. Trent's word is worth its weight in gold. I'm just glad he stepped up and saved the day. I hated the thought that anyone associated with Preston might have the winning bid."

"Me too," Kate said.

That silky voice that was equal parts cool satin sheets and teasing siren lured him from the mudroom into the kitchen. "Ladies."

Sitting at the bar, each with a half-eaten piece of cake in front of her, they turned their heads toward him but their expressions couldn't be more different.

Carol wore a bright, welcoming smile and Kate looked like she'd seen a ghost. Unfortunately, the expression didn't make her look any less appealing. She'd changed out of the dress she'd worn during the auction. The casual sundress she'd exchanged for the gown only made her look more accessible and down-to-earth. Touchable and way too tempting.

Time to finish up business and run as fast and as far as he could.

"Molly's set and she looks comfortable with Charley next door." He walked over and handed Carol the check he'd written out in the truck. "I'll get out of your hair and leave her to you." When she pointed to her cheek, he obligingly leaned down to give her the kiss she always required.

When she pointed to a mountainous covered plate sitting on the counter, he picked it up. No doubt there was enough food for three grown men beneath the foil.

"Ladies." He felt like a boy dodging a face washing before dinner as he nodded and turned to leave.

Carol knew him too well. "So, Trent… About your winning bid? I was thinking for your date—"

"Ah, that's okay. I'm happy to make the donation and let Kate off the hook. She's been such a good sport, so there's no need—"

Carol interrupted before he could dole out a lame excuse. "Oh, no you don't. When was the last time you did something fun?"

Here comes the lecture. There were only two women on this planet he'd allow to mother him—Sandy Walker and Carol Mitchell. He was screwed. "I've been busy and you know I like working with the horses. It's not work to me."

Carol kept right on going as if he hadn't spoken. "How about the art gallery? They're having a show next Saturday."

"I can't do Saturday, Carol. It's my best day for sales this time of year," Kate said. He looked over in time to see her take one last bite of cake before she pushed the plate away. The beauty queen held a job? Had she fallen on hard times since the divorce?

"Well, I have tickets to the symphony next Friday evening that Stephen and I won't be using. I'd hate to see them go to waste. You can take Kate."

He hadn't wanted to tuck his tail and run this badly since he and Justin had trampled Sandy's flowerbeds looking for their lost football when they'd been ten. "That's not necessary, Carol. I appreciate it but I'm sure Kate would"—

"Kate, do you still have that lovely black and white sheath that you wore last year? You'll wear that. Trent will pick you up at six. I'll text him your address and expect a full report."

Shit.

"Don't you move." Carol left the kitchen leaving the room in a heavy silence as if the kitchen itself waited with bated breath to hear what he'd say to Kate.

His tongue tied itself in knots. What did a man say in a situation like this?

"So, you trained Molly?" Kate's quiet question settled him.

"I did, if you want to call it that. She's such a good tempered filly, she practically trained herself."

"She is a sweetie. How long have you worked with"—

The door opened and Carol came through in a whirlwind of energy. "Here we go. I'll give them to you now so you don't have to make another trip out." She kissed him on the cheek and all but shoved him out the door before he could argue.

The symphony? With pageant queen Kate MacDonald? Really?

Shit.

"So, that's Trent Dawson? I've heard the name, but never met him in person." She watched the tall, seemingly shell-shocked male retreat.

"He's a good man. He just prefers to keep to himself. You won't see him unless you head out to the Walkers' stables. Other than making an occasional appearance because Sandy bullied him into it, he spends all of his time with his horses. He doesn't care for crowds."

When Carol took a bite of cake and beamed at Kate with a cat that ate the canary smile, Kate froze.

Oh dear God. She'd been suckered in more ways than one. No one ever escaped Carol's matchmaking.

Chapter Four

Gravel crunched in Kate's driveway, and she didn't know whether to be relieved that Trent hadn't stood her up or disappointed because she had to actually go on the farce of a date. Even though Trent seemed to be a completely different breed of man than her ex-husband, she was in no way looking for a relationship.

Apparently, he felt the same way. At the barbeque, when Carol backed him into the corner, he'd gone right past reluctant and straight into unwilling. She couldn't say she blamed him.

She took a deep breath and reminded herself to look on the bright side. At least at the symphony, they wouldn't have much time to make small talk. Thanks to years of pageants, social appearances and charity events during her year as Miss Kentucky, she could make small talk with even the shyest or most boring of guests.

Not that she enjoyed it, but she could.

She grabbed her clutch and wrap then resisted the urge to check her clear lip gloss one last time. She hadn't worn more than minimal makeup two or three times in the past year, but old habits died hard. In her previous life, appearances had been everything.

Heavy footsteps sounded from the porch, and she opened the door.

Dear God.

He'd been handsome in faded old jeans on the night they'd met, but in a tux he stole her capacity for intelligent thought. His dark blond hair had been brushed into shining waves that reached his collar. A black jacket framed broad shoulders that somehow seemed even larger than she remembered. He filled her doorway with raw power, his formal clothes doing nothing to subtract the masculinity from his presence.

Her mouth dried and parts of her that had slept for the past year awoke and took notice. They became anything but dry.

He stared down at her for a moment and then he blinked, seeming to shake off his stupor. Yet he didn't say a single word. Could he be that unhappy to go out with her?

"Hello." If he wouldn't talk, she'd have to.

"Hi." His expression—or lack of expression—gave her no indication of his mood or thoughts. *Great, just great.*

"It looks like it's going to be a nice evening. It's almost a shame to spend it indoors."

He held out a hand for her keys. When she handed them over, he locked her door and double-checked it. Keeping her keys, he took her arm in his other hand and silently led her to his truck. The calluses of his palms rasped over the skin of her elbow in a light whisper.

He opened the door, waited until she got inside and shut it for her. A moment later, he joined her, dropping her keys in the console and they were on their way in a silence so heavy she could choke on it.

"I apologize for bringing the truck. I would have brought my car, but a friend is in town on business and borrowed it for the week."

"No problem. You really didn't have to come all this way to pick me up. I wouldn't have minded meeting you at the symphony hall or at a restaurant. I wouldn't have even told Carol on you." She gave him her best cheeky grin.

"Not necessary."

Okay. So her pitiful excuse for a joke hadn't worked. He kept both hands on the steering wheel, shoulders stiff. She hated that he'd been put in an awkward position because he'd done her a favor. A *huge* favor.

She still couldn't believe that he'd bid ten thousand dollars for a night with her. What had he been thinking? Clearly, he hadn't been trying to get into her bed. Though he'd been a perfect gentleman at every point in their brief acquaintance, he seemed to want to put as much distance between them as possible.

Why?

Accustomed to men suffocating her with charm, she didn't understand him.

She watched the alternating sections of dense trees and rolling green fields go by and wondered if he resented her. Had he only bid out of some sense of duty or honor?

Of course he had. Why else would he have bid so much?

Stop.

This was one date. If she continued overthinking his motivations, it would turn into the longest and most excruciatingly boring night ever, which wasn't fair to him.

"So how long have you known the Mitchells'?" Her upbringing insisted she at least make another attempt at polite conversation.

"Nearly as long as I can remember. Sandy and Harlan Walker raised me, and they've been close friends with the Mitchells since the dawn of time, I think."

She remembered Carol mentioning they'd taken in a friend of their son's and how he'd had a natural affinity for horses that outshone even Harlan's. Considering how many parties and charity events she'd attended over the years, it seemed odd that she'd never bumped into him somewhere along the way.

Had she been that self-absorbed? She didn't think so. Then again, she she'd spent her time being the perfect wife to a man who hadn't deserved the effort, let alone her love.

"Was it Harlan who taught you how to breed horses?"

"Breed, train, buy, sell, you name it. Harlan knows his business, and it seemed to be a natural fit for me. He's always said I have it in my blood." He smiled, but was it doubt she heard in his voice?

"What about their son, Justin? Was he as interested in the horses as you?"

Quiet filled the cab until she worried that she'd stumbled upon an off-limits topic. She hadn't, had she?

Oh no. Shit. Shit. Shit. How could she have been so careless?

She had and didn't know whether it was better to apologize or change subjects and let the painful topic rest. Finally, he answered but, if possible, his hands gripped the wheel tighter and a muscle twitched in his jaw.

When a sad smile cracked through his tension, her heart melted. "No, no matter what Harlan tried, Justin never did click with animals, especially the horses. With Sandy and Harlan as parents, one would have thought that he'd be the damn horse whisperer, but no. He didn't care for them, and they didn't care for him. He just wanted to be a soldier. I miss the idiot something fierce."

"I'm so sorry. I forgot he passed away. What a way to put a damper on a date. Usually I'm great at the small talk thing, but my skills must be getting rusty. I don't use them much anymore. How about a nice, simple topic? Something other than the weather though, since everyone talks about the weather." God, now she was babbling. How low could a beauty queen sink?

"Why don't you turn on the radio and choose something you like? I'll listen to any song by a group with a guitar player in its crew." He looked straight ahead as he drove out of Riley Creek and toward the highway, but she swore his lips twitched with a hint of amusement. Well, she might feel like a dumbass, but his amusement was light years better than her previous attempt.

Plus, it seemed to have lessened the strain in his shoulders, so it was a definite improvement.

"There aren't any guitars at the symphony." *Great job, queen of the obvious.* She mentally smacked herself in the forehead.

"No, I don't believe there are." Was he biting the inside of his cheek to keep from laughing at her? But, you know what? He already thought she was a goofball, so she might as well go along with it. Even her making a fool of herself was better than their awkward beginning.

"So, do you even like the symphony?"

"No, not really. Not at all," he said with a shrug.

She hadn't thought so. She hated to make assumptions about people, but she would have pegged him as the type to listen to country music and drink a cold beer in the shade. "Does Carol know this?"

"She does."

Which didn't make any sense. Suspicion swelled. Carol said he didn't like crowds or people, so why would she expect him to take her somewhere she knew neither of them liked?

Though it seemed improbable, she asked anyway. "Can I ask, is it the music itself or the concert hall?"

"I have nothing against music of any kind, but sitting cooped up indoors in a suit is not the way I prefer to spend my downtime." He shook his head, both hands in a death grip on the steering wheel signaling the return of his earlier tension. "What is she plotting?" The question seemed directed to himself as he cocked his head as if in thought.

As they neared the freeway entrance that would take them to the city, he flipped on his turn signal. The highway sign near the interstate showed an arrow pointing left. Were they really going to sit for a couple of awkward hours in a place that neither one of them had any desire to be?

A mixture of dread and resigned duty filled her until she forced herself to shake it off and remember that the auction could have ended far worse. So she'd be bored when she would have rather stayed home with Bonnie. She should be thankful that Trent had bailed her, a stranger, out of a bad situation, and leave it at that.

Trent came to a stop and the turn signal tick-tick-ticked as they waited in silence.

"Change of plans. Go right." They hadn't actually promised to go to the symphony and were under no obligation to do so. Though, they both felt an obligation to go on this silly date. "I wish we could go riding. I figure that's more to both of our liking, but that's out thanks to this damn dress." She was a very capable rider, but unless she wanted to pull the tight sheath up to her hips and flash her ass at Trent, riding was a big fat no today.

"You're wish, my command." He quirked an amused grin her way. "Lead the way, beauty."

She matched his grin with one of her own, making his even brighter and, dear lord, could he get any hotter? A total one-eighty from Preston's polish that demanded acknowledgement, his rugged earthiness said take him as he was or leave him.

Warmth blossomed in her chest and spread to some very unexpected places. She shifted her legs and turned to take in the intersection before them.

He checked to make sure the traffic was clear and made a right turn.

"Chicken for dinner okay? No! Wait, how about garbage pizza? I'll call it in and we can pick it up on the way. I haven't had Pop's pizza in years."

"Sure. I'll eat anything. Even…garbage pizza." Bless his heart, he didn't even look surprised or confused by her odd behavior. Preston would have overrode her suggestion they skip the formal plans and he probably wouldn't even have acknowledged her choice of greasy pizza with anything but a scathing look of disdain.

"It's just a pizza with the works. It's messy, but so very good. I promise."

A sudden fit of nerves threatened to steal her momentum. Feeling as if she'd fallen down a rabbit hole, she didn't know what to do or what to say. She'd never hijacked a date before.

She gave herself a moment to get her nerves under control.

She couldn't leave the evening this way with the two of them roaming the city aimlessly.

"Okay, so here's the plan. What do you say we go and sit by the lake and have dinner? We can tell Carol that we had a picnic by the lake, which will be true and get both of us off the hook. We don't have to stay long. There's a quiet, private place I know."

He didn't voice his opinion, but his grin was back and the sight of it brought her a mountain of relief. Immediately, she relaxed at the thought of sitting and listening to the water lap at the shore.

Using her smartphone, she found the number and called in their order, sat back and smiled. She started to question how something so basic could make her this happy, but she stopped herself. The whys didn't matter. The only thing that did was enjoying the happy when it came her way, no matter how large or small.

And she suspected that Trent could use a shot of happy too. How did she make a gruff, quiet man, whose only concern seemed to be his horses, smile?

"You know what? I haven't done this in forever. I wished I'd thought ahead and worn real clothes."

"Real clothes? No offense, but the dress you're wearing must have cost a small fortune. How is something so expensive not considered real clothing?"

"Uhm. Yeah, it was no bargain. It's an old one from before I moved out. My cousin insisted I bring all my clothes with me. I nearly refused, but if you knew Leigh Ann, you'd understand why I caved. What I mean by real clothes is something that I would wear every day."

When his features twisted into a look of utter bafflement, she burst out laughing. "What's that look for?"

"I'm just trying to picture what a ten-thousand-dollar beauty queen wears everyday if a seven-hundred-dollar dress doesn't fit the bill."

"Old jeans and T-shirts. Cowboy boots."

He turned his nose down at her as if she were delusional.

"No. Really. When I left my ex-husband I took very little aside from the clothes. Even then, I didn't have anything practical to wear. He thinks I've sunk to the farthest depths of humanity by leaving him and coming back home to live in squalor." She made air quotes around the word squalor.

"What do you think?"

"I think he's selfish and only concerned with climbing the ranks of politicians and bluebloods. His opinion of anything in my life is the equivalent of cow shit."

"I don't know about that. Even cow shit can make for some pretty good fertilizer." There was that half grin he liked to hide. She needed to reevaluate her plan to make Trent smile, right here, right now. Those slow, lazy grins were going to be her undoing. Coupled with his slate gray eyes, he was downright swoon worthy.

She gave him a fake gasp. The quirk of his lips turned into a full blown smile and she contained her reaction, barely. "Was that a joke, Trent Dawson?"

Instantly that killer smile turned off. Sad to see it go, she poked him in his bicep. *His heavily muscled bicep.* "Hey. I'm just pla—"

The corner of his mouth twitched as if he fought back laughter. "You know, for a proper beauty queen, you're an awful lot of trouble."

"That's former proper beauty queen to you. I think I'm finished with that part of my life. I was always the good girl and always did exactly what everyone expected of me. I think that's how I ended up with Preston and in the unhappy world that I allowed to swallow me. I was content to float along and let everyone make all my decisions for me."

"So what's next?"

"I haven't figured that out yet, but you can bet that it will be what I want to do, not what everyone else tells me I should."

"That's a damn good start." His words sounded like something a MacDonald would say. The realization made something soft and warm uncurl in her chest.

He pulled into the pizza joint's parking lot and just as he came to a stop she jumped out, called out a cheerful "be right back!" and hustled across the lot.

He really needed to break her of that habit, but how could he? The sight of those long, lean legs and her sweet, curvy ass hypnotized him as they walked across the lot in the sexiest sway of hips he'd ever seen.

Was she even aware of the group of teenage boys who were too stupid to hide their lust-filled looks? Did she have a clue that the slightly older man, who'd opened the door for her with a gentlemanly nod, turned to check out her ass after she entered?

Not to mention that he hadn't been able to pull his gaze away, and she wasn't his type. He had no room in his life for high heels and designer dresses.

Yet, he couldn't convince himself that Kate attracted that kind attention intentionally. He hoped that his brain hadn't been overrun with lust and had lost its ability for rational thought. He figured the odds were fifty-fifty at best.

The door opened and yet another unknown male, this one closer to middle age with a large beer gut held the door open and he wasn't surprised to see Kate walk out carrying a large pizza box and carryout bag. She smiled a thank you at the poor soul holding the door open and the sap's chest puffed up with pride. A few seconds after she passed, he released a sigh and his belly doubled in size as he relaxed.

Trent shook his head and went around to open the door and take the food. He set it in the backseat and resisted the urge to put his hands on her. He wanted to grip her hips and pull her close. He could have easily used helping her up into the truck as an excuse to get close, but his last few functioning brain cells warned him off.

He had no desire for a beauty queen or any of the surrounding drama and headache in his life. None. Especially one with a walk that made grown men swoon, a fondness for horses and a voice like warmed honey.

She smiled up at him with a sweet warmth that melted his resolve as he shut the door for her.

No.

He'd take her to the lake, eat some pizza and play nice. Then he'd take her home and it would be end of story.

He got in the driver's side. "I would have paid if you'd actually let me park the truck first. You gotta stop jumping out of moving vehicles. You've been in my ride twice and both times, you've hopped out like it was on fire. It's not that dirty."

"No, it's actually a very nice truck. I like it. You were in your spot. And this is my treat, since I kidnapped you."

"Kidnapped? You did not kidnap me." The thought of a curvy little beauty queen holding him hostage made him laugh. He couldn't wait to see what she'd come up with next.

"Yes I did. We had plans, and I hijacked them." She spoke of kidnapping and hijacking as if they were shopping at the mall.

"I repeat. You did not steal me away. I'm a grown man and can fight you off if you threaten my virtue, okay?"

Meant as a joke, his words had a greater impact than he'd expected when a faint blush covered her skin from head to toe. Images of a desire flushed, wanton Kate slammed him. His cock approved, but he did not.

"How do we get to this special spot of yours?"

"Follow the signs to the lake until you get to the last one. Go past it. The second road will be a little gravel lane. Follow it until it forks then take the right." As he watched the early evening traffic, he heard the happiness in her voice.

"How did you find this spot?"

"My dad used to come out here all the time to fish. It was one of his favorite spots. Every once in a long while, I lucked into a free weekend and he'd bring me with him."

"You lucked into fishing with your father? Not many young women would consider that lucky." Dirt, weeds, mosquitoes, worms and hooks didn't spell proper young lady by any means. He couldn't picture beauty queen Kate at a secret fishing hole.

"I did. Any time I had free time I spent it with Dad or Leigh."

"What kept you so busy?" He glanced her way and saw her watching the dwindling buildings and encroaching countryside.

"Aunt Jeannie and pageant prep. Daily dance lessons, gymnastics, and etiquette lessons given by Aunt Jeannie herself. She had very definite ideas on what made a respectable Southern woman. Dad was a widower and feared I'd get into trouble if I grew up without a feminine influence. He worried that a 'grumpy old redneck' his words, not mine, wouldn't be able to raise a daughter properly, so he enlisted his older sister's help. She'd never married or had any children of her own, so she took the role seriously. You would've thought she was preparing me to become the first lady." Disbelief and maybe even a trace of disgust laced her voice.

"Was it that bad?" Concern colored his quiet question.

"Yes and no. Aunt Jeannie's heart was in the right place, and she loved me very much. She was never mean or anything like that, I just didn't enjoy most of my time with her. Gymnastics and learning how to cook weren't so bad. But, with everything else, there wasn't much time for fun."

The image of a solemn little girl with masses of dark brown hair and sad eyes punched him in the gut. Yes, raised as a Walker, he'd learned all about work and responsibility, but he and Justin had been rewarded with plenty of free time. "What was your favorite thing to do when you were young?"

"Work in the stable with Dad. We had two old horses, both of them grades without any papers. Dad won them off an old gambling buddy. He couldn't care less about their lack of traceable breeding. He got them when I was around seven and I had the same silly dream that many little girls have. I wanted a pony desperately. When he brought them home, I was so excited. I remember he beamed with pride when he unloaded them. Neither one of us cared that they were a little small, plain and thin. We pinky promised that we'd take good care of them. They were ours so, to me, they were the greatest horses in all of equine history."

He found the fork in the road that she'd described and drove down a short distance. As she'd described, visible between a gap in the tall trees, was the lake. He turned the truck around so the bed faced the water and backed close to the shore.

"Let's have pizza, and you can tell me more about your horses." Suddenly, her silly lake and pizza date seemed like a damn fine idea. "Wait for me before you get out." Surely she couldn't hop out and run off in heels on the soft ground, but he wasn't taking any chances. "I'll come around." He stepped out and tested the ground as he headed to her side.

Though the rough driveway itself was well-worn, the grass hit him at mid-calf. He didn't care how talented she was, unless she had super powers, she wasn't going anywhere in heels. How the hell was he supposed to keep her damn dress clean? He opened the door of the crew cab and pulled out an old blanket.

"Don't move." He dropped the tailgate and unfolded the blanket, shook it out and covered the truck bed. It wasn't great, but it was the best he had. He returned for Kate. Her tight, knee-length dress would cause problems. He stamped down the grass by her door and helped her to step down. As soon as she set both feet on solid ground he scooped her up with one arm under both her legs and the other behind her back. Caught off-guard, she put her hands on his shoulders, her slight weight a solid, sweet heat against his chest.

Shit.

He took her to the tailgate, sat her down as if she were a hot potato and retrieved the food. She took the bag and removed paper plates, napkins and bottled drinks. He moved the pizza box to set in the bed behind them and opened it.

He'd never been in this kind of situation before. What were the rules? Was there some sort of guy code that said he should serve her or wait until she took the first bite before he— well, that answered that question. Before he finished his thought she'd grabbed two of the larger pieces, plopped them on her plate and then took a hearty bite.

"Oh God. Sorry, you'll have to excuse my teenage boy manners. I haven't had Pop's pizza in years. I don't know why this wasn't the first thing I ate after I left Preston." Somehow, even as she scarfed down pizza like a champ, she still looked like the perfect lady.

"I've never tried it. Dare I ask why you couldn't have it while you were with the asshole?" He filled his plate and took his own bite. Damn, it was good. He had to hand it to her, the lady knew pizza.

"As silly as it sounds now, he simply would have turned his nose down at me, like eating peasant food was beneath us. I hated it, because this is where I grew up. Did that mean some part of me wasn't worthy? I struggled with that thought for years. Too many times I smiled and nodded when inside I felt like crying. I wasted years of my life. I'm sorry. Let's change the subject. Tell me about your first horse."

"The first horse I owned? A yearling named Knight. Harlan and Sandy gave him to me on my thirteenth birthday. I lived with the Walkers full time by then, and spent as much time down in the stable with Harlan as I did in the house or yard with Justin. Like every year prior, Sandy woke me up and fixed my favorite breakfast. She wished me a happy birthday and left it at that. Justin gave me a new video game and other than a tousle of my hair and terse 'Happy birthday, Trent, my boy,' Harlan stayed silent. He'd barred me from the stables the night before and I thought for sure that I had done something stupid and was in trouble.

"The thought of being banned from the stables terrified me, so when Harlan finished eating and stood with a look that was one hundred percent business, I just knew that I'd screwed up big time. 'Let's go, Trent. I've got something to show you.'" He paused and took a drink of his soda. He remembered the look on Harlan's face well.

Chancing a glance at Kate, he figured she'd be bored out of her mind, but she waited with kind eyes as if she'd listened to every single word.

"I got up and followed him out. When I saw Knight, I instantly knew he was a special colt. Love at first sight, but I still didn't have a clue why Harlan had brought me out. I'd never seen the new addition and hadn't even had a chance to screw up around him yet. Harlan stood there with his arms crossed over his chest and asked 'So, what do you think?' I told him that he was the best looking horse I'd ever seen. Real calm, like he was talking about the day's chores, he said 'That's good, son, because he's yours and I expect you to treat him like he's the most valuable horse in the world.' I had to replay his words in my head three times before they registered." He used a napkin to wipe the grease from his fingers. "I wouldn't go in for lunch or dinner that day and Sandy was adamant that her boys eat a proper meal, three times a day. She never, ever let us miss a meal, except that day. Harlan had to threaten to take away my stable privileges to get me to leave and that was two hours past bedtime."

"Bonnie filled me with that same feeling of instant love. No hesitation, no questioning it, she became mine the moment I saw her." She twisted the lid off her drink.

He nodded his agreement. "The next morning I was so eager to get back to Knight that I ate my breakfast even faster than a normal teenage boy and couldn't sit still. Sandy finally gave up and gave me the one word I needed to hear. 'Go.' She thrust a sack lunch at me as I ran out the door. Thankfully my birthday is in early June. I had the entire summer to fawn over him before school started." Had he really spilled the entire story with her? Apparently he had, yet he couldn't face the understanding in her soft brown eyes.

He took another bite of pizza and washed it down with his soda. Then he took another bite and watched the silvery water lap at the shore.

Her husky voice merged with the lapping water, a soothing balm on his tension. "Dad and I had to switch horses. The smaller gal was named Miss Priss and seemed like the obvious choice for me. Dad's horse, Jack, was a tall, solemn fellow. You would have thought by looking at them they were a match made in heaven, too, but Miss Priss set her eyes on Dad and that was all she wrote. She'd let me ride and care for her, but she preened and made doe eyes at Dad whenever he came near. Of course, he melted. He always pretended to be a big gruff redneck, but he had the softest heart, especially for animals and kids. He used to say that he always wanted a big family, but since he couldn't have one, God made up for it by giving him the prettiest girl in the world. He was always so damn proud when I brought home another crown and sash. I loved the way his big, barrel chest swelled and his eyes lit up."

Was that moisture in her eyes? *Damn.* This had become one of the sappiest, yet best dates he'd ever been on. He needed to slam the brakes before they went further down memory lane. Soon, they'd be talking about losing their virginity or something equally embarrassing.

"The sun's getting ready to set, and the mosquitoes are looking for dinner. What do you say that we pack it in?" He hated the look on her face. It said she saw the wisdom to his words, but didn't like them.

"Can we watch the sunset first? I think it's going to be a pretty one."

"Sure. I'll have some more of Pop's pizza, and do my best to keep the bloodsuckers away. Let's at least cover your arms." He took off his tux jacket and held it while she slid her arms in the sleeves. "It'll be warm, but it'll make decent armor."

"Thanks." Her quiet voice held a wistful note as she watched the sun set beyond the far edge of the lake. He cleaned up their impromptu picnic and, with nothing to do but wait, he watched the sky's colors shift as if it couldn't make up its mind which bright nightgown it wanted to wear for bed. It finally changed from a pale pink to the deep purple of dusk as they sat in a comfortable silence.

"All right, Miss Kate, let's get you home."

"Okay. I should get back to Bonnie soon anyway." Her blissed out, sleepy tone could very well push him over a line he absolutely did not want to cross. The new challenge—getting her back in the truck without kissing the sleepy, kitten-like look off her face.

He pictured his high school gym teacher's beer gut as he lifted her from the tailgate. When the soft, subtle scent of woman hit him, the gap-toothed, bowlegged, cranky old Mr. Johnson evaporated, leaving another image—one of a sexy as sin Kate walking across the parking lot in those killer heels.

A woman who put family first with her animals not far behind, who liked to fish and the simpler things in life but looked like a million dollars had to be too good to be true, didn't she?

Chapter Five

A weak trace of light blanketed the field around her home as Trent pulled into the long gravel driveway. Joe had been out with his tractor to help her cut grass a couple of days ago, so the place didn't look half bad.

Shifting in her seat, she released the seatbelt before saying, "Thanks for picking me up and bringing me home. It really wasn't necessary, but I have to admit that the evening turned out much better than I expected."

"Me too. I'll take an evening by the lake and pizza anytime. The company wasn't so bad, either." When he poked her in the arm, mimicking her earlier in the evening, she turned and gave him a genuine smile.

And as she turned her head back to the view of her farm, two things hit her back-to-back.

The first? She realized that she had two kinds of smiles. The pageant smile that she gave to anyone and everyone and her real smile. It was the one she shared with Leigh, Joe and had given her Dad. She'd given it to Preston in the beginning, but it wasn't long before she took it back. That should have been when she packed up her stuff and left, not after years of condescension and heartache.

And now she'd given the smile that she felt to the tips of her toes to Trent Dawson.

Then the second shock came as the truck slowed near the house, freezing her lungs. All the air in the truck disappeared.

"No! The barn's open!" Filled with equal parts fear and white-hot anger, she bolted from the truck and kicked off her heels.

"Kate! Stop! Damn it, wait!"

She heard Trent's words, but couldn't care less about their meaning. She had to get to Bonnie. If someone had taken her or, worse, hurt her baby, she'd commit murder.

A strong arm wrapped around her middle and lifted her.

"Stop." Trent said, low and serious, in her ear.

His words didn't matter. She had to get free and get to her horse. *Now.* The panic flowed through her in an uncontrollable, torrential flood. Some minute, sane part of her understood Trent wouldn't hurt her, so she shamelessly used that knowledge against him. She fought and squirmed to break free. Tumbling to the ground and to her knees, the only thing she cared about was what did or did not lie beyond the dark, gaping doorway. The knowledge that something wasn't right scared the ever-living hell out of her.

She crawled forward on her hands and knees, prepared to run again. Once she'd managed to almost get back on her feet, he pulled her back against the steel of his chest. She wriggled and got nowhere as his arms wrapped around her.

"Kate, baby. Stop it. Just stop." Low and calm, his deep voice rushed through her.

The iron bands held her immobile as his breath heaved in her ear.

"Listen to me. I get that you're worried about the foal, I promise." He turned her around and carried her the wrong way. Craning her head, she looked over her shoulder. She wanted to weep as the dark doorway grew farther away with each long stride. "You have to use your head. If someone's been here, they might still be inside." He put her into the corner made by the truck's open door but continued to hold her tight. Each word was a harsh push back to reality. She stared ahead but didn't see beyond the speck of dust on the truck's window.

"If they've done something, it's already done. If they're still there, you've made enough noise to ensure they know that you're here and know something's wrong. They'd be waiting for you, and you were running into an incredibly unsafe situation in nothing but your fancy dress and heels. Oh wait, you don't even have shoes on. It's dark now. With the light of the moon spotlighting us, they have the advantage. Damn it, Kate." His words were harsh and unyielding in her ear.

He set her down and, with a gentle tug, turned her until they were eye-to-eye. "Look at me. I won't let you go into an unsafe situation. It's not happening. I'll hog tie your ass and throw you in the truck bed if I have to."

His gray eyes boiled with a thunderstorm of intensity. He meant every word.

Defeated, worried, and scared, she dropped her head to his chest in defeat. At a loss, with nowhere to turn, she crushed his shirt in her tight grip.

"I need to know. I must look like a mad woman to you, but she's mine. I need to know."

He smoothed a hand over her hair. "Let me handle this. Promise me you'll stay here and wait for my call and I'll go check it out. I know what I'm doing and you're too upset to be cautious."

"Okay." It wasn't much more than a whisper, but she knew he'd heard it by the unconvinced scowl he gave her.

"Promise me you'll stay put. If you move from this spot, you'll divide my attention and that won't be safe for me, you, or Bonnie."

"Okay. I promise."

He leaned into the truck and reached beneath the driver seat. Something clicked and a small black drawer popped out. He pulled out a wicked looking handgun and removed it from the holster. Thanks to her father and uncle, she was no stranger to firearms, but her surprise must have shown on her face.

"Much better than a pair of high heels for nabbing intruders. Stay put." When she met his concerned gaze and saw nothing but a soldier staring back, she settled with the knowledge that he meant every word he'd said.

She had every confidence he had the situation under control.

Then he leaned in and kissed her forehead before turning and jogging to the barn.

She'd had a single thought—to get inside and find out what had happened to her foal. Nothing beyond that mattered. If someone was in there, she would have run headlong into danger. But Trent didn't go straight for the open doorway. He walked around the back, with his gun in a two-handed grip pointed downward but ready. He moved quickly, but seemed totally aware of everything.

As she waited for his signal, she didn't know whether to be relieved that he believed her or worried that the threat might be a legitimate one.

She knew she'd shut everything up after she fed everyone earlier that afternoon. She remembered her guilt for leaving Bonnie for the evening and chiding herself for it as she'd latched the door.

Who would do this? Bonnie might be her heart, but she wasn't anything special to anyone else. She had no papers, no traceable lineage. Tom's only concerns were probably about how much prison time he'd get or how he'd find a fix in jail, not about the horse.

She didn't have anything of value. Who would want to take from her or cause her trouble?

Shit.

Preston.

He wasn't above causing trouble. No matter how polished and perfect an image he'd crafted, he couldn't cover the truth of his heart. The man was pure selfish greed. How her little foal factored into his mess, she had no idea, but she wouldn't put it past him to do something out of pure spite.

He'd want to teach her a lesson.

Trent came around the far corner of the barn and went into the open doorway. She held her breath and, with no other way to occupy her time, she counted off the seconds. She got to eighty-nine and, just as she thought anxiety would get the better of her, he whistled.

The tightness in her chest eased, but her hands nearly shook with tension. What had he found?

"Kate? It's all clear," he called from inside. The light flicked on just as she entered the doorway. "She's fine. Come see."

Her knees trembled with relief.

"This isn't the way you left things, is it?" He questioned her as they looked around.

"No. It isn't. She was in her stall with the door shut and latched. I'm certain of it." Now her little girl stood there in back of the aisle, staring at her and Trent if it were perfectly normal for her to get out of her stall on her own. Full grown horses had been known to perform magic and escape their stalls, but there was no way her little girl could reach the latch on the outside of the door. Her box now stood open and empty. "You didn't see anyone, did you? I'm not crazy. I can retrace my steps this afternoon. I remember my exact thoughts as I closed up."

"I believe you. I'm just relieved she's here and okay. Now I have to figure out who was here and why. Let's put your little girl up and go check out the house." Trent rubbed a thumb over her cheek. The night's breeze sent her a whiff of his scent. Masculine and a little bit dark, she couldn't resist breathing more in.

"Trent, I appreciate this, truly. And you were right. It was stupid of me to rush in without any idea of what I was running into. Thank you. But you don't need to stay. I take care of everything on my own all the time." Grateful for the distraction, she pulled away and patted Bonnie's neck.

"I'm checking the house before I leave. No arguments. Let's put your girl to bed for the night. How long have you had her?" Then, as if he slipped out of soldier mode and became the horseman, he looked over Bonnie's accommodations.

She knew what he was doing. Trent was trying to put her at ease by talking about her baby. How many men would do that? He'd already gone beyond the call of duty by not only tolerating her date changeup but participating and helping her to make it enjoyable for them both. He'd carted her around because of her heels, protected her from mosquitoes and unknown trespassers. He hadn't complained once.

And, to think, he'd paid a small fortune for her at the auction.

The man deserved a medal *and* a cookie.

In no time at all, they had the foal back in its stall and shut up everything else. As they exited the barn, once again the world spun as he swept her up into his arms.

Slightly breathless with surprise and the heady scent of him, she managed, "Trent. You've carried me around all evening. This is getting ridiculous. Put me down."

"Nope. Carol will skin me if you get a splinter, and who knows what could be lurking in the grass in the dark? We're almost back to your shoes. I'll let you down there." A moment later, he turned his words to action. He held her hand as she brushed off her feet and slipped her heels back on. He walked slowly by her side, not letting go, as they returned to the truck where he retrieved her keys.

"Stay here," he ordered.

This time she didn't argue. Not just because the house only contained things, nothing living, but because the last thing she wanted to do was add to the headache she'd likely given him.

She gathered her clutch and wrap, then tried watching the stars. She failed miserably. She watched the house and began counting again. When she made it to two-hundred and fifty, she stopped and stared up into the night sky. Then she started counting stars.

Finally, the front porch light turned on, and she carefully made her way to the house. He pushed the door open and, without hesitation, she stepped into his arms.

"Everything seems fine to me, but I'll stay a moment while you go through and make sure nothing looks out of place or missing." He gave her space but stayed with her the entire time.

"Would you like something to drink? I can't thank you enough for everything. Bailing me out at the auction, putting up with my silly lake date—at every turn tonight you've humored me. Thank you."

"You don't have to thank me. I enjoyed the evening. To be honest, I dreaded the date but ended up having a nice time. Will you be able to sleep? Everything's secure, but will you be okay when I leave?" Trent raised his hand as if to reach for her, then put it in his pocket.

"I'll be fine. I grew up here, and I have Dad's guns. I have ammo and know how to use them." She'd worry about Bonnie being in the barn, alone. "He taught me to keep a shotgun loaded and ready at the front door and a rifle ready at the backdoor just in case I have to flee." She prayed she wouldn't need either weapon, but if push came to shove, she wouldn't hesitate to protect herself.

"You're sure?"

Okay, he was way too polite. What should she say or do? Nothing had gone according to plan, and there were no rules for this in the former beauty queen handbook. Her mouth spoke before her brain acted. "I'm certain. I've known how to use them since I was sixteen and started dating. Dad was big on making sure I could take care of myself. Would you like to go out again sometime? My treat, as a thank you?"

Where had that come from? She didn't want a man in her life. The last one made an utter mess of her world, and in the beginning she'd thought he hung the moon.

"Ah. Like I said, there's no need to thank me. Take care, beauty." Seeming to come to some sort of difficult decision, he kissed her. Soft and warm, his lips caressed hers in a slow, sensual dance.

Then he pulled away, turned and left while she stood at the door frozen in place like a total idiot.

He sat in the corner booth of the sports bar and waited on his client. There were smarter ways to handle these meetings, but this fool refused to take his advice. So he sat in a crowded public place, filled with potential witnesses.

He'd covered his own ass, but doubted Preston had. He seemed to think the world spun on his timetable and, if he thought it, then it must be so. Of course the fucker was fifteen minutes late when he walked through the door and flashed his best smile at the hostess. He looked her up and down, as if he were appraising a horse, then smirked as if she was the one who should be impressed by him. Waving her off as if she were beneath him, he looked around the bar and missed how she rolled her eyes behind his back. No doubt he imagined her pining away without the grace of his presence.

If he were a decent man, he would have stood and waved him over, but he stuck to the shadows and waited.

He bowed to no one.

After several minutes Preston finally saw him and made his way through the fifty-cent wing night crowd. He looked over the booth's seat as if searching for dog shit before he finally slid in.

Preston picked up a menu and frowned at it, seemingly disappointed by the offerings. When a waiter came by to take his drink order with a smile, the prick waved him off with a dismissal worthy of a stuck-up Hollywood socialite.

"I've been thinking about the best way to accomplish our goal. I agree that Kate is a stunningly beautiful woman. I married her, after all, didn't I? Her do-gooder habit will be an added benefit, as well as her former pageant title. By all appearances, if she can be persuaded to ditch the country bumpkin lifestyle, she'll be a perfect fit for our needs."

He stayed silent and waited for Preston to talk his way back to his point. He had an agenda of his own. For the moment, his and Preston's desires aligned—which was the only reason he'd agreed to work with the grasping moron. It was no wonder that Kate MacDonald divorced his ass.

He'd done his homework and, by all accounts, Kate was a smart, decent woman. Everyone made mistakes, so he wouldn't fault her for falling for whatever bullshit story Preston had likely conned her with. The only thing he couldn't fathom was why she'd stayed with him as long as she had.

Eventually, even the brightest and truest loves combusted under pressure.

The waiter brought his burger and asked Preston if he would like anything. The pompous ass turned his nose down and waved him off yet again. He didn't even consider telling him that by not ordering a meal or at least a beer he'd stand out.

People might not remember the average Joe, but they always remembered jackasses.

He took a bite of his mediocre burger and washed it down with a drink of beer which, thankfully, was cold. There wasn't much a cold beer couldn't fix.

"I've made an outline of how things should be done. It's all detailed in here. Look it over thoroughly and make sure you understand everything before you act. I won't tolerate mistakes."

He washed down another bite with his beer and pinned Preston with his stare.

"Are you even listening to me? You haven't said a single word. Bailey assured me you could handle our plan, but if not…"

"If not? What then?" He was beyond tired of listening to this idiot's delusions of grandeur. He'd actually written an outline? "My services are coming to you as a favor. Remember that. I owe you nothing. I don't work for you. I'm not your friend. I am not your colleague. If I can assist you with whatever hare-brained scheme you've come up with, fine. But that's all you get from me. Nothing. More. Are we clear?"

It was a rare breed of imbecile who remained within striking distance of a poisonous snake and believed himself immune. Apparently, he'd found such a creature. He finished his beer and reminded himself that there was a greater reason he was cooperating with Preston.

But that didn't mean he had to play nice.

"Are we clear?" He kept his voice quiet so the young couple in the booth behind Preston couldn't hear him. When Preston paled and his eyes widened he knew he'd been understood.

"Yes. Ah. Here. Here are my thoughts on what it will take to maneuver Kate where we want her." With a shaky hand, he slid a manila envelope over next to his plate.

"Tell me this. What do you get out of *maneuvering* Kate, as you call it? You had her, couldn't keep her, and by all appearances, she wants nothing to do with you now. What gives?" He pointed the mouth of his beer bottle at Preston and locked gazes with the weasel.

"She's not as perfect as everyone believes. Everyone feels so sorry for the poor beauty queen. Well, I suffered too." Preston straightened his arm and folded one sleeve without meeting his gaze.

"You suffered? I need to hear this. Exactly how did she make you suffer?" He leaned back and looked down his nose at the prick.

"Everyone thinks I'm the bad guy. Nearly half of my clients left and everyone looks at me like I'm a pariah." Typical non-answer, delivered in an almost nasal whine. Why he'd bothered to ask, he had no clue. It was no surprise that Preston refused to take any responsibility for his actions.

He'd had all he could stomach.

He picked up the envelope and, without saying a single word, stood and walked away, leaving Preston Michael Hayes to foot the bill.

Trent pulled around the driveway's last curve and cursed at the sight waiting for him. A dull glow shone through his living room curtains. Only one person had the know-how and the balls to essentially break into his home and make himself comfortable. The rich playboy had some unique skills. Rick Evans would be sitting in Trent's recliner, drinking Trent's beer and waiting for details on the date.

After all, what were friends for?

He'd happily loan Rick his treasured '69 Camaro anytime the man asked. He'd even take a bullet for him, but he absolutely did not want to suffer through a third degree interrogation about his night with Kate. When had they turned into teenage girls, staying up all night and sharing date stories? Suddenly, the thought of turning around and heading to the closest bar sounded like a damn fine idea. Unfortunately, it would only prolong the inevitable.

Rick Evans took relentless to a new level.

He unlocked the door and disarmed the security system, which seemed asinine considering the man who sat in his favorite chair. Rick had more money than God, but what had he chosen to do with his time? Golf or sail? Travel? Nope. The man's brain never stopped working, so when they'd left the military after Justin's death, he'd spent all his time learning how to become an even better soldier. He'd claimed he'd become a security expert, but that was like naming a tiger Kitty.

Trent believed guilt over Justin's death might have been his friend's biggest motivator. Maybe it was from some subconscious need to always be prepared for the worst possible scenario, but Rick would only deny it and claim it was just his latest hobby.

He swore Rick did it on purpose, just to irritate him.

He shut the door and went straight to the kitchen, ignoring his closest friend as he set his keys on the counter. He retrieved a beer from the fridge, took a drink and returned to the living room. "Can't you afford a hotel room? You have more houses than I have horses. Surely you could find one to stay in when you're in town."

"This place is huge, and I like your TV and recliner. Plus, there's the hassle of checking into a hotel. I'm not interested." A crowd cheered through the TV, drawing Rick's focus.

"You mean, you'd rather check up on your hermit friend and make certain he hasn't started talking to himself yet?" He walked into the living room and pointedly stood next to his chair.

"Well, yeah. That goes without saying. There's pizza, if you're hungry." Rick watched the game and ignored his presence.

"I've already eaten." He'd seen the pizza box on the counter. The smell reminded him of things he wasn't ready to face, at least not in the presence of his friend. He took the remote from the arm of his chair beside Rick, then flipped the channel as he sat on the couch.

"I was watching that." Rick didn't move, not even to turn his head. Trent couldn't tell if the man was exhausted or preoccupied with whatever random project he'd likely taken on.

"I know. Now you're not. So, what's the story? Are we taking the job or not?" Trent took a long drink of beer and put his feet up on the coffee table.

"Haven't decided yet. Tell me how things went with the beauty queen, and I'll tell you what I know about what Todd Hill wants." Rick turned his head and pinned him with his stare, one dark eyebrow arched in question.

"Todd Hill? Sounds familiar, but I can't place the name." He ignored the "beauty queen" comment and attempted to steer the conversation toward a safer subject.

"He's the distant cousin I mentioned. Todd is a real estate agent and the youngest brother of the late Mrs. Marilyn Bailey. What possessed you to finally go on a date?" Unsurprisingly, like a dog with a bone, Rick stayed on what he considered the more interesting topic.

"I accidently bought her and had no choice." He'd catch hell for the story, but Trent had nothing to be ashamed of. He might as well get the entire story out and finish up the interrogation. Then maybe they could get on with business. He'd been up since well before dawn and was exhausted.

Tapping his fingertips on the arm of the chair, Rick grinned. "I know we've skirted the law a few times, but you don't have to resort to prostitution. If you need…uhm…companionship, I can set you up."

He didn't even respond to Rick's dry sarcasm other than to flash him a middle finger and then continue. "It's funny that you mentioned Senator Bailey. I found him standing by in the Mitchell's stables while Kate's ex-husband put his hands on her. The dick squeezed her arm with a white-knuckled grip. I broke things up and sent them on their way. I only caught bits and pieces of their conversation, but what little I heard sounded awfully suspicious. The only thing I was sure about was that Kate wanted nothing to do with either of them. Then, at the Mitchell's charity auction, it became apparent very quickly that Bailey wanted Kate and was willing to pay almost anything for the date. Before I thought better of it, I stepped in at the last minute and placed my own bid. Thankfully, Stephen named me the winner and ended things. Unless I wanted Carol Mitchell's disapproval from now until the end of time, I had to follow through."

"So how much did you pay for this date?"

He coughed the muffled words into his hand. "Ten thousand dollars."

Rick laughed outright at that. "So, that's why you're dressed in a monkey suit. Where did you go?"

"We ate Pop's pizza in my truck bed at the lakeshore."

"You had pizza for dinner in your truck while wearing a tux? You really know how to treat a girl. I bet she swooned right there on the spot, just before the mosquitoes attacked. She's gonna beat down your door for another date." Dripping with dry sarcasm, the big man downed his bottle of water.

"The lake was her idea, and there's not going to be another date."

Steepling his hands and leaning forward, Rick honed in on the interesting tidbit. "Was she that vain or crazy? Clingy?"

"When did you become so jaded? What did your last date do to put your panties in a bunch? Considering the odd circumstances that threw us together, things actually went pretty well. She seemed like a nice enough woman." He had met very few over the years that preferred fishing and horses to a night on the town. Unless she'd picked the lake out of some sense of guilt or as a way to earn points with him? It certainly wouldn't be the first time a woman in heels had feigned interest in horses or the outdoors in order to get close to him. It probably wouldn't be the last. Money and social status caused some people to act in strange ways. Though well cared for, her small farm couldn't be very profitable. It was highly possible that she'd run into financial trouble since she'd left Preston.

Could it be that the beauty queen was tired of cutting her own grass?

"You're not going to go out again?" Rick's dubious expression matched his tone.

Trent shrugged. "Nah. She seemed nice, but I'm not interested. She offered to take me out as a thank you, but I declined and split."

"You mean you tucked your tail and ran?"

"Yep. Still not interested." Even as he said it, part of him knew he lied.

Rick took a deep breath and sat back before he spoke. "Well, that could be seen as a shame or as a bonus depending on your take on things. I figured out how you can help."

Dread snaked in Trent's gut. "Shit."

With a nod, Rick said, "To echo your words, yep. I'm taking Hill's case, and I think there's some benefit to having someone nose around in Kate's world to see if we can find out why Bailey has a sudden interest in her. I want you to get a little closer to her to see if you can dig up anything. I have a guy who owes me a favor or two. I'll have him start the background searches on Kate, Phillip and Marilyn Bailey, Todd and Preston. It's doubtful that everything is connected, but it seems awfully coincidental to me."

Unfortunately, Trent agreed. Phillip Bailey and Preston Hayes stank, of that, his instincts were certain. Whenever Kate MacDonald came onto his radar, the force he always listened to went screwy. Did that mean he'd be going into an unknown world with faulty radar? He sure as hell hoped not.

Rick continued, unaware of his worries. "Why don't you give her a call tomorrow? Tell her you changed your mind, play nice and see if you can get in her good graces. You already have one foot in the door, and she can't be that bad looking. She was a Miss Kentucky, after all."

"Actually, she's one of the most beautiful women I've ever seen." To him, it seemed to be a natural beauty, not the silicone, Barbie doll type.

Clearly not understanding the problem, Rick advised, "So take her out to a fancy dinner, and put it on my tab. That should be a quick way to her heart."

Trent shook his head. "No. I don't think a fancy dinner will do it. I have something else in mind. But if she tries to sink a set of gold-digging claws into me, I'm siccing her on you. I'll show her pictures of your houses and bank account."

"You wouldn't."

Trent finished off his beer and smiled.

She backed her rattling and coughing truck into a parking spot at the feed and general store. In her typical routine, she parked in the spot closest to the loading door. She could carry the supplies herself, but old Mr. Peterman would insist on helping her. She knew he had a bad hip, and she hated to have him carry her order any farther than necessary.

Her father's old truck shuddered and groaned when she turned it off in a rush. She had cold groceries behind her seat and wanted to get back to Bonnie as soon as possible. She knew she'd be fine on her own but finding the barn open the prior night had shaken her. If it hadn't been for the simple fact that she needed food for Pudgy and Bonnie, she wouldn't have left home.

She hopped out, and a strange presence standing across the street under a tree at the diner caught her attention. When she looked again he'd turned his back and put his phone to his ear. She didn't have time to people watch. Brushing the odd sensation of being observed away, she hurried inside. Mr. Peterman would have her order ready, so all she'd have to do would be pay and load.

She pushed open the door and smiled at the silly mechanical "Mooooo" sound. The shopkeeper's grandson rigged the door alarm, and the old timer liked it so much that he'd kept it.

"Have a look around, Katie Marie. I'll be with you in just a moment. My story is almost over. Then I can help you load."

She looked at her watch. *Damn. Five minutes.* Eager to get home, she'd rushed through the grocery store and had arrived too early. He watched his favorite soap opera religiously, and she'd be stuck until it ended.

She wondered through the aisles and heard the mechanical cow announce someone else's arrival. She made it halfway through the store when she turned the corner and almost bumped into someone.

"Kate. What a pleasant surprise. How are you today?" Phillip Bailey stood before her, his business attire out of place. His dark, fervent stare and oily smile sent chills racing through her. What was he doing in the feed store, of all places?

"Hi. I'm doing just fine. You?" She heard the signature music that accompanied the closing credits to the soap opera.

"I'm good. You're looking...well. How are your animals?" He looked down at her old jeans as if they might contaminate him with some imaginary infection spread by only the lower class. Then he pasted on a plastic smile, and she knew smiles. There was something off about his.

"They're good. Uhm...do you have any animals? I mean you're in a feed store, so that must be a silly question. What do you have?"

His pretended embarrassment fell flat, miles away from sincere. "You caught me, my dear. I was across the street and saw you come in here. I wondered if you might do me the honor of dining with me?"

"Ah. No. I'm sorry. I'm flattered, truly, but I can't. Thank you. I need to be going." She walked around him quickly. At the counter, Mr. Peterman stood beaming, his round cheeks bright. All the cheer in the county couldn't banish the feeling of having holes drilled into her back by Bailey's eyes.

"Thank you. I can get this, really." It was their routine. Always she made an attempt at carrying her order out on her own, but he always refused. She'd even taken to buying more of the smaller bags instead of the larger, more economical ones because she didn't want him carrying them. It would take them more trips, but at least she wouldn't worry quite as much.

"Kate, you know my policy." Policy-shmolicy. Every man that came into the store carried their own purchases out. "Besides, your father was my friend. I can't allow you to carry so much. He'd turn over in his grave." Again, that wasn't necessarily true. Her father prided himself on his work ethic and taught her to do the same. He'd be proud to know that she could take care of herself and her animals. But there was no point in arguing. He simply wanted to do what he thought was the right thing.

"I appreciate it. I've got cold groceries waiting on me, and I need to get back to Bonnie." They walked in and out several times, loading the mountain of bags into her truck and talking about her new baby. The entire time, Phillip Bailey stood in the same spot, staring.

She waved Mr. Peterman off and closed the tailgate with a forceful shove. She looked down at the uneven pavement as she walked to her door and dug her keys from her pocket.

"Kate. Or is it Katherine? We'll use Katherine, that's much more fitting. I really need to discuss a few things with you." His too-perfect, too-handsome face beamed at her, but his eyes were just…wrong as he stood beside her truck, blocking her door.

"No. It's just Kate. I'm sorry, but I have to be going. I have animals to care for and groceries to put away before they melt. Another time." *Or not.* Her gut instincts overrode even Aunt Jeannie's lectures on manners.

"That's a shame. You deserve a more refined name, not a nickname." Had he not heard her or was he crazy? She was betting on the latter. And she was done.

"It's not a nickname. It's the name my father gave me, and I like it just fine. I don't know what you're after or what Preston has told you, but I'm not interested. Goodbye."

His smile disappeared as his features hardened. Anger flushed his cheeks.

"Katherine, if you would listen I can get you out of here. This place is beneath us. We were meant for bigger and better things."

"I'll repeat myself one last time, and if you don't listen, I'm calling Joe. He drives a shiny black and white police car and, if I tell him you're harassing me, he won't care who you are. I am not interested. I'm sorry if Preston sold you on some grand scheme. He's good at that. I'm happy here, and I'm not interested. At all. Goodbye." Something in her tone must have got through because his eyes widened and he backed up a step. She snagged the opportunity to open her door and climb in.

Just like it knew she needed a hand, her truck started on the first turn of the key.

What was wrong with him? Would Preston ever quit causing her trouble? If her ice cream became soup by the time she got home, she would not be happy.

Damn it.

The tension in her shoulders didn't ease until she gotten home, checked on Bonnie and basked in the warm sun for a few short moments before unloading.

She'd just put away the last bag when her cell rang.

"So, finally I get a few minutes to ask about your date. How did it go?" Leigh hadn't bothered with a single *hi*, *hello*, or even a *what's up?* in years.

"Okay." Even as she gave the one-word answer, she knew Leigh would want more information.

As expected, Leigh said, "Honey, okay's not going to cut it. I demand details. All the details."

Sighing, Kate brushed her hands off on her jeans with the phone tucked between her shoulder and face. "There's not much to tell. I have to install a new lock on the barn this evening and don't have a lot of time."

"Why does the barn need a new lock?" Both a blessing and a curse, Leigh never missed a thing.

"The door was standing open when Trent and I got back from the lake last night, and it has me worried. I—" The hole she'd fallen into only grew deeper as she spoke. There'd be no escaping Leigh now.

"The lake? I thought you went to the symphony. And what do you mean the door was open? You'd never leave it open and leave. I'm coming over tonight." Her determined tone left no room for argument.

"Leigh," she began.

"I'll be over in about an hour. Get your chores done." Leigh disconnected the phone before Kate could argue.

True to her word, she pulled up just under an hour later as Kate brought in a load of laundry.

She set the basket on the couch and opened the front door while Leigh carried in a couple of large paper bags.

"Did you buy out the store? What do you have in there?"

"After we hung up, it hit me that we haven't had a true girl's night in forever. We're past due for takeout and strawberry wine. We should have done it when you first came home or shortly after, but you weren't in a good place. It's been almost a year since you left that no good loser. It's past time we celebrate."

She had to admit that her cousin's plan was a damn fine one. "Okay. I'm in. So what did you bring? Something smells good."

"Chinese takeout, Myer's double-chocolate brownies and cheap-ass strawberry wine."

Kate opened a cabinet in the kitchen only to have Leigh look at her as if she'd gone crazy. "Don't bother. We can eat out of the cartons and I have a bottle for each of us. It'll be like old times. We can gorge on junk, get drunk, sick and you can tell me all about Mr. Trent Dawson from Bourbon County."

Oh boy. Where should she start? There was so much and so little to tell. She opened the carton that Leigh handed over.

"What did you wear? Something appropriately sexy? I know it was classy. You don't know any other way."

"Sexy and classy? I don't know about that. I wore the black and white sheath and the matching heels."

Leigh spoke around a mouthful of food. "Yes, you, my dear, define the words sexy and classy. It is possible to be both, and you rock it like granny with a newborn."

She turned her head and just missed spraying Leigh when wine erupted from her mouth followed by choking laughter.

"So the wine's that good, huh?" Leigh winked at her.

God, why had she tolerated her ex's bullshit for so long? She'd wasted years of her life.

"The wine is wretched." And it was, the same brand they'd drank before they were legally allowed to purchase it. On her nineteenth birthday, she'd sweet-talked Joe into buying it for them because he'd only laughed in Leigh's face when she'd asked. On one of her rare free weekends, they'd built a bonfire out back, drank and talked boys. She suspected her father knew what they'd been doing, but allowed it. Between college and pageant prep with Aunt Jeanie, she'd been so busy. She took another bite and then washed it down with another swig of the vile stuff.

She loved it.

"So, continue. Is Trent a stud or a dud?" Leigh waved her own bottle, encouraging her to get on with the details as she used the phrase from their years in high school.

"Definitely not a dud. He showed on time, showered and dressed to kill. His suit probably cost more than my old truck is worth." She threw in the showered bit to reference one of Leigh's worst dates.

"So he has at least one more point than Dirty Harry. God, that boy stank. That was the first and last time I let Shirley set me up on a blind date. She married Dirty Harry's brother, you know?"

"No. I didn't. At least one good thing came out of that disaster, then."

Leigh's raised eyebrows let Kate know that she didn't think sitting beside Dirty Harry for a double feature at the drive-in had been worth Shirley's good fortune.

"What kind of rust bucket did he pick you up in?"

"His truck. He said a friend had borrowed his car." Before Leigh could reply with a sarcastic dig, she held up a hand and clarified. "His truck was nearly new, a smart choice for a horse farmer, and mostly clean. And I believed him about the car. I think he's an honest guy. He tolerated me hijacking the date really well."

Leigh's brows went up. "Exactly how did you hijack the date? You couldn't hurt a fly. You didn't use tears, did you? I've done that before. It works, but as expected, is a total buzz kill."

"No." She'd learned her lesson and waited until after Leigh spoke before putting anything in her mouth. When the coast was clear, she fortified herself with another bite and drink, then she finished the tale.

The look on her cousin's face scared her.

"Katie, you do realize that you may have met your perfect match, right?"

"No. Absolutely not." Leigh was totally mistaken.

Snagging her arm, Leigh squeezed it before continuing. "He must have a good heart somewhere beneath the gruff exterior or else he wouldn't have bid on you in the first place."

With a shake of her head, Kate discarded the idea. "Not necessarily true. Senator Phillip Bailey bid on me repeatedly, and something tells me he wasn't doing it because of a kind heart. I saw him today, by the way."

"Trent? Or the senator? Here in BFE, Potter County? I heard through the work grapevine that he's looking to open up an office of some sort here, but something stinks. I'd stay away from him if I were you."

"I plan to. He came into Peterman's to find me. Of all the places, that's the last place I would have expected to see him." Though she could easily picture Trent in a place like Peterman's loading heavy bags of feed into his truck with those broad shoulders of his. "He looked down on me like he might catch a disease from my clothes."

"What's wrong with them?"

"Nothing at all." Kate looked down to her faded jeans and old tee. Yes, they were old, but they were clean and comfortable. She couldn't be expected to feed her animals in pearls and heels, could she?

She was fed up with being looked down on by those from her old life who seemed to think that because she preferred animals to jewelry and cowboy boots to heels that she was beneath them.

"It's your life to do what you want with. I may give you a hard time, but if you don't want to do something, you need to speak up and tell me, or whoever, to stuff it up their asses. If you never want to wear a fancy dress again, then don't."

"You're right." And at the heart of it, Leigh would support her. Kate could cuss her up one side and down the other and her cousin would likely laugh it off or think she'd lost her mind. Likely the latter, but she would always be family.

"What's next on the agenda?" Leigh asked.

"I need to take care of some things. I'll be right back." Deep inside her, a flame of resolve sparked. She may have taken a huge step in leaving her ex, but it had only been the first step in getting her life back. She'd been content to sit idle and tinker around her the farm. Yes, she'd needed some time to heal and get her head straight, but that didn't give her the right to simply float along aimlessly and not participate in life.

Her father wouldn't do such a thing. No matter how big or small, he'd always had a plan or a goal. If he wasn't working at his job or on their little farm, he was often at a neighbor's helping them build something or tear something down.

It was past time she took her life back.

She rose, went to her old bedroom and looked around. She hadn't been in the small space often since she'd moved back. She given it a quick cleaning but then shut the door and left her old life in the dark. She moved the few things she'd brought with her into her father's old room, since it had a small attached bathroom.

Where was it? She knew she had some ages ago. Faded carpet in mixed shades of blue met her feet as she looked around, thinking. Above her bed hung shelves that her father made to display her crowns, but a layer of dust had stolen their sparkle. Posters of her favorite country musicians still covered the walls. Heroes with long hair, tight jeans and guitars looked down from above.

She looked in her old dresser drawer and thumbed through stacks of old faded tees. Several of them bore images of those guitar wielding knights. At the drawer's bottom, she found what she wanted and pocketed the small box, hoping the item still worked.

Her father had left everything exactly the way she'd left it when she'd moved out. She wondered if...of course it was. There on the top shelf sat her old hat. She pulled it down and looked it over.

He'd given it to her for her fifteenth birthday. Mostly cream, with a little chocolate brown around the band and the edges, he said it matched her freckles and she'd better wear it whenever she worked with him outdoors or Aunt Jeannie would skin them both alive.

They'd joked that her aunt counted the sparse scattering of freckles across her cheeks and they'd catch hell if a single extra appeared. She hadn't given one damn about the freckles on her face. She'd wanted to be in their corral with her father and their horses.

She hadn't stood up for herself. And because she hadn't spoken up, she'd lost years with her father and she'd spent those years in misery with Preston. Yes, he'd been an utter ass, but she'd accepted it.

No more.

It was past time that she took control of her life and did what she wanted.

She put her hat on, gathered a few things from her other room and headed out to the old fire pit.

Leigh watched as Kate came back down the hallway with clothing in her arms. She grabbed her wine bottle and looked over.

"Are you coming or not?" She turned on her booted heel and headed out back without another word.

Leigh followed but was afraid to hope. She'd worried over her sweet and far too giving cousin for so long.

She stepped out into the dark back yard just in time to see Kate fight with a match and smile when the flame caught. The smile warmed Leigh's heart. Equal parts steel and fire, it matched the flames that flickered in her cousin's eyes. Her face blushed with heat and her jaw set with determination. Tendril's of the gorgeous hair she'd always envied waved in the breeze.

And that hat. She'd always loved that hat on Kate. Silly as it might sound, it looked as if it had been made for her. She was the picture of a strong, beautiful farmer ready to kick ass.

Hot damn. Katie Marie MacDonald was back. A wicked smile spread across Leigh's face. It was about time.

"What are you doing, chick?" The pitch-black night hung in a heavy backdrop studded with rhinestone stars.

Kate took another drink of her wine, set the bottle down and picked up a piece of clothing. *What in the world?* Had she been wrong? Had Kate cracked?

"I'm pretty sure this dress is ruined anyway, but it's going in the fire." She held up the dress she'd worn yesterday and, sure enough, it had grass stains where the knees would have been.

"You could at least try and have it cleaned. Albert, the new owner at the dry cleaners is a miracle worker."

Her cousin threw the dress into the flames without blinking. "I actually liked that one but Preston always gave me the look when I wore it. I think it wasn't revealing enough for his taste. Too many bad memories." She held up another dress, blood red and clearly made from far less material. "He picked this one out for me, and I hated it. I felt like was auditioning for a 90's music video and I would be expected to dance on the hood of a car at any moment." Into the fire it went with a puff of sparks.

"I've wasted far too much of my life trying to make others happy. It's fine to give, but I didn't have to give them every single piece of myself, did I?"

Not sure if she should answer or not, Leigh waited. When Kate looked at her from across the fire with those eyes of strength expecting an answer, she gave it.

"No, you didn't. You've always tried so hard to be the good girl."

"What did it get me? Years of heartache. I'm done. I just want to be me."

"Then be you. I'll stand by your side and cheer you on."

"I know you will, and I can't tell you how much that means to me."

Leigh did the only thing she could. She walked around to hug her cousin close. "Now. No more sappiness. I like the fired-up, ready to kickass Kate, better."

"Me too."

Chapter Six

"I'm getting another coffee? You want one?" Rick pointed a thumb at the next booth in the county outdoor market.

"You've had three this morning. Your heart's going to burst if you have another espresso." Trent shook his head in disbelief at Rick's caffeine consumption and scanned the weekend crowd.

"I didn't ask your permission. I asked if you wanted one." Rick stopped at the window and placed his order.

"No. I'm good." Rick had called him late the prior night and talked Trent into coming along to Riley Creek. They'd been following Bailey for about thirty minutes. Todd Hill had called to let Rick know that the Senator was looking at office property in the area. They couldn't tell if the grieving brother was onto something real or grasping at straws. Trent agreed that it seemed odd that an up and coming politician who had more money than God would have such a marked interest in a little known dot on the map.

They'd worried that following Bailey through the crowd unnoticed would be difficult, but it hadn't taken them long to see differently. He appeared to have a specific destination in mind and when a small toddler wondered away from his grandfather, Bailey almost tripped over the poor little guy. He barely spared the little boy or the apologetic grandfather a glance as he continued on his path.

What was Bailey after?

"Nice to see the good Senator is such a caring man, huh?" Rick appeared at his side full of dry sarcasm and coffee. "Let's go see what's got him by the balls. Something has, that's for sure."

They followed him past the tables filled with old electronics and DVDs. Another makeshift booth had used books, yet another offered baby items.

"Any news from your new tech guy?" Trent thumbed through a crate of used DVD's and watched Bailey from the corner of his eye. When the senator rounded the corner, they followed.

"So far all I've gotten from him is a bunch of grumbling and promises that if there's dirt, he'll find it." Rick shielded his eyes as they turned the corner booth filled with colorful quilts.

He arched a brow at Rick's unusual tolerance of a delay. Typically, when the man wanted something, he demanded perfection and he expected it yesterday.

"There's a story there, but it's a long one. He's worth it." When Rick wouldn't meet his eyes, Trent decided to let it go for the time being.

He immediately regretted his kindness when Rick brought up his least favorite subject. "So, I bumped into Lindsey the other day." Rick paused to let his words sink in. "She asked about you."

"I bet she did. Did her latest mark run out of money?" Her money hungry ways had always disgusted Trent.

"Ah. I think this one died before she managed to get his ring on her finger." Rick's amused grin made him wonder if living in the upper echelons of society made Rick more accustomed to gold diggers.

He wished he could laugh at the story like many people would; instead, it made him nauseous with revulsion.

He would never understand how having mountains of money to spend on things, which would only be deemed "last year" a few months after you bought them, could be so important. Was an expensive house or designer jeans so necessary that a person would scheme and even stalk others for a chance to climb the social ladder?

When he didn't say more, Rick asked, "Aren't you going to ask what she said?"

"No. I don't want to know. If I never hear her name for the rest of my life, it will be too soon." Trent's revulsion ran deep, rooted in bad memories.

"Well, I won't go into the conversation we had, but I will warn you she's on the prowl. I wouldn't be surprised if she accidently bumped into you soon." Rick browsed through a selection of used lawn equipment while they waited for Bailey to decide which direction to turn at the row's end.

"Why me? I don't get it? The only thing I have that she wants is money. I don't have expensive taste, and I'm no pushover. Batting eyelashes have zero effect on me."

"Even money hungry sharks have a libido. She looks really good, as you know. Do you think it's possible that she grew up? We were all really young, man." Rick put down a shovel and turned to follow their prey.

He shuddered at the thought. "I'm not interested, even if she somehow miraculously grew up." He would never, ever forget the devastation on Justin's face as he lay in the hospital bed. Lindsey tossed out a few careless words and incinerated what little bit of remaining fight his friend had after he'd been brought home. In a few seconds, he'd gone from a wounded but determined to live soldier to a devastated ghost of a man.

He would never, ever have room in his life for a social climbing princess, no matter how beautiful she might be.

They came to the market's end where the local produce store had been set up—row after row of tables filled with handmade crafts, cherries and strawberries.

He stopped, cursed and pulled Rick's hat from his head and put it on his own.

"Hey thief, I need that. Get your own hat."

"That's Kate, you idiot. I'll stay back here and watch. You go on." Trent ducked his and turned back to them.

"Where?" Instantly, Rick became alert and all business. Rick craned his neck in the direction he indicated with a discreet head nod.

"The booth at the far end."

Sure enough, Bailey made his way directly to Kate. Her faded green pickup was backed up to a popup awning and table. Trent stopped at the last flea market table and feigned looking at some used hunting gear to watch from his periphery.

"That's your beauty queen? Helloooo, Miss Kentucky. She's hot as hell, but I don't see her as a simpering princess." Rick's brow's rose in disbelief.

Dressed in a snug, green T-shirt and a pair of faded jeans, she smiled at a young woman who'd walked up to her stall. Kate held her index finger up in a "one moment" gesture and turned her back on her customer. She was gone for a minute beneath the shade of her canopy before she returned carrying a large, low-edged box that held containers of strawberries. The box had to weigh at least twenty pounds, yet she smiled and acted as if it were something she did every day. Her arms looked toned as she bent to set the box down and positioned it on her table. She repeated the process with another box, just as big, this time filled with what looked like jelly jars, which had to be even heavier.

The young woman made her selections and paid. Kate made change, looked up and froze, shocked to see Phillip Bailey standing in line as her next customer.

She smiled again as she handed over the young woman's change, but her smile seemed forced.

Trent wanted nothing more than to go to her and put himself between her and Bailey, but he knew it would be unwise. "Go over there and see if you can hear anything. I don't like this at all."

"Man, I can't get too close. It's possible that he'll recognize me." Rick rubbed a hand over his jaw and watched Bailey.

"She will definitely recognize me and she'll either figure out that something is up or she'll think I'm stalking her. She'd never buy that me showing again to interfere with Bailey's appearance is a coincidence. Trent clenched his fists in frustration.

"Go, before I make an ass of myself." Shit, with that one sentence he'd revealed to both himself and Rick what a mess his head was over this woman.

Shockingly, Rick didn't argue, heading over to intercept.

There was something about watching her sweat in the sun, selling berries and jam for what probably wasn't more than a few dollars, that tugged at something in his chest.

He'd assumed she worked in the mall or in some fancy dress shop when she'd mentioned her sales being better on the weekend. Yet she smiled like she genuinely enjoyed herself as she worked for pennies.

Maybe she wasn't as stuck up as he'd thought.

"It's our anniversary tomorrow. I think I'm going to make chocolate covered strawberries for Jim and take the blackberry jam to my mom. It's her favorite, but she's not able to make her own anymore." Jan's smile was sad as she paid Kate for the berries and put them carefully into her large tote.

"Yum. It's been forever since I've had a good chocolate strawberry. You'll have to tell me how your mom likes the jam. I'm just getting started this year, but I hope to add a few new flavors soon." In fact, she needed to track down her mother's old cookbook and look through it. It had been years since she'd seen it, but she knew her father wouldn't have parted with it. Kate's jam was pretty damn good, but everyone swore her mother's had been the best.

"I will. I'll let you know when I come back next weekend."

Kate smiled as she counted out Jan's change but when she looked up, she felt the smile fall from her face. *What was Senator Bailey doing here?* First the auction, then the feed store and now the farmer's market? What did he want with her?

She waved Jan off and, in a habit that had been all but beat into her by Aunt Jeannie, she smiled again. "Senator? How are you today?"

"Good, very good, Katherine. How are you?" Sweat beaded on Bailey's upper lip as he smiled a slightly crooked, plastic smile.

"I'm fine, what brings you to Riley Creek again?" She placed emphasis on the word *again*, though he didn't seem to catch her point.

"I'm looking into buying or renting property here and setting up an office or two. I stopped by to see if you had reconsidered my offer from the other day."

"Offer?"

"To go out to dinner. We have things to discuss." He started as if baffled by her response, looking at her like she was a dimwit.

Her basic unhappiness and confusion swelled and grew into concern. "I'm not sure what you have in mind, but I'm not looking for any kind of relationship right now. My life is in flux but I'm happy where I'm at. I'm flattered but not interested."

"My dear—"

A large man in a baseball hat, camouflage jacket and matching backpack jostled Bailey, nearly knocking him over. She caught a flash of dark blond hair at the man's collar. The temperature had to be at least eighty degrees in the midday sun. Before she could give the odd clothing choices any more thought, a second man drew her attention with his silly smile.

"Hello, there. You have the most beautiful berries I have ever seen. May I have a taste?"

What? What kind of cheesy pickup line was that? Tall, leanly muscled with coal black hair, he'd stop traffic.

"Sure." Long used to politely thwarting advances, she picked an enormous strawberry and stuck the entire thing in his mouth. She was more interested in catching another glimpse of the man with the backpack than whether or not he actually liked it or if Bailey stuck around to finish his sentence.

"My dear, we need to—" Bailey attempted to enter the conversation, but couldn't keep up.

"So, gorgeous..." The new guy, with his dark hair and mirrored glasses finished choking on the berry and again interrupted Bailey. "That's definitely the best berry I've ever tasted. How much?"

Annoyed that the man in the hat had disappeared, she pointed to the old chalkboard where she'd written her prices.

"Katherine, we'll talk again." Bailey left in a huff, apparently giving up at the continued interruptions.

She proceeded to sell a ton of berries and six jars of jam to the guy in the glasses. She wasn't above taking advantage of a man's lust-addled senses when it came to business.

Unable to shake the image from her mind, she kept watch for the rest of the day for the man she'd seen in the heavy coat, but he'd disappeared.

A few hours later, back at home, she'd just finished unloading her little bit of unsold stock when Pudgy's tail wagged and his ears twitched. His telltale signal alerted her to someone coming up the driveway. She looked out the window and saw a black Mercedes crawling up the gravel lane. *Preston.* He'd be terrified his precious vehicle might not only get dirty, but somehow infected by the "white trash world she lived in."

Crap. She'd had a good day and hated to have it tainted by his general assholishness.

What did he want now?

She walked out the door, crossed the yard and waited at the driveway's edge. She wanted to tell him that no matter what he did, the gravel dust would coat his car but he'd only turn his nose down at her. It was the only thing he'd ever done. No matter how perfect she'd tried to be, he'd always found her lacking.

There was not a damn thing wrong with her. After years of marriage to a man who drilled insecurity into her psyche, the hard won truth finally settled into place. Her only regret was that it took her so long to figure it out.

He parked and opened his door. He probably expected her to come around to the driver side, so he wouldn't have to get out.

He'd be wrong again.

After a pause, he stepped out as if she'd burdened him. The golden boy walked around his car, watching the yard as if it were covered in land mines of the canine variety. The sun glinted in his salon-highlighted hair and his suit was immaculate, as always. No matter how perfect the image he created might be, his appeal to her had long since died.

"What do you want? Whatever it is, I can tell you now, you've wasted your time and gas coming out here." She put her hands on her hips and let her disgust fly. She didn't have to take his shit any longer.

"Potter County is a pretty enough place. It's no hardship to drive out here." The derision on his pretty boy face belied his words.

"Cut the crap, Preston. You've never in your life been interested in scenic drives. Tell me what you want, so I can say no and then you can be on your way. I have animals to feed." She could see him fighting to contain the curl of disgust at her mention of animals.

"Kate." She absolutely hated the patronizing tone he so frequently used and today was no exception. "I came all the way out here to offer you an opportunity that any woman would be thrilled to receive. The least you could do is act civil."

She didn't bother wasting her breath with a verbal response. She crossed her arms and waited for whatever "favor" he was trying to con her into.

His gusty sigh proved she wearied him with her lack of enthusiasm, a bid for pity she wasn't willing to acknowledge. "I swear, Kate, I don't know why I even bother. I'm starting a new charity, and I think it would be a good fit for you. It would give you something productive to do. I worry about you wasting yourself out here with nothing but a bunch of animals to talk to."

"What kind of charity are you planning, exactly?" Whatever it was, she knew the reason behind it would be either publicity or monetary reasons. He didn't have a generous bone in his body.

His long, silent pause told her all she needed to know. "You haven't even decided, have you?"

He surveyed her property and stopped on Pudgy, who sat by her feet. When he directed his focus back to her with a calculating look, she braced for trouble. "We're putting together an animal rescue. We think you'd be perfect to head it."

Damn him! He'd chosen his words specifically to draw her in, but no matter how hard he tugged on her heartstrings, she wasn't falling for it. That path lay filled with frustration and heartache. "I'm not interested."

She turned her back on him and prayed he took the hint and left. The last thing she wanted was to get tangled up in anything that had his fingerprint on it.

And, you know what? She could start her own animal rescue. She and Leigh had joked about it, but why the hell not? She waited inside, watching, as Preston awkwardly turned his car around and left. Then, with the spark of righteous determination glowing bright, she made a phone call.

"Hey, chickie. What are you up to?" Leigh answered immediately.

"I just packed up my leftovers from the farmer's market. Business slowed down a little early today, so I headed home a bit earlier than usual." She tucked the phone between her ear and shoulder then pulled her stockpot out of the cabinet.

"How did you do today?" Her cousin's genuine interest never failed to warm Kate's heart.

"Pretty damn good, actually. Things were looking kinda slow until some sucker in sunglasses came by and hit on me. I conned him into buying thirty dollars' worth of jam and strawberries." She smiled as she waited for the large pot to fill with water.

"Way to go, cuz." She suspected Leigh's excitement had more to do with her fleecing the man who'd hit on her than the few dollars she's earned at the market.

"There was only one problem. Phillip Bailey showed up again." After she retrieved her bucket of blackberries from the fridge, she began to wash them at the sink.

"That's creepy." Revulsion rang clear in Leigh's voice.

"Definitely. He stayed until the guy in sunglasses appeared, then he left."

"What else happened? I can hear it in your voice." Leigh's tone softened in concern.

"Preston just left. He tried to con me into heading up a charity that, according to Preston, he's starting with Bailey. I told him no, but I think it's odd that they both showed up on the same day." She'd be a fool if she didn't suspect they were up to something. Did they think her name or title could benefit some scam of theirs? How? Her days in the spotlight were long gone.

"It is. Have you talked to Joe?" Leigh might poke at her brother on a daily basis, but when it came down to it, there was no one more trustworthy than Joe.

"It's a little weird, but I don't think it's anything dangerous. I won't bother him over ex-husband drama. He's too busy." Her cousin was the busiest man she knew, but then again, he was a MacDonald.

"You know he won't mind." As his sister, Leigh didn't think twice to add more to his list of responsibilities, but Kate couldn't make herself bother him over something that only annoyed her.

"I do. He'd want me to call, but with work, his farm and Kylie, he's running himself into the ground." She pulled a bag of sugar from the cupboard and set it on the counter.

"What are you going to do?"

"Feed my animals, shower, treat myself to a candy bar and a put my feet up while I research animal rescues. I know we mentioned it in passing when you brought me Bonnie, but I think I'm serious.

I've got plenty of space. I've wanted to do something productive with it since I came home. It feels right." She might not be willing to let Preston or Bailey use her name, but she damn well would. It belonged to her after all.

Chapter Seven

She lugged her dad's old ladder out of the storage shed and carried it across the yard. Why had the shutter come loose in last night's quick and angry storm? The constant banging against the outside wall kept her awake most of the night.

She'd rather spend the entire day cleaning out the barn than climb up to the second story for two minutes. She'd never been fond of heights but, unless she asked someone else for help, the chore was hers.

The sun slid down the sky toward late evening and she wanted a quiet night's rest. With another storm rolling in, strong winds were predicted for another night. The barn door incident from a few days ago only added to her unease, so she didn't need another night of rattling and banging on top of it.

She set the ladder just to the left of the shutter and tied her long hair into a ponytail. With a screwdriver in one pocket and a hammer in her belt loop, she climbed and kept her feet to the rungs' outer edges. She'd always teased her dad that the ancient wood would break under his large frame, but it had always held strong. Plus, it was the only thing she had tall enough to reach the window level.

She hoped she could fix the damn thing but would settle for removing it completely and asking Joe to come out and hang it later. He'd only give her a small amount of grief for her fear of heights.

She slowly climbed higher and cautiously reached up, knowing that she hadn't climbed high enough but hopeful there'd be some sort of miracle. With one arm fully extended, she still had at least a foot and a half to go. She raised her left foot and lightly placed it on the next rung. She eased her weight onto it and then raised the other at a shaky snail's pace to the next highest rung. She repeated the procedure, testing the ladder's will to hold her aloft with her foot on the rung. When it held the majority of her weight without too much complaint, she raised the lower foot and set it beside the other.

She took a deep breath, braced herself the best she could and reached for the shutter. A strong gust of wind caught it and blew it away from her with a loud thwack. When her hand fell about ten inches shy she wanted to bang her head against the wall. She pulled her hammer from where she'd hooked it and repositioned her feet. She leaned out farther and reached out with the handle hoping to use the claw to pull it to her.

A loud crack split the air and she fell while the world spun in a dizzying whirl. She braced, holding her breath.

With dark, angry clouds on his tail, Trent pulled his truck into the MacDonald driveway. The humidity had been high for days, but in Kentucky, the resulting storm could last hours or minutes. Turning off the truck, he heard nearby music. He stepped out, glanced at the house and paused.

What in the world was she doing up there? Her height on the ladder gave him a prime view of her ass in a faded pair of jeans that looked soft enough to wrap a baby in. And, heaven help him, just below her left cheek was a frayed tear a few inches wide. She stepped up with her left leg and the tear gaped wider. The peach blush of her skin taunted him through the hanging threads as he got closer.

Damn it all. The ancient, wooden ladder had to be older than he was. Suddenly, he wanted her down from there. Yesterday.

She stood on the third step from the top of the ladder and leaned over toward the window with a hammer in one hand outstretched to hook the shutter's corner. His stifled his need to yell at her to get down. One, he didn't want to startle her. Two, he doubted she'd hear him over the radio blasting a loud, old honky-tonk song he knew well.

A loud crack sounded, the step splintered beneath her feet and she fell through the air.

Without thought, he dove for her.

They landed with a jolting thud against the grass. His head hit the ground, making him see stars. If the fall hadn't knocked enough air out of his lungs, the slight weight of Kate's body landing atop his abdomen finished the job. Tight and hollow, his chest burned with the emptiness. A sharp, stabbing pain struck in his upper chest.

When his deep draw of breath pulled in the faint scent of peaches and woman, the pain almost seemed worth it. He couldn't understand how someone so small made contact with so much of his body. Tied up in a tangle of arms and legs, with her on top, they put the old kids' twister game to shame, with his one hand on the back of her thigh, the other on her waist. One of hers was around his bicep and the other caught between their lower bodies. He had no idea where his legs began and hers ended.

Somehow, his hand had found its way to the back of her thigh, the very same one with the rip. The hole felt a good deal wider than when he'd seen it. Though he couldn't see it, he felt the silk of her thigh beneath his fingers.

"Hi." Kate lifted her forehead from his chest to give him a shy smile. She was plastered tight against him, filling him with her scent and blanketing him in the sexiest sort of heat. His brain had been lulled into stupidity while his body came alive, raring to take what it wanted.

He forced his fingers to stop the slow sweeps it made over her skin and focused on their situation. When he thought of what could have happened if he hadn't shown when he had, his temper flared hot and bright. "Hi. Question. What the hell were you doing? Do you have a death wish? You could have been killed. Don't you know better?"

"Excuse me? I was doing just fine on my own, so you can just go on and get out of here. I don't need your help." She'd gone from sweet to defensive in a flash of anger.

"Don't need my help? Honey, you almost got yourself hurt, badly. That doesn't look like someone who knows what they're doing to me." Asking for patience, he laid his head on the ground and took a deep breath, then another. He might never get the memory of her falling out of his head.

"Let me up. Now." Her jaw barely moved as she spoke through gritted teeth. She tried to move her leg making the skin beneath his fingers move.

He couldn't stop his grin. "Sweetheart, you're on top of me."

"Your fat leg is on top of my ankle. I'm stuck." She smiled serenely, but damn, she was pissed.

Had he hurt her? He'd tried not to, but the only other option was to let her fall, and he couldn't do that.

He tried to feel around to ensure it wasn't broken, but didn't know where to start. "Which leg? How badly are you hurt?"

"My left knee and ankle are trapped under your right leg." She spoke to him as if he was an idiot. Maybe he was? Why had he let Rick talk him into coming out here again?

She pulled her arm free and raised her chest a few inches off his.

When the fire of her bright eyes met his and two of his fingers swept over her thigh again he had no idea what she was talking about.

"How do we untangle the human pretzel we've made and get up? My ankle seems to be trapped under you knee. It hurts a little." She repeated herself slowly and reminded him that he was being a dumbass.

Shit.

He'd yelled at her, mooned over her pretty eyes and snuck a sample of the silken skin just below her ass and she was hurting. He was an asshole.

He raised his right leg giving her room to move her foot. She'd been laying low on his thighs and the shift in position tipped her forward to fall, returning flat against his chest with a quiet whimper. She shifted and both her legs were spread wide over his pelvis and lay just outside his. And he'd only moved his fingers farther into the rip of her jeans as he'd attempted to steady her.

Damn. Was that the bottom edge of her underwear at the tip of his fingers? It had to be. His finger slid up beneath the elastic feeling the supple under curve of her ass. His palm tightened on her upper thigh, squeezed.

A hot, soft, wet dream lay sprawled atop him. A perfect match for his, her smaller, softer body stirred his baser instincts. Desire surged to life.

"Are you okay?" Her voice registered, but her words didn't make sense to his lust-addled brain.

"Yeah. Why wouldn't I be?" Not even thinking of why he shouldn't be there stopped him from realizing he couldn't think of a better place to be than underneath Kate.

"Because I just did my best impersonation of an anvil falling on a coyote when I landed on you. What about your ribs? Are you sure you're okay?" Her soft fingertips began a careful and teasing exploration of his ribs, leaving him gritting his teeth at the added sexual provocation.

"I am. Let's get you up and check your ankle. Does anything else hurt?" He still had his hand in her pants and couldn't seem to make it move away like a gentleman's hand should. And he couldn't make himself care.

At least until she moved her leg and released a soft hiss of pain.

His hand regained its manners and retreated to the curve of her hip. Taking her waist, he lifted and gently turned until they were side-by-side. Shifting, he sat near her feet and pulled them into his lap.

Thunder rumbled and a cool, damp breeze blew the scent of rain across his face. "Change of plans. Let's get you inside." He stood, helped her to her feet, then scooped her up against his chest just as the first drops of rain fell. Thunder cracked announcing the quick arrival of a vicious summer storm.

"Trent! I can walk... I think." Her fingers gripped his shoulders as he ran to the porch. "Put me down."

"This is becoming a habit, beauty." He opened the front door and set her on the couch. "Do not move."

"I'm fine, you don't need to—"

"Hush. Let me take a look." He sat beside her and put her feet on his lap. Comparing the two, he saw that her left ankle was noticeably larger than the right. He ran his hand over it and watched her carefully. Other than a small wince, she handled it well.

"I promise, it's okay. It's sore, throbs a little, but I really don't think it's broken. I'll ice it and be fine."

He stifled the urge to argue and let her feet go. He wasn't her keeper, and she didn't need him to take care of her. She'd told him as much. But he couldn't leave her like this. He went to the kitchen and looked through her freezer. It was older than dirt, but everything was neatly arranged inside. He pulled a bag of peas out and returned to Kate.

"Put these on there and stay put. I'll be right back."

"Wait. Trent, let me look at your shoulder." He made sure she did as told, ignored her concern and then headed out to the porch. As soon as he'd shut the door, he pulled out his phone and called Rick.

The crack he'd heard as she'd fallen had been a lot louder than he would have expected from splitting wood. And it hadn't echoed like thunder.

It was just as well that Trent insisted she stay on the couch. If the shaking of her hands was any indication of how her legs would function, she'd be another heap on the ground if she attempted to stand.

But the stubborn, frustrating man had ignored her concern. He was bleeding. His dark gray tee had a rip in the shoulder.

She must have hit him with the hammer or screwdriver when she fell. They were probably lost in the yard now, and she'd have to find them before she cut grass the next time. She put her trembling hand to her forehead and sighed. Either or both of them could have been hurt so much worse. If Trent hadn't arrived when he had, she would've had a whole lot more than a swollen ankle to worry about.

God, she'd known better, but this was her farm now, her responsibility. And, yes, she had people she could call on, but it had seemed silly to ask Joe to drive all the way out there for a chore that would have likely taken him all of ten minutes.

Still, she'd almost hurt herself badly and hurt Trent when he'd only been trying to help. Again she told herself that her upset nerves were a result of the fall and had absolutely nothing to do with the way Trent's hands burned against her in a most delicious way.

She might never forget the feel of his fingers rubbing over the back of her thigh when they'd unerringly found their way into her jeans. She didn't know whether to trash her old favorites or preserve and frame them. Even now, the sweet heat of his touch lingered, a reminder of the firm grip he'd had on her flesh.

Of course, his grip had only been a happy byproduct of his catching her midair and had nothing to do with any feelings or desire for her. And that was fine. She had no need for a relationship—not even with a man who smelled like sin, behaved like a southern gentleman but looked like a cowboy and cared more for horses than people.

Nope. No interest at all.

But no matter how chaotic her feelings were, she owed it to him to at least make sure he was okay. She stood, tested her ankle for pain and decided she'd had far worse injuries. Looking out the window, she saw him talking on his phone.

She'd thought he'd been mad at her when she'd fallen on him?

His anger then had been a low simmer compared to the tight, tense fury she saw in his face as he told whoever was on the other end of the phone to "hurry the fuck up." She might not have been able to hear his words, but she read his lips clearly.

Deciding against interrupting his call, she settled for gathering a few first aid supplies and setting them on the counter beside the sink. When he didn't come back inside, she went to the window again. Then she opened the door and hurried out to the porch.

"What are you doing?"

"I want to look at something before it gets any darker." The stark anger in his face scared her. Not knowing how, she knew it wasn't directed at her, but something wasn't right. She followed him down to the yard.

Without hesitation he walked straight to the fallen ladder and righted it.

"You can't use that ladder! If it couldn't hold me, how do you expect it to hold you?"

"I'll be quick and then I'll explain. Bear with me."

She watched with her heart in her throat as he set the ladder up in the exact same place she'd had it. He looked up above with a dark expression as the rain dampened his hair and clothes. The gray cotton of his shirt clung to every ripple and ridge of muscle. The faded denim molded thick, muscled thighs.

"Honey, as old as it looks, the ladder is sound. It's strong. I'll be quick."

She watched with her heart in her throat as he climbed. It wasn't enough that he climbed an old, rickety ladder and weighed a good deal more than she did, he had to do it in the slick rain. She held her breath while he carefully climbed. With each step he took, her chest felt tighter. He stopped when his head was level with the busted rung. Instead of focusing on the ladder, he stared at her wall and then poked a finger at it. Then he pulled his phone from his back pocket and took a picture of the spot he'd poked.

"Are you aware of any damage to the siding on this wall?"

"No. Not unless the shutter did something while blowing in the wind."

"I don't think so. This spot is too low for that."

"As far as I know, everything was in good shape when we painted the house last fall. All we had to do was clean and paint. Joe and Leigh helped and they would have told me if they'd seen anything odd."

He quickly climbed down, grabbed her hand, frowned as if he just realized she was walking on her ankle and pulled her to the door. "Come on. We need to stay out of view."

"Trent, what's going on?" This was not the quiet, easygoing guy who she'd met at the barbeque or shared pizza with at the lake.

This man was all stone-cold, serious soldier. Hyper-alert gray eyes glinted in the dusk and surveyed her farm and beyond. When his focus returned to her, no less serious, her heart caught in her throat.

He took her face in his hands and met her eye-to-eye. "There's nothing wrong with the ladder. Someone shot the rung out from beneath you. I don't know if was intentional or on accident but, unfortunately, I'm betting on the first. Accidents like that are far too rare."

She shook her head in disbelief. "What? Shoot at me? As in tried to kill me? No. This is Nowheresville, USA. Out here in the county everyone has guns and learns to shoot before they learn to drive. It was probably a freak accident. How can you be certain that it was a gunshot?"

The grim lines of his face didn't change. "There's a bullet hole in your wall at almost exactly the same height as the busted rung. I'm betting there's a bullet imbedded in your wall. That's not a believable coincidence." He tugged at her again.

With the late evening light fading fast, she followed him inside. A sinking feeling warned that her world was about to change again. He shut the door and her curtains. Then he faced her with worry in his eyes. "Are you okay?"

Her hands shook, but she said, "I'm fine. I'm still processing everything you've said and don't know what to think, but I'll be fine. I need to look at your shoulder and see what kind of damage I did."

His baffled expression would've amused her under other circumstances. "My shoulder? You're the one who's hurt. You should have your feet up."

"My ankle is fine. Trust me, I've had my fair share of sprained ankles over the years and this is nothing. But, you need to take off your shirt and let me look." She pointed at his shoulder.

He ran his hand over it and seemed surprised to see blood on his palm.

"It will only take a minute. Who did you call?" She gestured to the counter where she'd set everything. He stripped off his wet shirt and hung it on her barstool. When he walked over, all bare muscles and brawn, she fought to remember her plan.

"Fine, but if you insist on seeing to me, then you do it from here." He put his big hands on her waist and set her on the counter then he stepped in between her legs.

"If you're so worried, I can stand on one foot while I patch you up. This is not necessary." *Not to mention too tempting, by far.*

"I'm sure you can, but I won't have you hurting while you're taking care of me." He swallowed, and she watched the tight muscles in his throat work. As if he didn't know where else to put them, he settled his hands at her waist.

"So, princess, how many sprained ankles did you have over the years?" His low tone didn't hold a single trace of scorn or sarcasm, but she couldn't help but bristle over his use of the title princess.

"I lost count. Between at least eight years of cheerleading and gymnastics? Several. You don't know the meaning of pain until you have to complete a dance routine in front of judges on a bad ankle with perfection and grace. To top it off, you can't forget to smile. Ever. The smile is everything. No matter who's talking trash behind your back, stealing pieces of your routine or how badly you're hurting, the pageant must go on." She met his eyes with steel of her own for a brief moment and then got to work.

Picking up the wet washcloth, she carefully wiped the blood from his upper pectoral muscle. She'd revealed a shallow gash not much more than a couple of inches long. Dabbing some antibacterial ointment on it, she met his eyes again.

"Thank you." He really had saved her ass, and they'd both lost their tempers, likely due to the adrenaline rush and fear.

"No reason to thank me for doing the right thing."

The air grew thick and hot as she focused on the wound in his upper chest. "But you were hurt because of me. Thank you. I don't know why you came when you did, but I appreciate it. I probably shouldn't have climbed up there alone, but I couldn't stand the thought of listening to the shutter beat my house to death another night. I haven't slept well since we found the barn door open and the noise last night only made it worse."

When she mentioned the barn door, his eyes darkened as if an ugly thought occurred to him. "Patch me up quick, Kate. We need to get moving." He pressed a quick kiss to her forehead. His jaw tensed with impatience as he waited.

"Are you going to tell me what has you so upset? Or am I supposed to simply follow like the good little girl?" She couldn't help but feel irritated by being left in the dark.

"All right, I know this is asking a lot, but you have to trust me. I need you to pack enough clothes and items for at least a few days. You're going back with me." He paused to get her attention, his stony gaze bored into hers, all too serious.

"What? Why? I can take care of myself." She covered the wound with gauze and tape.

"I don't doubt that you can, but you're not staying here alone. We're going back to my place." He gave a small shake of his head and touched her cheek.

"Trent, I'm sorry, but I won't leave my animals. I refuse and, short of literally tying me up, you won't get me off my farm without them."

"They're coming with us." There was no anger and only pure determination in his tone.

"What about Bonnie? I don't have a trailer, I'll have to call Joe and it's too late for him to find a sitter for his daughter." She couldn't believe he expected her to pack up and blindly follow his lead.

"I have a friend bringing a trailer. I have everything your animals could need at my place and it's safe. I'm not budging. I don't want to, but I will make you if I have to. No lie."

She looked at the firm line of resolve in his jaw and ran her hands over her hair. She believed him. She pulled out her hair tie and fixed her ponytail and looked at him again. His eyes met her in a battle of wills.

He sighed, leaned in and tucked her under his chin. "Kate. There is a bullet hole in your wall. Someone shot at you. Someone broke into your barn."

Putting her hands on his muscled shoulders, she looked up into his eyes. The solid strength beneath her palms and steady gray gaze anchored her. "Aren't you overacting?"

"When a person's life is in danger, there is no such thing as being too careful." Subtle vibrations from his deep voice rumbled through her in reassuring waves.

"Are you certain? Why? How?"

"I know this is asking a lot of you, but just know I'm certain. The why, I don't know yet, but plan to find out. I can't say for sure if this was an accident or intentional, but I'm not taking any chances. I promise to tell you more the moment I know you're safe, but my gut is telling me we need to get out of here." His face softened as he fingered a lock of her hair and tucked it behind her ear.

What should she do? Believe that her string of bad luck was just that or trust someone who cared more about his horses than he did anyone else?

"Okay. I'll go with you." It was a quiet acceptance, but she gave it.

"Good. Let's get you packed, and I'll explain what little I know on the way to my place. I'm going out to my truck for a minute and I'll be right back." He squeezed her waist once before turning away. He wasn't acting like someone who was happy he'd gotten his way. He acted like someone who was hip-deep in a mess.

Somehow oddly reassured by his lack of enthusiasm, she eased off the counter and tested her ankle for pain. The dull throb pounded with each step, but she hadn't lied when she said she'd had far worse injuries. Thankful neither one of them had been seriously hurt, she packed for herself.

Not truly caring whether her clothes matched or not, she threw jeans, tees and underwear into a large duffle bag. She threw in a sweatshirt for early mornings, grabbed her bathroom items, a hairbrush and called it done.

She carried the bag out and found Trent in the kitchen making sandwiches.

"Are you picky?" His attention shifted to her slight limp as she walked into the living room that opened into the kitchen, but he didn't mention it.

"No, but I'm not hungry. Fix whatever you want."

Standing at the bar, he quirked a brow at her, lifted a sandwich as if to say, "too late" and took a bite. He quickly put another one together and brought it to her in the living room. "Sit and eat. Put your foot on the coffee table. I won't tell Ms. Manners. We'll be on the road soon and then busy getting your critters settled at my place."

Not knowing what else to do, she did as she was told. In the amount of time it took her to force down one entire sandwich, he ate two. He carried her bag out to his truck and quickly returned. He dug through her freezer again and brought a bag of corn over. He sat beside her and patted his thigh.

"Let me see your ankle again." She set her foot in his lap and he tested the swelling. He seemed to bite his tongue but gave her a look that said he wasn't pleased with what he saw.

Instead of repeating that she was fine, she leaned back against the couch's arm and closed her eyes. Knowing they'd be shaky if they held them up, she stuffed her hands under her hips and took a deep breath.

"What's wrong with your hands?" Apparently, he paid more attention than she'd hoped.

She felt the makeshift cold pack against her ankle. "What? My hands are fine."

His eyebrow quirked up. "Then why are you hiding them from me?"

"I'm not hiding them from you." She bit her lip and refused to meet his eyes.

Not bothering to argue any longer he shifted, leaned over and pulled them out. He looked them over and looked at her with suspicion.

"They're shaky, okay? I'm tired of feeling them tremble. That's all."

"Come here." Without actually giving her the chance to obey, he grabbed her waist and sat her on his lap so she faced him. "Why are you so stubborn?"

How did she answer that? She didn't consider herself stubborn. She'd simply decided that she would no longer buckle beneath anyone else's demands.

She…lost all thought when he took her face in his palms, the rough calluses rasping over her flesh sending ripples of heat through her.

What had she been thinking?

"I'm not stubborn," she repeated. "I just know my own mind and don't see any reason to give in to what everyone else wants."

His only response was to shake his head and kiss her. When his mouth touched hers, the world fell away. He held her in place as if he owned her, licking into her with a ferocity that should have scared her. She accepted him with the knowledge that if she wanted to break away, she could. But as their mouths melted into each other and warm, liquid pleasure spread through her, pulling away was the last thing she wanted to do.

He drew back and met her eyes as if looking for something. Making some sort of determination, he cupped her nape, tangling her hair in his hands. He nipped her bottom lip and returned, kissing her and stealing her breath.

Running her hands up the damp heat of his chest, she gloried in the solid, reassuring warmth of him. Her world had tilted on its axis and, for just one brief moment, it felt so right to lean on Trent. She stepped back from the ledge and stole a shot of pleasure for herself.

His hands slid down her back, urging her even closer to the comfort she craved with shocking need. His fingers gripped her belt and held tight as if fighting the urge to go beyond a boundary from which they couldn't return. Then, as if giving up the fight, he pulled her tee from her jeans and ran his palms up her abdomen. He slid his thumbs beneath her bra and she sighed, the air in her lungs leaving in a heavy rasp. Their breaths mingled and their mouths tangled in a wicked dance.

"Kate, the things you do to me? I've never felt anything like it." He stared into her eyes, locked in a fiery embrace she felt to the tips of her toes. Without looking away, he shifted his thumbs to brush over her nipples. Sharp and electric pleasure arced through her.

Her body tightened. Her panties dampened. The muscles in his bare chest flexed, rippled.

The sound of breaking glass slammed her back to reality with bone-jarring force. One moment she was lost in Heaven, the next Trent wrapped his arms tight around her and rolled her to the floor, pinning her beneath his body.

"Fuck me. Do exactly as I say, when I say." The authority in his voice reminded her of the night they'd found her barn open, only ten times harsher.

Heat washed over her and she caught the flicker of orange from the corner of her eye.

"Can you run? We need to get out of here, make a dash up to the tree line. I'm sorry, but we need to get out of sight. Let's go. Stay by my side every step of the way and, if I say drop, you drop flat to the ground. If I say stop, then you become a statue." He didn't bother waiting for her agreement. Taking her hand, he pulled her to her feet and she mimicked his low to the ground posture. He drew her to the backdoor and out into the dark of night.

He paused as if listening and, suddenly, as if the hounds of hell were on their heels, he pulled her into the yard and ran. Running as fast and as hard as she could make her legs move, she fought to keep up. Knowing he slowed to keep pace with her only drove her to push herself harder, despite the sharp pain lancing up her calf with each step. Pushing herself to keep up, she drew on her prior years of experience. She could do this, she told herself as another jolt shocked through her ankle.

Then the moment they entered the dark of the forest, he stopped with a lurch. She struggled to catch her breath. Each gasp ripped in and out of her chest with jagged tears. Her heart thundered in her ears. Logically, she knew she wasn't making much noise, but her adrenaline-fueled fear made her hyper-alert to every rasp and wheeze.

With pain screaming up her leg, it was all she could do to stay upright and still while Trent watched and planned.

After a tense moment of him doing nothing but listening and surveying everything, he leaned close to her ear and spoke in a near-silent whisper. "How well do you know this area? Is there a good place to hide, or anything to at least put our backs against?"

She nodded and drew him with her. Just a short distance into the treed hollow, she took him to a cluster of enormous boulders. The instant they came into view, he gave her a thumbs up and drew her beneath the largest one. He sat beside her and pulled out his phone.

Below them, orange flames flickered and waved, stretching out of the front windows as if reaching for the sky. Smoke billowed.

Her home burned while she sat powerless and hoped the fire didn't spread. She stared at the distance between the house and the locked barn and prayed it was enough to keep Bonnie and Pudgy safe. She'd fought the urge to run straight for the barn, trusting Trent to do the right thing. The barn and her animals appeared safe, but she didn't know what she'd do if the danger spread.

He tucked Kate beneath the largest boulder. The behemoth would cover them from behind, above and left. He'd put himself on her right side, leaving the front as the only exposed side. It was far from ideal, but would have to do for the moment.

What had she gotten herself into?

He'd had strong suspicions when he'd called Rick to bring a horse trailer and to come armed and ready, but they'd just been suspicions. Too many odd coincidences stacked up to draw an ugly picture.

Now the danger had become three-dimensional.

He spared a brief glance to the fire below as he drew his phone from his pocket and dimmed the touch screen's brightness. He hated to make noise, but he couldn't let the fire get any larger. He made a call to 911 and told them a quick, vague story about the fire's origin. They assured him they'd notify the fire department immediately. The moment he disconnected, he dialed again. He needed to warn Rick that they'd run into more trouble.

The sound of squealing tires pealed through the quiet night. A dark, sleek sedan flew down the road.

"Where are you? You should have been here already." He couldn't help the abrupt words, worry overriding his usual cool control.

"Sorry, man. I had a little trouble with the trailer, and I had to borrow Bill's truck. Harlan isn't back yet." He heard Rick's frustration, even through the crappy connection.

"Tell me you at least came packing heat? We have a situation." Trent always kept a gun in his truck and had it on him now, but he'd feel better if he had more than one 9mm as backup.

"I'm prepared for war. What's up?" Rick's quick reply eased his tension.

"Kate's house was just firebombed about two minutes ago. We're both okay and took cover in the woods behind her house."

"I'll be there in about twenty minutes." The cell connection weakened and Rick's voice sounded garbled.

Trent ran his hand through his hair with impatience. "Okay. I think the dickhead just ran, but I'm not moving her until I'm certain it's safe."

"No shit. Watch yourself. If it weren't for this damn trailer, I'd already be there. I'll be there as soon as I can."

Trent disconnected and continued his survey. The night around them was quiet and heavy, but the flames had only grown larger and brighter.

Tapping his shoulder, she snared his attention. "Let me call my cousin Joe. He's a sheriff's deputy, so if he hears my address over the radio, he'll kill himself to get here and raise half the county while he's at it. He won't be happy, but I need to let him know I'm okay."

He understood her need to let her family know, but he hated the idea of alerting anyone that something other than an accidental fire had occurred. They needed to keep their suspicions quiet until he and Rick knew exactly what was going on and who was to blame.

"Call your cousin and let him know you're okay. Don't say anything else until I get a better handle on things. For now, we don't know how the fire started." He wished he could be happy that she'd listened and done exactly as he'd asked, but there was nothing simple about their situation.

"Fuck, I know you're hurting. The last thing I want to do is drag you back down to the house, but we can't let anyone know you have bigger trouble brewing." He had to weigh which danger was greater. Was someone watching them now? Or had the only threat just fled into the night? Would she be safer when the fire department arrived?

He recognized the confusion on her face before she asked, "Why? Joe's as good as they come."

"I'll explain everything, I promise. We just need to get through the next little bit safely and then back to my place." He was asking too much from her, but she seemed to accept his control of the situation. She'd handled a fire-bombing and a mad dash through the night on an injured ankle without complaint and she'd nearly been able to keep up with him as they made their way to safety.

How many women would do that without asking any of the hundred questions that had to be swimming through her mind? While she made her call, he carefully pulled her legs and set them in his lap. In the dark, he couldn't do much more than check for swelling. He felt both ankles and compared their size. His gut clenched with guilt when he felt the obvious difference. He looked to Kate. The stubborn woman waved her hand at her ankle and gave him a thumbs up.

"Joe? It's Kate. Hey listen. I'm okay, but there's been trouble at my house. I wanted to let you know I'm okay before you get a call." Quiet and steady, she spoke to her cousin as if they were discussing the weather, without a single tremor in her voice.

How could he not admire that?

"There's a fire in the house. Yes, I'm out and where we built our forts as kids. I don't know, but from here it looks like it might be bad." She paused again. "No, uh, I'm with a friend and he pulled me out quick. You don't have to. What about Kylie? I promise, I'm okay. I love you, too. Bye."

She handed his phone back and pulled her knees to her chest. He heard the faint howl of the fire department's horn. He tucked her into his side pressed a kiss to the top of her head. What if he hadn't shown up tonight?

"My friend should be here in about fifteen minutes. As soon as he gets here, we'll load your animals and head out." The sooner he could get her on familiar territory the better. He and Rick had some serious digging to do.

Red lights flashed in the distance. He drew her to her feet and once again pulled her into the night. He'd put their backs to the barn and hope for the best.

Despite seeing a car flee, he couldn't help but feel pinned beneath a sniper's scope as they ran back down to the yard.

"Open the barn, stand just inside and set this somewhere out of sight." He pressed his gun to her palm. He'd rather have it ready, but it would bring too many questions that he wasn't ready to answer.

Sirens wailed louder and then the yard filled with what must be half the county's volunteer fire department. Red and white lights flashed, setting the night aglow. Though he dreaded the questions he knew he couldn't answer, he relaxed a fraction.

If the shooter had even one functioning brain cell, they'd back off as long as witnesses surrounded them.

He pulled Kate to his side and spoke low. "For now, we don't know what happened. We were on the couch, occupied, and then there were flames. That's it. Bear with me a little longer, sweetheart." He held her hand and pulled her into the yard as Rick finally pulled in and drove across to park near the barn.

"It's about damn time. Can't you hitch and pull a trailer?" Trent's worry for Kate's safety threatened to unleash his impatience.

"Uh...actually no. I had Ray help, though, so it should be right." Faced with admitting Trent found what might have been the one thing that he couldn't do, Rick turned his head to take in the flicker of flames and billowing smoke.

"Good. This is bad and I want to get her out of here as soon as possible, but with this circus, it'll be a while yet."

"What the hell happened?" Rick turned to him for answers, worry evident in his dark eyes.

"What didn't happen?" He ran his free hand through his hair and scanned the chaos surrounding the house. Kate squeezed his hand. "Sorry. Kate, this is my friend Rick Evans. Rick, this is Kate MacDonald."

Trent's friend? Then why did he look so familiar?

"Nice to meet you, Kate. I wish it were under better circumstances." He smiled and tipped his head to her, but the smile didn't make it to his eyes. Then he turned his head back to face Trent, all business.

When she saw the steep slope of his jaw, recognition slammed her.

"You're the sucker."

Both men looked to her as if she'd lost her mind.

"Sorry, I mean you were at the farmer's market. You bought six jars of jam and a mountain of strawberries." An odd feeling squirmed in her belly. "And that's not a coincidence, is it? What's going on?"

"Ah. Kate, I'll explain but—" Rick rubbed the back of his neck, guilty.

"I'll explain everything. I promise, but not here. I need you to trust me for just a little longer." Trent interrupted, his friend. *Why?*

"Katie Marie!" Their heads turned in unison as the fire chief called out and headed over. Then both men looked back to her. A humid breeze blew through and ruffled Trent's hair against this collar.

"You. You were there too. You knocked into Phillip Bailey and then ran. Why?"

127

"Yes, that was me, us." Trent cupped her neck and touched his forehead to hers. "Who's coming over?"

Was he avoiding her question or did he genuinely want to know? "That's Bill. He heads up the volunteer fire department."

"You know him well?" Why was he suspicious of everyone?

Confusion slowed her speech. "A little. He was three years ahead of me in school. He's a good guy. Smart. Why?"

"Just remember what I said, okay? Rick, stick to her like glue, I'm going to take care of Bonnie."

She told Bill what little bit she could, feeling completely helpless. She'd grown up on the farm and, though it might not appear to be much, her house was filled with so many memories. Her throat tightened as she watched the water pouring in as smoke fled through the broken windows like ghosts in the night.

"Katie!" She turned at the sound of Leigh's voice and ran to her cousin's open arms. "You're okay? Promise me."

"I'm good. I promise. Confused and a little heartbroken, but physically I'm fine." Kate hadn't realized how tense she'd been until the familiar comfort of her cousin's arms hugged her close.

"Joe called. You'll stay with me." A straight-up order, there was no arguing with Leigh, but she was going to have to and neither she nor Joe would like it. He ambled up, beside them and pulled her from Leigh's arms into his. She rested her head against his chest and felt the steady rumble of his heart beneath her ear. His tall, familiar presence steadied her.

"You know you're welcome at my place as well. Kylie would be overjoyed, and we can easily make room for your menagerie of animals." His eyes took in the chaos and they never missed a thing. She pulled herself away and straightened her spine.

"I know. Thank you, but I'm going with Trent." All four eyes shot to Rick who stood nearby, watching silently. He towered over everyone, reeking of macho protectiveness and nearly smothering her with it.

"You're Trent Dawson?" Joe looked him up and down, assessing.

Rick shook his head. "No, I'm a friend. Trent is loading Kate's horse."

"I really think she should stay with family." Joe wasn't budging. When Leigh stood shoulder to shoulder with her brother, Kate knew it was time to intervene. One MacDonald could be a terror, but two? By some weird law of familial physics, the effect only quadrupled when they teamed up.

Trent stepped from the shadows and drew her into his side. "Not necessary. Thank you, but Kate's going home with me. I have more than enough space for her animals and we've already made plans."

Apparently, she'd become a human pinball, bouncing from person to person. It had to stop. *Time to take charge.*

She put a light hand on Trent's uninjured shoulder and stepped forward, meeting Joe and Leigh head on. "I love you both and appreciate you checking on me. I'm staying with Trent."

They both looked at her as if she'd lost her mind, and it was quite possible she had. But everything that made her a woman insisted that she listen to him. "I don't know if my phone survived the fire. It's doubtful, but I promise to get another soon and will keep in touch with you both daily." She leaned in and gave Leigh a hug and a kiss. Then she repeated the same with Joe. Then she looked him in the eyes and vowed. "It's good, I promise. We'll talk soon." The only response he gave her was a tightening of his brows, as if he were afraid he'd say something stupid if he opened his mouth.

She turned to Trent. "Is she settled?"

"She is and we need to get you off your feet." His jaw tightened with impatience.

She placed her hand on his stubble covered jaw. "Thank you."

"Kate, can I speak with you a moment?" Bill returned and Trent squeezed her hand in silent warning. She wasn't the least bit surprised when he followed her over.

"We've almost got it extinguished, but you're sure you don't know where it started or why?" Bill's kind, tired features pinched in suspicion.

"No, I'm sorry. I was, uh, distracted. The poor house is ancient, but I hope it can be saved. The thought of losing it breaks my heart." Tired, overwhelmed, she just wanted to lie down and block everything out for a few minutes. She girded up and pasted on her good girl smile.

Bill's eyes softened. "Don't you worry, Kate. We'll get to the bottom of this." Bill took her hand in his and patted it.

Trent bristled beside her, but remained calm, cool, as if this were an everyday event. "Here. Take my number. You can reach Kate through my cell until we get her set up with a new one. If it's okay, I'm going to take her home. We need to get her animals settled, and Kate's exhausted."

"Of course. You go right ahead. I'll be in touch." Bill put the business card in his shirt pocket and nodded.

Trent ran his hand down her spine and settled it at her waist. "We appreciate it."

After they walked away, he leaned down to speak into her ear. "Does that always work for you? Of course it does, I don't know why I even asked."

"What? Does what work for me?" Confused, she looked up at him.

"You flutter your eyelashes and men crumple at your feet." He shook his head and grinned.

"Oh. That. Well, it worked, didn't it? I figured the shorter the conversation, the better." She smiled and fluttered her lashes at him in play.

He laughed and walked her over to the truck that Rick had driven. Rick leaned against the door. When Trent held out his hand, they traded keys.

Trent opened the door, hoisted her up then closed her in. She couldn't tell if it was to help her or speed her up. Through the window, she watched the smoke billow from her home. The last of the firefighters rolled up their hoses as Trent pulled out of the driveway and onto the blacktop.

Chapter Eight

Rick turned toward Trent's ride. As soon as the last fire truck pulled out and cleared the way, he'd follow Trent and Kate. He didn't expect they'd have any trouble on the way home, but stranger things had happened.

He nearly bumped into Kate's cousin, Leigh. She stood with her back to the driver's door, arms crossed and enough attitude sparking in her green eyes to reignite the undoubtedly soggy house.

He took in her long, willowy form and grinned. Clearly, the beauty queen genes were a family trait. "Can I help you?"

"Do you want to tell me what's going on with my cousin?" Suspicion rolled off her as she stayed still, as if refusing to let him leave until she got her answer. Her voice was quiet, but laced with steel.

Hoping to charm her, he smiled. "I don't know what you mean. We all just want what's best for Kate and she won't be parted from her horse. She'll be in good hands. Trent's the best guy I know."

"Why should I take your word? And the safest place for Kate is with family. She's had a rough couple of years and she deserves happiness, not more drama." Intelligence bled through the suspicion. Leigh MacDonald was no bubble-headed beauty.

"You act like Kate's in danger. This was just a freak house fire. Nothing more. She'll be back in Riley Creek before you know it." Rick reassured Kate's cousin.

If anything, her suspicion only increased at his words. He smiled when her green eyes crinkled at the edges. He wasn't fooling her.

"There's been an awful lot of strange interest in Katie lately, and I don't like it. Her ex-husband is a loser, and I wouldn't be surprised if he's causing trouble. I won't have him putting her in danger." She cocked her head and leaned as if to look at something behind him. An odd expression crossed her face then, like a rabbit, she bolted around him.

What the hell?

Without the faintest idea what he was doing, he followed as she flew around the barn's corner on long, lean legs. Her dark hair trailed behind her, a witchy shadow in the night. At the barn's second corner, leading to the pasture, he was on her heels. He came around the corner just in time to see her reach for the hood of a smaller person with arms and legs pumping as if their life depended on escape.

Wait, was that a small adult or a kid?

"Stop. We won't hurt you. Come here, damn it." Breathless, Leigh tried to reason with the small figure.

"No. Thieves. You're all horse thieves." It came out on a sobbing wail as the kid broke away and lengthened the distance between it and Leigh.

Had the kid started the fire? Why?

He put on more speed, stretched his legs and passed Leigh. In a few second's time he caught up with the fleeing figure and grabbed it around the waist.

"No! Let me go!" He caught a kick to the shin and an elbow to the chin as he wrestled with the lightweight octopus all the while, trying not to hurt it.

"Stop, damn it. Stop. We're not going to hurt you. Stop now. You see that tall guy over by the house, with a ball cap on? Yep, he heard you and now he's coming over. He's a cop. If you don't settle down, I'll throw you to him. Chill." The light weight in his arms stopped squalling but continued to squirm.

"Hey. Ignore the big ogre. Listen to me. I only want to help." Leigh's voice broke through the storm, a calm cool breeze, washing away the upset. "If I ask the ogre to put you down, will you promise not to run? You're not in trouble. I just want to make sure you're okay and ask you a question or two. Okay?"

The reply came, both soft and mulish. "Okay."

"Good. Ogre? Put her down so we can talk."

He glared at her insult and slowly set the kid to her feet, though how Leigh knew its gender, he had no clue. All he saw were dirty jeans, ratty-assed shoes and a baggy sweatshirt. The moment her feet touched the ground she made a hop as if to get away, but then stopped as if remembering their bargain.

"Will you tell me your name? I'm Leigh Ann. This is…" she looked to him with an imperious lift of her brow, waiting for him to fill in the blank.

"Rick." He didn't bother to hide his irritation or suspicion. It couldn't be a coincidence that they'd found this kidding nosing around just a short time after the fire. No way.

"Uhm…Mary. My name's Mary."

"What are you doing out so late?"

What Rick wanted to know was why the kid was on Kate's property and if she had a lighter in her pocket. He put his patience to the test and waited while Leigh tried to ease Mary into conversation.

"I saw the fire and wanted to check on my…uh…the horse. Is she okay?" The trembling voice squeezed something in his chest. But why did the kid think the horse belonged to her? How did she know that Kate had a horse?

"Bonnie, Kate's foal, is just fine. Kate and Trent have taken her to another farm so she'll be safe until things are fixed here." Leigh reached forward and tipped the kid's hood back. A pale face, with long, dirty, hair and enormous gray eyes looked up tentatively. Her hair had been braided, as if in attempt to make it neat, but there was no hiding the simple fact that she was overdue for a shower or three.

Poor kid. Where were her parents?

"You promise?"

"I promise." Leigh radiated kindness and reassuring warmth. "Kate loves all animals, but horses have always been her favorite. She loves Bonnie very much. How old are you?"

There was a pause and her eyes tightened. "Eighteen."

He wanted to call bullshit. He was no expert, but he'd be surprised if the girl was over thirteen. He had a question of his own. "Do you have any idea how the fire started?"

Fear flickered in Mary's eyes. "No. I didn't see anyone or anything. I just saw the flames and had to make sure the horse was okay. Horses and fire are bad news."

"Where are your parents, honey?" Leigh's voice infused with the comfort of cookies and milk.

"Uhm. At work. They work nights. I snuck out. I should be getting back. Thanks!" She backed away as if to leave, but he stopped her.

"I don't think so, young lady. It's well after midnight. We'll give you a ride home and make sure your parents know you're okay." He looked to Leigh for agreement, somehow knowing instinctively that she'd give it.

Her nod was brisk. "Absolutely. There's no need for you to walk anywhere. These roads aren't safe at night."

Mary wouldn't meet their eyes. She looked down, seemingly at the holes in her shoes and nodded.

Joe made his way over, a million questions written on his face. He turned his head toward Leigh and, with one nod, she appeared to answer at least a few of them.

"Joe, this is uh, Mary. She stopped by to check on Bonnie when she saw the fire. Mary, this is Joe. He's my brother." Leigh continued on as if all of this was a family picnic.

"Nice to meet you, Mary." Joe looked to his sister, as if following her lead. The two seemed to share some sort of silent sibling communication.

"Rick and I were just going to give Mary a ride home. I'll check in with you in a bit, okay?" Hidden meaning filled Leigh's words as she put her arm on the girl's shoulders in a friendly gesture.

"Sure. Do that." The tense line in Joe's jaw belied his easy words.

"Let's go, kiddo." Rick gestured toward Trent's truck and held the door open, watching as the kid acted like she headed to the gallows for sentencing. He shut her in and got in the driver's seat. Leigh climbed in, buckled her seatbelt and made sure Mary had done the same. "Where to? I'm not from around here, so you ladies will have to tell me what to do."

"First, if you don't care I need to make a stop. I'm starving and could really use something to eat. How about you?" She directed the question to him, but anyone could see the poor kid had missed more than one meal. His gut twisted as he thought about what it must be like to be a kid and not know when or where your next meal would come from.

"Yeah, sure. Just point me in the right direction." He followed Leigh's directions until they came to an all-night convenience store.

"It's the only thing open this late. I'll just run in and get us a few snacks, okay? I'll be right back." *Smart move.* Chances were good that if they left the kid alone for a second, she'd run. He just wished he knew whether it was from fear or guilt.

"Yeah, that works for me. How about you, kiddo?" He shifted the truck into park and tapped his fingers on the steering wheel.

"I really need to go to the restroom. Can I go in?" The girl's quiet, hopeful request filled the cab with worry.

"Sure." Unease tightened Leigh's features.

"I'll just stay here and watch the truck." He looked to Leigh to see that she got his meaning and she quickly agreed. He'd watch the front entrance in case Mary ran out the door.

"Perfect. You want anything?" Leigh asked as she opened the door and stepped down.

Their gazes met and locked. He answered with a husky voice. "No, I'm good."

"I'll be right back!" Mary climbed out and practically ran into the store and Leigh went right behind her.

Five minutes later, a heartbroken Leigh came back out, empty-handed. He didn't even ask what happened. The worry on her face was so easy to read.

"There's a door in the back where the bathrooms are. I asked the clerk, and she told me there were no other exits. Then when Mary didn't come back I went to look. There was a door. The clerk thought I meant a public door. She thought because it said employees only, that it didn't count." She climbed up and sat back, devastation written on her beautiful features.

"It's a shame we don't know where she lives." He ached to wipe the worry from her face, but their situation had no easy fix.

"I think I know where to find her, but there's no point in chasing after her in the dark. She'll know this area better than Joe and I combined."

His throat stayed tight at the pain in Leigh's voice. He'd never before felt as if he were standing on such uneven ground. He'd always known his next step until now. "Do you want me to take you home or back to Kate's?"

"Give me a minute, and I'll let you know. I'll be quick." She pulled her phone from her pocket and dialed. "Hey, it's me. Yeah, she gave me the slip at the gas station. All I wanted to do was put some food in her belly. Please tell me the Caudill's place has been decontaminated."

Decontaminated? What the hell?

"Thank God. I'm going to go out there tomorrow. Do you have time to go with me? Shit. Okay, but I'm not waiting. I'll figure something out. I know. I promise I won't go alone. Love you too. Bye." She disconnected. "Turn left up at the stoplight. It's only about ten minutes to my place and Joe's got to get back so he can send Mom and Dad home. They came over to watch his daughter while he checked on Kate."

A sick feeling coiled low in his belly and twisted. "No problem. What did you mean by decontaminated?"

"I'm certain that Mary lives out at the old Caudill place. Her father, Tom was arrested for making meth. That's where we found Kate's horse. The mare died of neglect, and Kate took custody of the foal. The meth has a distinct smell, so it's not uncommon for meth cookers to keep horses and use the manure to mask the aroma." She smacked the dash in frustration. "God, it makes me sick to think she's been living out there all this time. There were signs that a child was living there, but we've been out there twice and haven't been able to find her. No one is missing from the elementary, middle or high school. The worry was bad enough when I only thought there might be someone hiding out there. Now that I know for sure, and have a face to go with the knowledge, the worry is going to make me sick."

"And you're going back out there tomorrow? To look for her?" He couldn't grasp the idea that the girl, that any child might live in such a place.

"She'll hide from me. It's not like she's a wild animal I can set a trap for. I'll have to see who I can get to go with me. Joe usually goes, but he has to be in court tomorrow. He'll sic Dad on me if I go out there alone, and that is not a pleasant experience." She visibly shuddered.

"I'll take you. What time should I pick you up?" He had a million things on his schedule tomorrow, including sleep and digging into Kate's mess, but he'd make time.

"How about noon? I have to work, but can take a long lunch break. Turn in there, the last door in the row." She pointed to a row of neat, simple townhomes. "Give me your phone and I'll give you my work address." He handed over the phone and parked.

"Thanks." She handed it back, opened the door and vanished like a witch in the night.

Kate rolled her shoulders and laid her head against the back of the plush couch. A wide yawn stretched her face as purple rays of dawn peaked through the curtains. She'd been awake for nearly twenty-four crazy, chaotic hours. Once they'd dealt with the drama at her house then made the drive to Bourbon County, unloaded Bonnie and gotten her settled, night had come and gone.

She didn't expect to have much time to rest today either. Joe would be breathing down her neck for an explanation. He knew something was up and would only give her a minute grace period before he demanded answers.

She'd have to check in with the fire department and see if and when she could go inside to see what, if anything, could be salvaged. She'd have to contact her insurance company and figure out how to manage her berries. The county fair was closing in and she'd already made plans to share a booth with a local crafter. Now she might not have any stock to sell. An endless list of errands replayed in a dizzying loop.

She leaned down to remove her shoes and groaned.

"You okay?" Trent's fatigue roughened voice whispered through her.

"Just sore. I'm sure it's from the fall. My ankle is a little tender and my muscles are stiff, but I'll be fine after a hot shower and some sleep."

"Here." He sat beside her and carefully tugged off her shoes. A dull ache spread and throbbed as she tested the sprain. It was sore, but she'd had worse. "It's a little swollen, are you sure?"

"Yes. I promise. Now, when are you going to explain what's going on? I find it awfully difficult to believe that you, your friend and the senator just happened to show up at the farmer's market on the same day. And if it was just a coincidence, then why did you hide from me?"

"You caught that, did you?" He gave her a half-hearted smile and rubbed a hand over his head. She wasn't sure if it was a touch of guilt or exhaustion.

"I didn't at first. I thought it was odd to have Bailey appear in Riley Creek and find me more than once. Then when you bumped into him, all I caught was a flash of your hair and your shoulders. There was something there that nagged at me, but between your friend and Bailey, I was too distracted to give it a lot of thought."

"Wait. What other time did you see Bailey?" She resisted the urge to smooth the frown over his brows with her fingertips.

"A few days ago. He said he was in town and wanted to speak with me. He makes my skin crawl and I brushed him off. He pretended to bump into me at the feed store, of all places. When I asked about his animals, he admitted to not having any and only wanting to see me. Then, when he showed at the market, the awful feeling returned. I guess it's possible he's just a lonely widower looking for someone to talk to, but he seems to be going out of his way too much for my comfort." She shrugged.

"No. For what it's worth, I think your feelings are on target. We were following Bailey, and he led us to you. We had no idea where he was going after his appointment. The Senator's former brother-in-law asked Rick to look into his sister's death. We had no idea you'd be at the market that day." He idly traced the seam of her jeans running up her calf.

"Which is why you used a shitty disguise. How much did Clay charge you for the used hunting gear?" She smiled as she pictured the gruff and often suspicious Clay haggling with a rushed Trent.

"A small fortune. He must have sensed my desperation." Trent smiled wryly.

"Probably. He doesn't like outsiders. Why all the interest in me? I don't understand." She'd spent the entire ride into Bourbon County thinking on it and came up blank.

"I don't know. You're a beautiful woman, that's obvious, but I don't know why he'd fixate on you, if that's what happened." His heavy palm rested on her knee and he raised his head to meet her gaze.

"Why would he try to kill me if he wants me? I don't understand."

"It may be that there's no way to explain it. All we know is that there are too many questions, and they all revolve around you." He tapped her nose with a finger.

"So...this is a job to you?" She had so many questions, but she had to start putting herself first. She owed it to herself.

"Yes and no." He sighed heavily.

"I don't know if it's the exhaustion or your words. I feel like a naïve school girl. Explain." Yes, he'd done so much for her, but she deserved answers. She couldn't bear living in the dark a second longer.

"After our date, I had every intention of walking away and never seeing you again. Your actions, your words, you? It was all too good to be true. But when it began to look like you could be in trouble, I couldn't walk away. When Rick gave me a suggestion on how to get in your good graces so we could both learn more and see if you were truly in danger, I shrugged it off, knowing it wouldn't work for you. I just knew. And there was not a chance in hell I could walk away if you were in danger." The sincerity in his voice knocked her off balance. He said all the right things, but should she believe him?

"And how did you think to get in my good graces?" She couldn't wait to hear his answer.

"Bonnie. Your farm." He knew her. She had to give him that, at least. But was the knowledge from true emotion on his part, or intelligent calculation? He'd shown nothing but care for her since the first moment they'd met. He'd helped her out of one bad situation after another.

"Do you have a white knight complex?"

"What?" Clearly exhausted, he looked back in confusion.

"You know, do you get off on saving damsels in distress?"

A blank look crossed his face and then he burst into deep, rolling laughter. The sound rumbled through her in waves.

"Sweetheart, you are the farthest thing from a damsel in distress I've ever seen. Damsels in distress don't manage a farm, big or small, all on their own. They don't do home repair or load shotguns. You are no damsel."

"That's all I've wanted to do, just take care of my animals and be me, I just didn't know it. I hate asking for help."

A crooked, wicked, little grin lit his face. A melty-warm, altogether lovely sensation spread low in her belly and something bright bloomed in her chest.

"If it makes you feel any better, remind yourself you never asked. I had to barge in and take over." He cupped her face in his big, rough palms. "You are a strong, capable, caring, and beautiful woman who has her shit together. That is sexy as fuck. The fact that you are in trouble and need help, does not subtract or add to the attraction I feel for you."

The brightness in her chest flashed and her breath hitched in a ragged stutter. Deep and powerful emotions gripped her. How could she know if she was capable of wading through them when her head was a mess and her body on the verge of collapse?

"All I know is that your evening started off with a bang and never really slowed down. You were hit with one catastrophe after another." Maybe it was childish, but she wasn't ready to deal with the heady feelings. So much had happened so fast, she didn't know which way was up or down. Maybe it would be best to save the rest of the serious discussion for another time? "Why did you come out to see me in the first place?"

"I had some extra tack that I thought might fit Bonnie. I brought it out to check for fit. At least, if we're being honest, that was my excuse. I came to check up on you and get closer for Rick's case." He shrugged as if his words shouldn't mean much to her.

"Ah. That makes sense. You didn't come to see me. You came to visit my horse and for work." She hoped a dose of sarcasm might lighten the heavy atmosphere.

"Yeah, that's it. I'm a sucker for the long-legged beauties."

She met his storm-gray gaze. A dense mix of emotions swirled there, revealing heat and hunger that inspired matching sensations in the deepest parts of her. "Good thing, I'm short then, isn't?"

"Sweetheart, from where I'm standing, there's nothing short about your legs. What are you? Five foot five?" His eyes surveyed her from toe to head in a slow sweep.

"Five feet, four and a half inches. Aunt Jeannie never quit despairing over my lack of height. She always held out hope that I would grow at least one more inch." She straightened her shoulders in her old habit of trying to look taller so her aunt would be happy. It never worked.

"Well, you've got enough leg to wrap around a man's waist and hold tight. That's all a man needs." Heated male appreciation stared back at her. Knowing he had noticed her legs or any other part of her body flooded her with languid desire.

Her long day and eventful night exhausted her. She lacked the energy needed to absorb the meaning of his words. And the heat in his eyes? She didn't know if she'd ever be able to accept or process that kind of passion.

Fatigue pushed her closer to sleep, making both her eyelids and limbs infinitely heavy. Her thoughts became jumbled, yet at the heart of it she knew there was something there she needed to concentrate on.

"So someone is trying to kill or scare me. I wouldn't have believed you yesterday, but there's no denying it anymore, is there?" She fought to string her words together with some semblance of logic.

"No. There's not. You're in danger."

She believed him. Sure, she'd be an idiot not to after everything that happened, but also because his sense of honor was stamped on everything he did.

"So you want me to stay here with you just because you're a nice guy. Is that what I'm supposed to believe?" The heat of his palm rested on her thigh.

"Sure. You can believe that if you want." At least for the time being he seemed to allow her denial. She'd have to face the more complicated decisions later when she could focus. She needed to turn off her brain and let exhaustion carry her off to sleep, but she couldn't make her mouth stop. Encroaching sleep slurred her words and she had trouble completing her thoughts.

"How about if I tell myself that you are only interested in my horse? Can I do that?" She closed her eyes in a slow blink and forced them open.

"Sure, princess, you go right ahead. My only interest is that pretty little filly out in the stables. Tell yourself that all you like." A lazy grin spread across his face and his hand patted her thigh.

"That's what I thought." Incapable of holding her eyes open a moment longer she listed to the side and leaned her head on his shoulder. A low chuckle rumbled through his chest.

All she needed was just a few seconds to rest her eyes.

Something shifted and she lay closer to warmth. A subtle rocking motion swept her away.

He lay Kate on the guest bed and covered her with a light quilt. She didn't move except to take in a deep breath and settle. While he was used to the long hours, he wasn't so sure she was. Yes, he'd learned enough about her, he could easily see her rising before dawn and putting in a hard day's work. To top it off, she'd do it with a smile on her beautiful face the entire time.

Still, he didn't see her having much experience with the stresses life-threatening danger brought. It had nothing to do with her being a woman or even a former beauty queen. No one as softhearted as Kate should ever have to learn how to deal with that sort of thing.

He closed the door and hoped she was able to get some solid sleep.

He'd just finished taking off his boots when a light knock sounded at his front door. He opened to find an equally exhausted Rick.

"Since when do you knock?" he asked.

Rick snorted. "Since you have sexy little beauty queens in your home. Did she make it to bed yet?"

Stretching his neck, he pointed toward the bedroom. "She finally settled and crashed a few minutes ago. Where've you been?"

"That's right, you missed last night's surprise." Rick grabbed a bottle of water from the fridge and slumped to the couch.

"What happened?" Concern deepened his voice, but he kept it low so he didn't disturb Kate.

After taking a long drink from the bottle, Rick answered, "A few minutes after you two left, Kate's cousin met me at your truck and gave me the third degree."

Confusion battled with exhaustion, so Trent asked, "Which cousin?"

"The pretty one."

Interesting. Rick never used the word pretty. Hot, sexy, fine, plain-Jane, yes, but he'd only heard the man say pretty once, in reference to a rare classic car. Rick then offered the owner nearly double what the car was worth and got denied. He'd been heartbroken.

He'd like to call his friend on the use of the word, but then he'd clam up. In the long run it'd be more fun to see where it went.

"I was in the process of telling her everything was fine—" Rick picked at the label on the water bottle.

"So you were lying to her." Afraid he'd fall asleep in the comfort of the couch, Trent leaned against the wall.

"Exactly, when she bolted like a fucking rabbit midsentence. Confused and wondering if she was crazy, I chased after her. Turns out she'd seen someone peeking around the barn's corner behind me when we were talking and chased after them." Rick waved a hand in the air, as if still baffled.

Trent rubbed his hands over his face, and his words came out muffled. "Who was it?"

"A damn kid. Filthy, scrawny and terrified. I caught her and have the bruised shins to prove it. We tried to take her home, but she gave Leigh the slip. Leigh wants to go to where she thinks the kid lives later today. Apparently it's a really nasty situation. Sad? Yeah, sad is probably a better word." Rick leaned back against the couch and laid his head on the back.

"Do you think she could have started the fire?" It couldn't be that simple, could it?

"My gut says no, but I'm not going to completely discount her. Kate has enough trouble surrounding her and I'm certain your beauty queen's tangled up in the case I took for Todd Hill. She sure as fuck doesn't need a vindictive teen adding to it. There was no denying the kid was upset when we found her. Who the hell knows with kids?" Rick had been an only child and raised in boarding schools. He'd gone all of his life without strong family ties.

Some things, not even money could buy.

"What could the girl have against Kate?" For that matter, he couldn't see why anyone could have a reason to be angry with her. She was too damn nice to everyone.

"When I caught her she called us horse thieves. It's likely that Bonnie was hers before her dad was arrested." Rick ran a hand through his black hair.

"Shit." The last thing they needed was one more person to investigate.

"Yeah. It's a hell of a mess and one more thing I'll have to sort out." Rick stood and pulled a set of keys from his pocket.

"So when are you going to pick up Kate's cousin? Leigh, is it?"

"I'm supposed to meet her at noon. How did you know I was going back to Riley Creek?" Rick cocked his head at Trent, full of suspicion.

"No reason." He just looked at Rick and grinned.

Rick stepped out of Trent's car and onto a driveway of more weeds than gravel. He shut his door and Leigh did the same, the sound loud in the quiet surroundings. This was where Mary lived? He prayed Leigh was wrong.

A small, ancient gray house sat amidst acres of knee high grass. The size or age of the home wasn't the issue so much as its pitiful condition. At least two windows were broken and the holes had been covered on the inside with cardboard. The screen door hung loose and Christmas lights that looked to be twenty years old wrapped around the sagging roofline. The nearly hollow shell of an old rusted car sat on blocks at the house's side and it looked like a village of ramshackle sheds filled the backyard. A small pasture sat beyond that, surrounded by fencing a stiff breeze could blow over.

Leigh met him at the car's trunk and barely spared him a glance as she took in the scene.

"Someone's been here recently." Her voice was filled with what sounded like equal parts heartache and determination.

"How can you tell?" He might be observant, but all he saw cried out with neglect and despair.

"The cardboard in the windows is new. It would have been taken when they decontaminated the place after Tom's arrest. Let's go." She hefted several bags from a local grocery and clothing store. He lifted a case of water and followed as she walked up the driveway and around to a backdoor.

"Stop. Let me go in first. I'll take a look around and let you know if it's safe. That's why I came, remember?" He set the water down and drew his gun.

"I really don't think that's necessary." Quiet despair laced Leigh's voice

"There's no telling who or what's in there. I'm with your brother on this one." He'd learned long ago that to never go into a blind situation unprepared.

"You don't get it now, but you will when you open the door. Go ahead and do your hero thing." She used the same resolved tone women used when a man was getting ready to do something stupid.

Curious, but more worried over the possible threat, he opened the door and looked inside. As she'd said, there was little to see. The place looked like an inside out skeleton. Nothing remained except for bare framing and flooring. Everything else was gone.

"Damn." He stepped inside the hot, stuffy house and looked around. Sadly, it was a quick survey.

"This is what happens when they decontaminate a meth house. When they're finished, there's nothing left but the bare bones. Anything that may have had contact with the chemicals has to go. Let's set everything over here."

He followed her lead and holstered his gun. He retrieved the water and put it next to the bags of food and clothing he'd purchased. She'd asked him to stop by the store and, when he'd realized what she was doing, he'd added to the cart and insisted on paying. After seeing the house, he wished they'd bought more. He'd told himself they were wasting money and time. There was no way anyone lived here, but when he spotted an old ratty horse blanket on the plywood floor, he was proven wrong. Beside the pallet lay a plain, lined notebook and a couple of pens and pencils.

He picked up the notebook and flipped through it. His gut clenched.

Drawings. Scenery, dreamy landscapes and horses. Pages and pages of horses.

Jesus, she was talented. The kid belonged in some fancy art school, not a hole in the wall shack with no food or running water. There was no one to care for her. What if she got sick or hurt? Who did she have to talk to? Did she have any friends? *Probably not.*

A gnawing hole opened in his chest. He didn't know whether to put his fist through the wall or cry.

Leigh's gasp whispered over his ear as she looked at what he held.

"Did you leave the phone and the note?" Anger and grief raced for the lead, setting his blood afire.

"I did. I set them on top of the water. I figure that's the first thing she'll take."

"We didn't bring enough stuff. She needs more clothes and food. What about the heat? We caught a break today, but when the temperature soars, this place will be a fucking hotbox. She'll need more paper and some real fucking pencils."

"I know." Soft and sad, Leigh's words weren't much more than a whisper.

"I'm coming back tomorrow. She needs a fucking pillow and…and a sleeping bag to lay on. No. Fuck no. What she needs is a fucking home with walls and water and electricity and people who give a fuck and worry when she's out at two fucking a.m."

"I know." The sweet acceptance in her voice only made his anger burn hotter.

"Why? Why the fuck are people such assholes? She's a fucking kid. Damn it." He fisted his hands at his side and barely resisted the urge to put both fists through the nearest wall.

Leigh stayed quiet beside him and he liked her all the more for it.

No excuses. No meaningless words.

"Let's get out of here. Maybe if she's nearby, she'll see us leave and at least put some food in her belly." He risked a look in Leigh's direction and she just nodded, eyes bright with unshed tears.

"I really wanted to be wrong, Rick. I swear."

He sat back in the fussy chair, not giving a fuck if the dainty thing broke. His uncle stood, staring at a painting on the floor, and leaned against bookshelves on the left wall.

"This is my latest acquisition. I'll have it hung over the fireplace after it's been appraised and insured." Bailey didn't bother to step aside to actually let him look at the painting. He stood in front of it as if transfixed by the image. "It was painted in 1962, almost a year to the date before he was assassinated."

He had things to do and really couldn't care less about Bailey's latest acquisition. He wanted to get the job done and move on, not wax poetic over antiques. "Look, if you're serious about this, I think it's time we do something about Preston. That fire idea of his only caused a bigger headache and there was no benefit. It was absolute panic with zero thought. Before that fire? There was no way to prove that Kate's fall was anything other than an accident. Now? It looks damn suspicious and it's only made Dawson pull her closer. If Preston's not careful, which he won't be because he's an idiot, he'll get caught and you know as well as I do, he'll squeal loudly. I get why you wanted to bring him in at the start, but he's a far greater liability than asset at this point." He glared at the old man's back, frustrated with his lack of response.

"He promised he could get me what I wanted." Bailey sounded like a child who'd lost his toy. He turned around and looked to him.

"Yes, he did and, in the beginning, I can see why you listened to him. But, if anything, he'll only make obtaining your goal harder." His patience wearing thing, he stood.

"You're certain?" He heard the doubt in Bailey's voice and it sickened him. If a man couldn't obtain his end goal on his own, then he wasn't a man at all. To rely on an idiot like Preston Hayes and expect them to deliver? It was laughable.

"Absolutely. It's time to cut him loose." At this point, he'd go behind Bailey's back and take care of things himself. He'd have to make it look accidental, but it would still work.

"How would you do this?" Bailey walked around and sat behind his desk. He ran his hand over the polished wood, lost in his thoughts. "This is a near identical match to his, you know. I haven't been able to track down his desk yet."

He shook his head in frustration at the old man's fixation. He didn't get it. "I know how to get rid of both your biggest obstacles in one clean move." In the process he'd have to go against someone who might actually pose a challenge. It had been too long since he'd had one, and it would be a good exercise. His skills were going to waste.

"Then do it. Just make sure I get what I want." Bailey, still half lost in his adoring trance, could barely be heard. "He died too soon. There's no telling what he would have accomplished if he'd been allowed to live out his full life. I've modeled my career after him and it's near time for my path to continue where his ended. My image is almost complete. The only thing I lack is the proper wife."

He looked at the painting as he rose to leave. John and Jacqueline Kennedy stared back at him. *Well, hell.* Maybe his dear old uncle wasn't as sane as he'd thought.

Chapter Nine

"What are you doing?" Trent spoke from somewhere behind her. She hefted the shovel and tossed the pile of horse manure into the wheelbarrow. Turning her head, she saw his silhouette in the barn's massive doorway, his fists planted on trim hips. She could just make out the ridges of muscle beneath a shirt that molded his chest and belly. Her mouth watered and her fingers itched to feel the strength of those muscles.

"Kate. Did you hear me?" She shook the lust-fueled fog from her head and focused on his words instead of his body.

"I did." She scooped up another pile and hefted it into the wheelbarrow.

"So, what are you doing?"

"I'm cleaning Bonnie's stall." Why she wasted her breath answering him, she didn't know. What else would she be doing in a barn with a shovel?

"Why?"

"Well, she's an animal and they make messes. Animal owners cleanup their animals' messes. I figured since you breed, raise and train horses, you would understand the reasons why horses require clean stalls."

"Yes. I do understand. We have stable hands. There's actually one just outside the barn now. Ray will be in and work his way down the aisle. He'll get to Bonnie's stall shortly. Her stall was cleaned not too long ago. It won't hurt her to wait a bit longer." Something about his tone grated over her nerves. Yes, she'd used the dry, smartass talking down to a peasant tone first, but that didn't mean he could use it on her in return.

Did it?

Yes, she had no doubt it wouldn't be long until Ray returned to make another round. She'd always admired the Mitchell's stables, but even her friend's spacious, over-the-top barn had been eclipsed by Walker Stables. Even when they'd brought Bonnie in during the early morning, well before sunrise, the place had been staffed. No one had blinked when Trent unloaded her little, mixed breed and he'd housed her alongside his most expensive horses. She believed he meant it when Trent said his horses' value went beyond the monetary.

Blowing out a breath, she leaned on the handle. "I was already here, and it needed doing. Horses make messes. It's not a big deal for me to clean up a few horse apples."

"There's no need for you to shovel shit. You're a…guest." Something in his pause made her stop and think as well. What was he getting at?

"I appreciate everything you've done for me, I do, but she's my horse. My responsibility. I don't mind taking care of her. I enjoy it." Why was he looking at her like he didn't believe her?

"I get it, she's your hobby."

Oh no. He'd brought out the listen here, little lady tone. She took a deep breath and scooped up the last pile of manure and pitched it. She would have rather thrown it at his head. She put the shovel nose to the ground and held the handle in one hand with the other on her hip.

"She's not a hobby. She's mine. It's that simple."

He looked at her as if she were from another planet. "You've seen this place. You won't find better care for her anywhere. I don't see what the problem is. There's no need for you to get dirty."

"I'm not questioning your farm's ability to care for her. I like caring for her. As for getting dirty? I've never minded. It's called work, and I'm not above it." What was his problem? Then it hit her. Anger made her see red. "Trent Dawson. You're a snob."

He looked at her, and it wasn't only like she was from another planet, but had grown two heads as well.

He looked down at his clothing and then back to her. "Are you blind? The only time I've put on a suit in the last year was for our date. I'm not a snob."

"Yes, you, in your dirty boots and with your calloused hands, are a hypocritical snob. You think that because I look good in heels and have worn a crown, it means what? I think I'm above getting dirty or doing physical work? Take a look, Trent." She held up her hand. "No chipped nails. I can do both."

He rubbed a hand against his hair, coming a bit closer. "I'm not trying to piss you off. I just don't understand why you're being so stubborn."

"Stubborn?" Her blood pressure went through the roof. "I am so over men calling me stubborn! Why is it that when a woman sticks to her guns, she's stubborn, but men are strong under the same circumstances? I can be strong too, damn you." She could. *She would.* Even against someone as strong-willed as Trent Dawson.

"Kate. Put the shovel down." He raised both hands in a calming gesture.

She tightened her fist on the handle and glared at him.

"What makes you think you can tell me what to do? Well, you can't, not with Bonnie. I mean if you want to be an ass and forbid me to use your stupid shovel, then fine. You can have your shovel. But you are not telling me what I can and can't do with my horse."

"Kate." *Was he fighting back a smile? The nerve!*

"I suppose you're going to tell me that even the manure belongs to you? Well, here. You can have it." She grabbed a handful and strode forward, not stopping until she stood toe-to-toe with him. Some small distant part of her warned that she was overreacting, but she was so fed up with everyone either looking at her like she was crazy or was somehow a failure because she was happy on her little farm in Potter County.

She was tired of everyone thinking they knew what was best for her when no one knew except her. Every man she encountered seemed to think they could step in and take over. Then, like a good little woman should, she was—for some stupid fucking reason— supposed to accept their will and smile prettily.

She was done.

She took the manure and smashed it into his chest.

And the bastard smiled at her like she was cute. *Cute!*

"Do you feel better?" The corner of his mouth twitched. Had the man lost his mind?

"Why would I feel better?" She didn't even feel bad for yelling the words.

"Because you just vented a year's or more worth of steam?" His words registered along with the fact that she'd just left a palm sized smear of horseshit on his shirt and he hadn't even blinked. He wanted to know if she felt better.

Did she?

Crap. She did.

She couldn't help it. She smiled.

"Oh no. You're not getting away with this. This is my favorite shirt." A wicked light entered his stormy eyes, and she stepped back.

Yes, she was already a mess, but she really didn't want to get into a shit-slinging fight. Before she could blink, he grasped her by the hips and pulled her flush against his broad chest then captured her mouth with his.

Her mouth parted on a gasp and he took full advantage, sweeping in and kissing her until the barn spun. Delicious, heated sin, his mouth tamed the remnants of her anger and replaced it with an altogether different type of fire.

Desire.

Liquid, warm and dazzling, it filled her every cell until her senses swam with need for him. Lost, she gripped his shirt and held tight. He groaned into her as his calloused palms swept up her sides to hold her in place.

He lifted her and palmed her ass as she wrapped her legs around his waist. The hard ridge of his erection rubbed against her core. Sweet, erotic, sensation bloomed, spreading through her. Needing more, she tilted her hips, seeking.

Stepping into the stall, he shut them in and pressed her back to the wall. Hungry, shameless, she laced her fingers at the back of his neck. Claiming hers in wild tempest, his mouth set upon hers, filling her with his dark, masculine, flavor. His hand returned to her ass, kneading and shaping. With his tight grip, he encouraged her rocking, rasping her flesh against fabric and heat until she grew faint with desire.

Hollow, aching, she needed.

"That's it, beauty, let it go. Damn, but you're beautiful like this. Hot, hungry, shameless. Fucking beautiful. Makes me want to take you right here in the stables." He nipped her bottom lip and held it between his teeth. He sucked the soft flesh into his mouth and let it go on a pop. One hand cupped her breast, thumbing the nipple through her shirt.

Meeting his eyes, she writhed, arched and her body tightened with an explosive release. Gasping, she held on, shuddering as it rode through her, white hot and consuming.

Trent touched his forehead to hers, breathing heavily.

"Katie Marie MacDonald, you are trouble."

She grinned and gave him her real smile.

"I do this all the time on my own. You really didn't have to come. No one's going to try anything in broad daylight. The weekend crowd will surely keep my drama away. Besides, I'm sure you have more important things to do with your time back at the stables."

Trent's glare said he hadn't believed a single word she'd said. Dark sunglasses, muscle and male attitude radiated forbidding protectiveness as they set up her stall at the farmer's market.

"Is all this really necessary? Couldn't you postpone it until we're certain of your safety?" There wasn't anything more than mild exasperation behind Trent's words as he helped her set up her table at the market but she was compelled to defend herself anyway.

"Yes, it's necessary. You insisted on coming along, so you'll have to suck it up and deal. It might not seem like a big deal to you, but I have customers who expect me." She straightened rows of jelly jars, wishing she could have added more to her meager stock. When she'd asked about picking berries out at her farm, Trent had given her a single look. No words had been necessary. "I don't want your money. I have money of my own in savings, but I'm choosing to live on what I make. If I'm going to open an animal rescue, then I have to be smart with my savings. Who knows what will happen with my house and whether or not the insurance will cover the damage? Right now, it's not looking good."

His eyes told her all she needed to know about his thoughts on the subject. Along the same lines of his offer to help her with money, he'd more than likely be willing to help her with her home.

Not happening.

She appreciated his generosity all the more because there were no strings attached, as it should be with a gift. Preston had always acted as if she owed him the sun, moon, and stars for everything they owned. Yet, when she'd wanted to work, he'd thrown a fit. Of course, he'd been more worried about what everyone would think if she took a job. Didn't she think he was capable of providing for her?

He never understood. She'd fought for the freedom and would do things her way.

"I'll be fine. You don't have to hover. We're in a busy public place and, with everything that's happened, they'll probably give things a rest for a bit." She turned into the heat of him and wiped his frown away with her fingers. "If you keep scowling, you'll scare all my customers away."

He growled, low and menacing, then dipped for a breath-stealing kiss. "I don't care. All the better to keep the assholes away, my dear." He returned for another taste, tangling his tongue with hers, only backing off once he made her toes curl.

"I wish I had more stock. If I can't salvage what's at home, I'll have to nearly double my time in the kitchen this coming week to make up for the loss." Just the day before, she'd been cleared to go into her house. The fire hadn't spread past the living room and it had been deemed structurally sound. After she finished up at the market, Trent planned to take her home to look things over and get a start on sorting out what would no doubt be a total mess. The Fire Marshall opened an investigation and still had questions, but there wasn't much she could tell them. All she could do was take the headache one day at a time.

She'd have to find an alternate solution until he decided she could pick the berries on her farm. Thinking about the waste, sickened her, but what could she do? She'd dipped into her savings and purchased a couple of flats at a farmer's market in Bourbon County, not too far from Trent's place. She'd worked double time to try and make up for the shortage, but she'd have to figure out a better solution for long term.

He sighed and looked up to the canopy above them but, wisely, he didn't comment.

And that was something she was getting used to and liking. He might grumble over her not wanting his help or be bossy when it came to her safety, but he'd never once looked down on her for doing something as simple at operating a booth at the farmer's market.

With her putting in long hours in his kitchen and him both tending his horses and working with Rick, they'd both been exhausted each night. They hadn't had enough time to do much more than have a quick dinner together and go to their separate beds.

She wasn't naïve enough to believe things would continue that way for much longer. He'd come in the day before to find her in the kitchen with her hands covered in a sticky mess. There wasn't a woman alive between the ages of eighteen and eighty who would misunderstand the raw desire in his eyes. His hands dived into the hair at her nape and he'd stolen a long, wet, panty-melting kiss.

When she'd grumbled it wasn't fair because she couldn't touch him, he smirked and whispered, "I know." He'd stolen another kiss, along with all the air in her lungs, then left.

She'd stood there, stupefied, her hands sticky with berry juice, likely looking like a star-struck teenager.

"Have you decided on a name for your rescue?" His question pulled her back to the present.

"No, not yet. I've been thinking, but nothing sounds right. I'm certain I want to at least include horses, if not focus on them. I'll come up with something. There are a million things to research and figure out, but I'm making headway." Not even the mountain of work waiting for her could dampen her happiness when she thought of her plans. She pulled the last box of jars from the truck bed and sat it on the table.

"Trent Dawson! How are you? It's been ages." An overly cheerful, borderline shrill, voice rang out through the crowd. Unable to stop herself, Kate stopped arranging jars to look up.

"Shit. Not here, not now. Who the hell told her where to find me?" Quiet, but undoubtedly irritated, Trent cursed beside her. Helpless with curiosity, Kate searched for the source of his anger.

Tall and slender with artfully applied makeup, she could have been a runway model. Pale, perfect porcelain features and miles of thick, auburn hair framed striking green eyes. Her expensive jeans were so tight, they looked as though they'd been painted on. Kate wasn't sure how the woman was capable of walking or even breathing in them. Her boots were new and probably had never stepped foot in real grass, let alone a barn.

"What are you doing here, Lindsey? Who told you were to find me?" Trent faced the redhead with his arms crossed and a frown on his face.

"I bumped into Ray at the Empty Horseshoe the other night, and he said you'd probably be out here today. I have a little favor to ask." She trailed a finger over Trent's chest and smiled. *Wow.* Kate had seen a lot of professional moves in her day, but this Lindsey chick had the simpering princess vibe perfected.

"How many drinks did you pour into Ray to get him to talk?" Trent's irritation edged toward anger as he pointedly looked down to the polished fingernail on his chest. "My schedule is full. I can't help with whatever it is. You'll have to find someone else."

"I'm looking to buy a horse. I need your help. You can't make time to show me around your stable? I'm sure you have something that will suit me." If the woman poured any more sugar into her tone, she'd draw bees.

"I'm not interested Lindsey. Not in you or your bullshit story."

"I miss Justin. That was the biggest mistake of my life. I panicked and ran. It was silly of me. Would you be willing to let me take you out to dinner, so we can talk about old times?" Big crocodile tears welled in her eyes, somehow only making them seem bigger and brighter.

"No. Goodbye, Lindsey."

"Well, here's my new number if you change your mind..." When she saw the look on Trent's face, she stopped mid-sentence. "Bye, Trent." As if she'd said farewell to her long-lost best friend, she turned and walked away without giving him the card she held.

Trent just shook his head and looked as if he wanted to throw something. He placed his hands on his hips, tipped his head back and closed his eyes.

A customer came up, so she chatted with them a moment and completed their purchase. While she promised that she'd be back with more jam the following weekend, Trent stayed silent.

Dark and heavy, his mood threatened to suffocate her. She couldn't stand the tension any longer. "Okay, spill. Before all the anger inside you explodes, let some of it out." She kept her voice quiet as she moved to stand in front of him. She met his eyes and draped her forearms on his shoulders. Her heart ached when she saw something other than blind anger there. It was so much worse. His eyes were full of pain.

She didn't know how to erase his misery, but she had to do something. "Okay. Let's start with the basics. Tell me her name and how you know Ms. Tightpants."

When he blinked and looked at her as if she'd lost a marble or two, she knew she was on the right track, so she continued. "Didn't her momma tell her that, no matter how tight your clothes are, it will never make up for a distinct lack of class?" She let every ounce of her Kentucky accent into her words. "I mean, she was sporting some serious camel-toe. It just screams shameless floozy, bless her heart."

He shook his head and smirked. "Lindsey was Justin's fiancée. They had plans to get married as soon as we finished our tour in Afghanistan. When he came home, wounded and facing a lifetime of surgeries, pain and the very real possibility that he would never be the same man again, she cut and ran. She couldn't face it."

Scrubbing a hand across his face, his lips took on a rueful smile. "I never liked her, Harlan and Sandy were never crazy about her, but her emotional abandonment cinched it. She lacked the basic decency in her heart to give it a little time. Why couldn't she let him gain some strength before she told him she wanted out? Before he was awake and out of intensive care, she snuck in and laid her engagement ring on the table beside his fucking hospital bed. She didn't have enough spine to give his ring back to him in person before she split. I watched him give up the will to live. I saw it fade right then and there. He kept up appearances for his parents, but he laid there and waited to die. It was the hardest thing I've ever had to watch."

He paused, seeming to collect himself before he continued. "Knowing Harlan and Sandy saw it as well only made him wasting away all the more painful to bear."

"You love them." She stroked a hand up and down his arm, offering the comfort of her touch as he recalled the obviously traumatic memory.

"I do. They're my parents. They claimed me for no other reason than they're good people and they raised me. I can't ever take them, or what they gave me, for granted."

"I'm glad they were there for you and that they had you throughout Justin's death. I know it hurt you all horribly, but by taking you in, they saved themselves, in a way. Were you two always close?" Her heart ached for the pain he must have endured.

"We barely knew each other when our worlds collided. He and I rode the same school bus together but never said much to each other. We were always lost in our own little worlds. When we were eight or so, an older boy from the middle school gave Justin a hard time. He kept calling him names and giving him hell for being a rich kid. Justin tried to ignore it, but things escalated. I jumped in when another middle school kid joined the first. They beat the snot out of us. When the bus driver had to pull over to break it up, I took the blame. No one at my house gave a shit about me. My mom probably wouldn't have even noticed that nearly half of my face was swollen. Why would it matter if I got in trouble? She wouldn't care." He watched the early morning activity, but she suspected he'd turned his thoughts far away.

Helpless, she wrapped her arms around his waist and laid her head on his shoulder. The rumble of his voice vibrated through his chest and tingled against the hand she'd placed over his heart. "Justin had the perfect life and hadn't done anything wrong. Why should he get in trouble for defending himself against a bully? When the driver came to Justin's stop, he insisted I get off with him. The driver didn't say a word when really I shouldn't have been allowed off without a note.

"Justin tried to sneak me up in to the bathroom, but Harlan caught us. He took one look then took us behind the barn to get the story. Justin explained, while I dug a hole in the ground with the toe of my shoe. I fully expected to be ran off their property, but Harlan gave us a boxing lesson right then and there. He swore us to secrecy. Sandy came out to call them for dinner and found all three of us with our fists up, pretending to fight. She acted like she didn't notice we were breaking her no fighting rule and took us in to clean up." He ran an absentminded hand over the length of her hair.

"I can't imagine the worry she must have felt when she saw you both so battered. I'd have been spitting mad." The vision of two little boys with bruised faces haunted her.

"She had to have been as well. That's the only reason she would have allowed the lesson. After dinner, Harlan gave me a ride home. He insisted on walking me to the door. When he knocked, no one answered. I tried to tell him it was fine, how I stayed by myself all the time. He refused to leave me. I knew what'd he'd find when he opened the door, and I tried my damndest to get him to go back home. He caught onto my panic and opened the door. He took one look, grabbed my hand and took me back to their place without a word.

"I knew without looking what he probably saw. Most likely my mom was passed out on the couch with a bottle of whatever cheap alcohol she could afford that day still in her hand. From that point on, I spent most of my days and nights at the Walkers. I know at one point they tried to get her to seek treatment, but she refused. About two years later, my mother died of liver failure. Harlan had his attorney draw up papers, and I don't know what kind of magic they worked, but they claimed me as their own." He turned her into him and kissed the top of her head.

"I've always known they were good people, but they are *really* good people." It was the right thing, something her father would have done.

"I owe them everything I am." He released her and walked to the edge of her market space and stared out into the distance. This time his eyes appeared alert as he scanned the area from one corner to the other. "So, yeah. Justin and I became inseparable, but it wasn't just because of my circumstances. We clicked. We were both outcasts of different breeds and it was a relief to be able to just be who and what we wanted to be with each other without judgment."

She set up her chalkboard and wrote out the day's inventory and prices. To fill the empty space where her fresh berries should have been, she drew a few berries and flowers. "You both needed that freedom, that connection in your lives."

"I guess. He always wanted to be a soldier. When Sandy got a little panicky over the idea, he settled for the National Guard to pacify her. The idea was he could eventually help run the business side of Walker Stables while I helped Harlan with the horse side. I went simply because Justin had joined, and I had nothing better to do. Being a stubborn teenager, I refused to let them put me through college, so I told them I didn't want to go to school.

"I came from nothing. I should have been the one to die. Never Justin. Never Harlan and Sandy's son. He was loved. He had everything in the world going for him. That bitch Lindsey couldn't see past her own little selfish bubble and, with one move, she shattered my family. Less than three months later, she married another man— much older and with more money. Gossip says she's on the hunt for, not her second or third, but her fourth rich husband. According to Rick, this time she wants one with both money and life left in him. For some reason, she's set her sights on me."

Her heart broke in two ragged pieces, but she didn't think he'd appreciate the knowledge, so she settled for a simple fix. She stood on tiptoe and kissed him. "Well, that's too damn bad for her. She can't have you."

Sometimes simple worked best.

Something soft whispered across his features and he patted her ass. "You've got a customer, babe."

He'd sent the idiot on his way, knowing that he'd do exactly what he'd been told. Even if he thought he was following his own plan, he wasn't. He'd been ridiculously easy to manipulate. All he required was a scene. A little drama played out in public forum would add another layer of suspicion on his target.

He adjusted his hat and surveyed the parking lot as he ambled through. *Just another good ol' boy out for a day at the flea market.* The early morning rush ended and it wasn't quite lunch time, so the traffic in and out slowed. He watched a young woman sit her little one into a stroller, load it up with baby crap and then she went on her way, leaving him alone.

One more pass and he decided it was likely his best chance. It only took a few seconds to unlock the truck. He opened the door and checked the glove box. It was empty, except for the usual paperwork and manuals.

He went to the center console, opened it, and found what he needed. It wasn't his first choice, but it would suit his needs.

Too fucking easy.

He slipped it into his backpack, closed up the console and locked the truck. He looked around and, other than an aging, feeble man pulling an old wagon near the entrance, the lot was clear.

With a little luck, the item wouldn't be missed for a couple of days.

It was more than he needed.

She looked up and swore. *What is he doing here?* Couldn't she have one day of peace? Why was that too much to ask?

Preston stood near the first table in the farmer's market and looked around. Seeing as he'd never stepped foot in any sort of outdoor market in his life, it didn't take a genius to figure out he came to see her.

Dressed in expensive loafers, slacks and a button up shirt, he stood out like a sore thumb. But when he walked through the crowd, he didn't come up to her as she'd expected. He headed straight for Mr. Peterman and his wagon.

Mr. Peterman came every weekend with his grandson, and they spent the day filling their wagon with junk. His junk collection neared hoarder proportions. He'd nearly filled his home and had begun to add his finds to the feed store. Today was no exception. He'd purchased a used television, and Trent had gone over to help him load it into the wagon.

Preston walked straight up to Trent and tapped him on the shoulder. *Oh no.* This had nightmare written all over it. Still in a crouch, Trent carefully set the television down and looked up. Recognition, irritation and disbelief flashed across his features. Even from her booth, she saw his eyes tighten. He nodded to Mr. Peterman and turned to face Preston.

"I heard you've been sleeping with my wife." Preston's voice was loud and obnoxious. He sounded drunk. He'd never been much of a drinker, and it was still early. Had he drank something to compensate for his lack of true courage?

Oh. Dear. God. What was wrong with Preston?

Trent arched a brow and looked down at her ex-husband. "Ex. She's your ex-wife. She left you. She divorced you. What she and I are or are not doing in a bed or elsewhere is none of your concern. Anything she does stopped being your business the day she filed for divorce."

Preston's voice changed to a whine. "How do I know she wasn't sleeping with you before she filed?"

"Man, what are you after? She's made it clear, she wants nothing to do with you. You were a lucky man. You had her first, but you fucked it up. That's all on you. I should thank you for being an idiot because it cleared the path for me to meet the sweetest woman I've ever met. But again, I repeat, what we do or don't do is none of your business. Did you show up here with the intention of starting trouble? 'Cause that's what you're doing, making an ass out of yourself." Trent stared down at Preston, his handsome features marked by a frown of irritation.

When she realized Trent was right, Preston was likely here just to cause trouble, she expected Trent's anger to go nuclear. But that moment when she'd forgotten that's not who Trent was only lasted a bare second.

Trent had the air of a man extremely annoyed by a pesky fly. She saw none of the testosterone-frothing rage she'd dreaded.

That was all Preston. That was the life she'd come from and not where she was headed. Noticing the contrast in the two men sealed her fate. On one side, she saw her past and all the resulting pain and heartache. The cause for most of it stood there, in his expensive clothes, looking down on the world around him. She'd lay a small part of the blame at her own feet simply because she'd tolerated it for so long when she shouldn't have.

On the other side stood a man in faded jeans and old boots who went out of his way to help an old man with a heavy television that would probably end up tucked into a corner of an already over-packed house. There was no doubt in her mind that later today Trent would get his hands dirty helping her clean up waterlogged trash at her house. Just the day before, at his ranch, she'd watched him patiently coax a skittish horse into a trailer using nothing but his soft voice and a great deal of time.

Night and day.

When she thought about her life, she realized she was happy. Or at least she had been until Preston arrived. She'd fought for her peace, and she would not stand by while he screwed it up. She was done with him and the headaches he caused.

She rounded her table and, before she knew it, stood between the two men. Her anger boiled white-hot as she pushed a finger into Preston's chest and lit into him with all the pent up anger and hurt she'd stored over the years.

"You. Get out of my life. I'm done with you and the headache of having you in my past. You have no place in my world, *none*. Go away." She stepped forward and pushed with her finger. In that moment, her finger had all the strength in the world and she was going to use it to crush Preston like a bug.

A strong arm wrapped around her ribs and a low voice spoke in her ear. "Kate, I've got this. I don't need you to protect my virtue." Was he smiling? He was smiling. She could hear the amusement in his voice.

"Why, I don't know, but he came here to pick a fight with you. I won't have it. I like you and I'm keeping you. He needs to get lost."

"Kate, I don't know what I ever saw in you. You're nothing but white trash. Coming back to Riley Creek has made you lose your mind." Filled with derision, Preston shook his head at her as if she had truly gone crazy. He turned and walked back the way he'd come.

She stared holes into his back until he disappeared from view. Then she realized what she'd done and what she'd said. *Oh no.* She never lost control and she never lost her poise or the smile that was everything.

She turned her no doubt bright red face to Trent and buried it in his broad chest.

"So. You're keeping me, huh?" Laughter colored his voice.

"Oh God. I'm so sorry. I saw him and I got so mad. I just lost it. Pretend you didn't hear that."

"What if I liked what I heard?" His words were murmured low, as if he meant them for her alone.

"You did?"

"I did." He kissed her lightly, but he didn't hide the desire in his eyes, letting her know without words what was on his mind. Desire, electric and potent arced between them. "Crowd's watching. Let's get back to your berries."

Trent disconnected his call with Rick and left his office. He found Kate in the kitchen washing more berries. Did the woman ever quit working? He doubted it. After spending half the day at the farmer's market, they'd worked at her house then came back to his place. She'd insisted on seeing to Bonnie herself, even though his employees would have handled the task easily. Then she'd showered and fixed a quick meal for them both. After all that, she had enough energy to make fucking jam?

She was either the hardest working woman he'd ever known or crazy. Possibly both.

"Won't those keep until tomorrow?" She really needed to give it rest for a bit.

"They should be fine for a couple of days, I think. Why?" She'd turned on the radio as she worked, and he watched her hips sway in time to the music. The volume was low and her movement so subtle, he wasn't sure she was aware she did it.

She wore a pair of pale blue pajama bottoms that had been washed so many times they hugged each curve and dip of her ass. He tried to focus on her words, but the sight of her heart-shaped cheeks snagged his attention.

"Trent?" She turned and caught him staring. Shit. Caught red-handed, there was no reason to hide it. He just grinned. "Does Rick have any news? I can only hold Joe back with vague answers for so long. Any day now, he's going to show up demanding answers and to make sure you're not holding me against my will. It won't be pretty, especially if I don't have something to give him."

He wished he could do the same—just show up on the senator's door and demand answers. It'd be so much easier, but he'd do anything to keep Kate safe, even go toe-to-toe with her overprotective cousin. He couldn't say he blamed the man, though. Call him old-fashioned, but every woman should have someone in their corner watching out for them. The time might come when they'd have to tell Joe MacDonald what was happening, but they couldn't take a single chance.

"Rick's had someone digging into both Preston's and Bailey's finances. According to the reports, the good senator made a couple of large deposits to an offshore account. Rick's guy is trying to find out who holds the account now." He leaned against the counter and crossed his arms.

"Exactly how much money is a large deposit?" She set a colander full of strawberries in the sink to drain and turned to face him.

"The first one was a hundred and fifty thousand. The last one was a quarter of a million dollars."

"I didn't think he was that wealthy. I mean, I know he lives comfortably and has some old family money, but that's almost a half a million dollars. Wow. What could it be for?" She walked into his arms where she fit, as though she belonged there.

"I don't know, but to me it reads as either paranoia or dirty dealings. Either one isn't good." He shook his head, wishing he had better news to share.

"You're probably right. I don't see him gifting the money to puppies or starving children." A shudder passed through her shoulders, and he smoothed his hands over them.

"Why don't you rest for a bit? Keeping up with you today has worn me out. You've got to be exhausted."

"I am tired, but it's a habit, now." She tucked a strand of hair behind her ear and he wondered if it was only habit like she said or something more. She seemed to have a near obsessive need to stay busy and work for everything she had. It was a trait he appreciated, even admired, but it could go too far.

"What are you making tonight?" Following the scent of berries, he moved closer. When she turned to him, her own vanilla scent mixed with the fruit, making his mouth water.

"Strawberries. I'll be sad to see them go. They're almost out of season now. Do you want one?" She selected one from the colander and took a bite. "These are sweeter than they are tart, which is great. I won't have to add as much sugar."

He grasped her wrist and pulled her hand to his mouth. Her attention shifted to him and her lips parted as he took a bite of the fruit in her hand. Sweet and juicy, the flavor melted over his tongue, but it wasn't what he wanted.

They'd danced around each other for days, and he'd tired of it.

"It's good, but I want something sweeter. Give me a taste, pretty Kate." Not giving her time to object, he dipped to touch his mouth to hers. Lord, she was soft as she released a breathy little sigh.

But he wasn't soft or sweet. His body had grown hard and hungry, starving for her. Unless she threw up a red light, he was taking what they both wanted.

For days she'd nearly tiptoed through the heavy, anticipatory air. They hadn't spent much time together, but each time they'd crossed paths, the weight in the air tightened until she'd imagined she felt the press of it against her skin. Somehow, without words, it hadn't become a question of would they or wouldn't they address the issue of chemistry, but a matter of when.

Apparently, Trent decided enough was enough. He touched his mouth to hers, igniting a firestorm of desire. She opened, letting him take until she saw stars. The rough tips of his fingers grazed her cheeks as he tilted her head and sucked her bottom lip.

Lost in the storm, her hands searched for an anchor and gripped the waistband of his jeans. They curled, the backs of her fingers meeting the warm flesh of his abdomen. She toyed with the button of his jeans.

He touched his forehead to hers. "What do you say we give those legs of yours a test run?" She met the heat of his eyes where dark and turbulent desire simmered. Something snagged behind her heart, squeezed and blocked her breath.

Well, if she couldn't speak or breathe then she might as well go back to kissing him, because the man could kiss. She tackled his mouth with hers, taking every bit as much as he'd taken from her and giving it all right back.

He gripped her hips in his hands and lifted, sitting her at his waist. The evidence of his arousal singed her through her thin pajamas, branding her with a fire she'd never forget.

The house moved by in a blur then they were in his room and on the bed, a tangle of limbs, heat, and desire. Lips, tongues, and teeth dueled in a passionate war where no one lost.

He pulled his mouth away and put his forehead against hers. His heart raced hers as he closed his eyes, appearing to give himself a moment to settle.

"I swear all it takes in one sweet little smile from you and my cock turns to steel. All I can think about is stripping you bare and sinking my teeth into you while every rational thought in my head flees. Let's see if we can slow this down a bit. A body like yours needs to be savored."

Slow down. *Slow down?* That was the last thing she wanted. She wanted to be pressed against him in a hot, bare, flesh to flesh clench. She wanted to succumb to the demanding, greedy inferno that threatened to claim them both. He felt the same as she did. She saw it in his eyes and heard it in his deep controlled breaths.

He stood, took the bottom of his T-shirt in both hands and pulled it up and over his head. Every ridge and shadowed hollow created by long days of work flexed. Taking in the sight, she forgot every thought. Fortunately, she didn't need brains. She could simply lie there and stare at the view until the end of her days.

"Your turn." His sexy half-smile turned her girl parts to liquid. The heat in her belly pooled, spread and engulfed her. "I showed you mine, now show me yours."

Without giving her time to comply, he took matters into his own hands. He raised her shirt by placing his palms flat to her abdomen and sliding them up her torso, removing fabric as he went. Pleasure followed beneath his touch and grew like a wildfire engulfing every cell. Her shirt disappeared.

A slow, wandering finger trailed from her shoulder, over her collarbone then to the upper border of her bra. "Pretty, but it's got to go."

Tugging her upright, he crushed her to his chest, unfastened her bra and whispered into her ear. "I can't tell you how many times I've dreamed of seeing your breasts. I told myself repeatedly to stop, that you weren't for me. Yet each night, when I closed my eyes, you insisted on haunting my bed." His voice, filled with wicked promise, rumbled in her ear. "Show me."

He laid her down and sat back, giving her a little space and waiting. Watching her, with those intense gray eyes. She couldn't count how many times she'd been near or completely nude in front of others over the years, but right then with Trent, it mattered. She knew that her body was decent, but she wasn't a twenty-something, perfect, pageant queen anymore. Somehow though, she knew that no matter what she revealed to him, he'd approve.

She slid the fabric shielding her breasts down her arms, baring herself. A hungry intensity sparked in the smoke of his gaze. As if they knew they were on display, her breasts grew tight, swelling and vying for his attention.

"Fucking perfect." His hands skimmed up her belly, lighted over her ribs and cupped the mounds, thumbing her nipples. Her hips arched in reaction, seeking contact of their own. "Not yet. We'll get there, but you hold still for now." One hand moved down to cup between her legs and put her where he wanted her without words.

He took one tight nipple into his mouth, drawing hard. When her hips tried to buck in response, he held her with that one hand, his eyes never once leaving hers. Working her until she was dizzy, he moved from one breast to the other. Sucking and tormenting with the sweetest of tortures, he drove her to the peak of madness without pushing her over.

Trent drew away and finished stripping her. As if awed by the sight, he stood and paused. He wiped a hand over his mouth then unfastened his jeans. Already low on his cut hips, the denim dipped even lower revealing a faint, dark blond trail of hair. In one smooth move, he pushed the jeans and underwear down, baring his everything. And, damn was there a lot of everything to take in. Cut muscle from head to toe and the kind of equipment that made women swoon, he was perfection. His cock stood straight and ready. Long and thick, it drew her gaze and made her hunger.

He'd stolen her ability to speak.

He opened the bedside table, produced a condom and slipped it on. He returned to her, sinking into the bed and her.

"Legs, sweetheart. Let me have them. Since I first saw you in that barn, wearing a fancy dress and old mud boots, I've been dying to try them on for size." Taking one ankle, he opened her and moved between her hips. He notched the head of his cock at her entrance and eased in, stretching her flesh with a delicious burn.

He met her mouth with his and kissed her until she saw stars. Then he moved. Once, twice, he eased in and out, rasping through her tightness. As if satisfied she was with him, he slammed home in a single plunge. He met her gaze with his, pressed a final passionate kiss to her lips and then let loose, driving in a steady, relentless pace. Again and again, he drove into her, each thrust a devastating pleasure-filled blow.

Something inside her swelled, tightened and grew with electric bliss. A bright bubble of ecstasy expanded with every touch of his body to hers. She wrapped her other leg tight around his waist, tying him to her. Tilting her hips, she met him more completely and his cock found that spot.

The spot that made grown women forget their names and beg for more.

He intensified his rhythm, somehow doing the impossible and making something that was perfect even better. She arched and tangled her hands into the hair at the back of his neck, hanging on for dear life as that bright bubble grew again. His hand slid down her abdomen then lower, finding her clit. A rough, calloused finger rasped over the straining nub and she exploded with a blinding flash of heat and pleasured agony. Her body bowed as her pussy clenched tight around his hard flesh, spasming and gripping him.

He wrapped an arm around her hips, thrust home in a brutal final plunge and groaned into her neck. She clenched his shoulders and felt the muscled strength of him stiffen as he held his hips close to hers.

He shuddered and met her eye to eye. Long moments of heavy, blissed out silence passed.

Then he pulled away on a low groan, walked to the bathroom and returned a moment later. He slid into bed, pulling her close.

"Beauty, I think those legs will work just fine."

Chapter Ten

A month ago she would have laughed in the face of anyone who told her she would fall into another relationship. She'd been determined to go it alone. As the first dim rays of dawn peeked into Trent's window and the solid comforting heat of him seeped into her, she wouldn't have it any other way.

She heard her cell ring in the other room, so she carefully eased out of bed. She grabbed Trent's T-shirt and slipped it on. The soft cotton fell to and brushed across her thighs as she went to answer. Early morning calls never brought good news. A knot of worry tightened in her belly as she answered.

"Katie!" The excited whisper did absolutely nothing to dampen the volume of the small, familiar voice that she adored.

"Kylie, is that you? What are you doing up this early?"

"I ate all my begetables wast night so daddy said I could go wiff him to feed the cattle this morning." She listened to her niece ramble on as she started a pot of coffee.

"So which vegetables did you have to eat?"

"Fwoccoli and cawwots." Her niece's disgust echoed loud and clear through the phone. She could easily picture Kylie's scrunched up nose and squinted eyes.

"That's great, honey, but I thought you liked carrots."

"I do, but I don't like the fwoccoli."

"It's broccoli with a b, sweetheart. So, is your daddy getting ready?"

"That's what I said, fwoccolli. No, he weft a while ago. Gwampa came over. He's gonna take me to feed the cows. He's looking for my lost boot now." *Poor Grandpa Robert.* Who knew where she'd left the stray shoe or how long it would take Joe's dad find it.

"Why's Grampa there?" Joe kept a strict routine and never veered from it unless he had no other choice. He had to in order to take care of Kylie, his cattle and his job, none of which he was willing to part with. They were his everything.

"Daddy had to go to work early. He told Gwampa on the phone he had bad news to deliver. Daddy had the sad face on. He doesn't like bad news." No, he didn't. And, with no thanks to his job, he had to deliver it often. Added to that, Kate suspected that each time he notified someone of a death, he was reminded of how he lost Kylie's mother.

"Did you eat breakfast yet?" Time to steer her niece onto a new topic.

"Daddy made me eggs and toast while he waited on Gwampa. He didn't get to eat any though. He weft as soon as Gwampa pawked his twuck." Yet again, her cousin put himself last and had a long, likely busy day ahead of him. Her heart hurt for him, but there wasn't anything she could do. He wouldn't let anyone help him. Other than occasionally drafting a family member to keep Kylie when he got called away, he insisted on doing everything himself.

Stubborn MacDonald man.

"Uh oh. I gots to go. I think Gwampa found my boot. Bye!"

As fast as she had called, her niece was gone. Kate shook her head and poured herself some coffee. She'd start both breakfast and the day. It might be early yet, but she had a long list of things to do.

After all the calories they'd burned last night, Trent would likely wake starving.

She was whisking eggs when heavy arms wrapped around her ribs and pulled her back against a muscled wall. "How long?" A low, barely understandable rumble whispered in her ear.

"Until food's ready? Fifteen minutes or so." She turned in his arms and drank in the sight of his sleep ruffled hair standing on end. Stubble the color of a sandy beach peppered his jaw. Bedhead and sleepy eyes shouldn't be so damn sexy on a man, but she could lick him up. His hands dropped to the hem of the shirt she wore and flirted with her bared skin. They trailed around and lighted on the bottom curves of her ass. Then as if he just didn't care, he cupped both cheeks and pulled her close against him.

"Hmmmm. Want you." He leaned in and nuzzled her ear making her knees wobble. "Shower, food, then I'm taking you again." Then he nipped her ear, patted her ass, turned and left her watching his low slung jeans shift on his hips as he left the kitchen. He must have slipped them on commando, leaving them unzipped. As low as they sat, there was no way he had anything on beneath them.

She fanned her face and turned. *Breakfast.* She was making breakfast, not making a fool out of herself mooning over Trent Dawson.

She'd just set the butter on the counter for toast when the doorbell rang, startling her. She heard Trent's voice from the hall, all business. "Don't answer that." She turned in time to see him head straight for the door, all traces of laziness gone. Then he cursed and looked to her. "Go put some clothes on. It's your cousin, and he does not look happy. Hurry."

Her cousin? Why was Joe here this early?

Then she heard Kylie's sweet little voice replay in her ear. "Bad news to deliver. Daddy had the sad face on."

Trent read the fear on her face and came to her. "Go get dressed, baby. We'll talk to him together, okay?"

She nodded and ran to do as she'd been told. She threw on clean clothes, ran a brush through her messy hair and made herself take a few deep, slow breaths.

She returned to the living room to find Trent holding the door wide open, but Joe continued to stand at the threshold wearing an unreadable expression. Another man she'd never seen before stood beside him.

"Kate, this is detective Bowie. He has some questions to ask you and Trent." A twisting, nauseating sense of despair took root deep in her stomach.

In reflex she went down a list. Obviously Joe and Kylie were both okay. Trent drew her into his side, sharing his strength, so he was fine. "Is Leigh okay?" Dear God, please don't let anything be wrong with Leigh.

"Leigh Ann's fine, honey. You need to speak with the detective." Something odd laced Joe's tone. It was cold, unyielding.

"Kate MacDonald?" The detective held up his badge. "I'm Detective Bowie. I'm here to inform you that your ex-husband is dead."

She dug her fingers into Trent's arm and sucked in air.

Son of a bitch. He had to call Rick immediately, but he couldn't leave Kate. She'd just had the rug pulled from beneath her feet. He wouldn't leave her to face the cops on her own. But, damn, did the situation stink to high Heaven. An ugly sense of foreboding sank its claws into the back of his neck, gripping tight.

Undoubtedly, Preston had been a royal pain in the ass, but this had trouble written all over it. He itched for his phone, but stayed with Kate as she answered the detective's questions one-by-one.

He knew what was coming next. Sure enough, the questions stopped aiming at Kate and redirected to him. He answered and held Kate, feeling the sting of her fingernails in his flesh. He focused on that little bite of pain and took solace in the fact that she was safe in his arms.

After what had felt like hours but probably wasn't much more than a few minutes, they left, leaving him with a visibly shaken Kate. He tucked her into the corner of his couch, pressed a reassuring kiss to her forehead.

She wrapped her arms around her middle and looked to him for answers. "This isn't a coincidence is it? Preston changed so much in the last year or two. We didn't get along anymore, but I didn't want him dead, I swear. All I wanted was to be left alone."

"No, I wish it were a coincidence, but it can't be. Somehow it's all tied to you and Senator Bailey." He wished like hell he could give her the answers and safety she deserved.

"What does he want from me? I've never done anything to him. I don't understand." She shook her head as her eyes shone with unshed tears.

"I don't either. Just promise me you won't go anywhere without me until this is settled. All right?" His heart sank when her only response was a single quiet nod.

"I've got to update Rick, okay?" She nodded again and straightened her spine as if realizing she'd allowed it to soften. Didn't the woman know she could lean on others?

He stood and paced as he called Rick. It took several rings before he finally picked up. "Lo?" Trent could barely make out the greeting over the crappy connection.

"Where are you, man?" It wasn't like him to not answer by the third ring. He was always on standby with his phone at his side.

"Sorry, shitty cell service out here. I'm out in BFE, Riley Creek."

"What are you doing out there again? This is what, the second time this week? You really have a thing for…" He stopped speaking and glanced up. He'd nearly forgotten Kate wasn't far away.

"No, it's not her. I'm looking for the kid we saw the night of the fire."

"She got to you, didn't she?" Rick had been given the nickname Granite, when they'd been in the desert. Nothing appeared to move him. It had taken Trent some time, but eventually he'd learned otherwise.

"No. You know how I can't stand loose ends. What's up?" The cell signal strengthened and his voice came through clearer.

"Joe MacDonald and a Detective Bowie just left here. They came bearing news."

"Shit." Rick's muttered curse echoed Trent's feelings.

Trent walked down the hallway to his office. Kate didn't need to hear his speculations, especially the more gruesome ones. "Yep. Someone found Preston dead last night. They wouldn't give us many details, but I got the impression it was messy. To say they were suspicious would be an understatement."

"He's the idiot troublemaker and someone's tying up their own loose ends would be my guess." Rick put two and two together.

"Mine too. No question, he was an ass, but I don't like this." He stared out his office window at the active farm.

"No shit."

Trent heard the low growl of his own car as the engine rumbled to life. "Are you ever going to get your own ride or just keep stealing mine?"

"Borrow yours. You never use it. A car this sexy and mean needs to be driven. How's Kate doing?" Rick's taunting turned to concern at the mention of Kate's trouble.

"Pretty well for someone with a soft heart who's just been notified that her ex-husband was murdered." He left his office and made his way back down the hall. He'd left Kate alone for longer than he liked.

"Damn." Rick's single word said it all.

"Exactly."

"I've done all I can do out here today, so I'll head your way. I have a friend who owes me a favor. I'll see if I can shake anything loose. Keep your girl close." He didn't dispute Rick's claim.

"Will do." He was past denying his feelings. He'd been shown time and time again how, in the blink of an eye, the sweetest dreams could become nightmares. He wasn't going to let Kate out of his sight. And her safety was only half the reason.

"Katie!" Delight squealed in a little girl's voice.

Trent placed his hand on Kate's back as a small whirlwind of dark curls raced toward her legs. Certain of a catastrophic impact, he readied to catch the cake she carried, but the little girl stopped a millimeter shy of ramming into Kate. "You came to my pawty!"

Kate's smile was warm and full of loving amusement. "Of course I did. It's not every year you turn six. Your hair looks pretty today."

"Daddy said I should have it fixed 'cause Gwamma will want to take pictures and it's a special day." Kylie scrunched her nose in disgust and her slightly crooked pigtails shook. Trent assumed having her hair fixed wasn't high on her list of favorite activities. "Did you make my cake? Can I see? You didn't make me a fancy pwincess cake, did you? My fwiend at school had a pink pwincess cake, but I don't like pink or pwincesses." She jumped up and down in a mismatched pair of boots, one brown leather and the other black with pink hearts. Her little T-shirt was green with a tractor stamped on the front and her shorts were red.

"It's a surprise. You'll just have to wait and see." He didn't have to see Kate's face to know she was delighted by her small cousin. Her voice rang with happiness and barely controlled laughter.

He softened and rethought his objections about coming to the party. He'd been as worried about her quiet, sad mood over the past week as he had her safety. Hearing laughter and life in her voice made him thankful she talked him into it.

"Who's that?" Kylie moved away from Kate and stopped with the toes of her tiny boots touching his tennis shoes. She looked up at him and squinted as if she were examining a bug in a tree.

"His name is Trent. He's a good friend of mine, so don't play any tricks on him, okay?"

"Okay." She drew the single word out until it had six syllables. He couldn't help but wonder what kind of tricks the little munchkin played on people. "Is he your boyfwiend, Aunt Katie?" The word *boyfriend* might as well have been *vegetable* or *chores* for all the disgust in her tone.

"Kylie Jane! Where'd you run off to?" Joe's voice yelled from somewhere in the house.

"I gotta go! Bye!" Then she was gone as fast as she'd come.

"Tricks?"

188

"You don't want to know. I'd like to keep you around."

He didn't bother telling her that he wasn't going anywhere. There was more than one way to make his point. He took the cake box from her hands and stole a quick, fierce kiss.

"Ahem. Where do you want to set up the party stuff Kate? You're better at this than I am." Joe spoke from the kitchen doorway, clearly not giving a damn if he interrupted them. "Mom and Dad will be here later, but I don't figure she'll feel like setting up."

"No, absolutely not three weeks after heart surgery. She needs to rest and watch Kylie enjoy her day. Leigh can watch over her. You handle the grill and I'll take care of the rest." She took the cake back and set it on the counter. Then she patted Joe's chest. "You man the grill and play nice."

He gave her a frown with *we'll talk later* written all over it.

Trent told Kate on the way over that he didn't have a problem with Joe's continued dislike. If anything, he found the worry and protectiveness admirable. She'd only rolled her eyes at him in a way that suggested he had become a member of the stupid caveman club. He didn't care.

The rapid *stomp-stomp-stomp* of boots echoed distantly through the house, followed by an aggrieved whine. "Dad. Do I have to? I don't wanna wear a dwess."

"She found the clothes I laid out for the party." Joe released a long sigh and left them alone.

"What can I do to help?" He prayed she'd put him to work, so he wouldn't have to stand around counting the minutes until he could get her back home.

"I'll show you where I want the tables outside, and then you can fill the coolers with ice and soda." It wasn't much, but he'd do anything to keep busy. Thanks to Kate's direction, the place went from a slightly messy farmhouse to birthday central in no time. She greeted each guest as if they were her favorite relative until the backyard buzzed with conversation. Kylie reappeared in jean shorts and a matching purple shirt, strutting into the backyard as if she'd won some sort of monumental battle.

"Gwammy!" She greeted her grandparents the same way she had Kate, still in her mismatched boots.

An exhausted looking Joe came to stand by Kate. "I tried to get her into something nicer, but short of sitting on her and wrestling her into it myself or outright spanking her, it wasn't going to happen."

"Joe, it's her day. Don't worry about the little things. She's clean, she's happy and she's surrounded by people who love her. That's more important than what she's wearing. You're doing a good job, you know." Kate patted his arm.

"I can't help but think back to when you and Leigh were little. You two were always the perfect little southern belles. Mom and Aunt Jeannie would have died if either of you went to a party in anything less than ruffles and Mary Janes." He watched his daughter run from family member to family member to greet them with a hug. Then she ran off with a group of kids to the swing set.

Kate snorted. "Joe, I was miserable in those dresses and shoes. I would have given anything to be able to run and play and just be myself. Ask Leigh. She'll tell you the same. There are so many more important things to worry about than whether or not her shoes match."

Trent's heart ached for the little girl Kate had been.

"I know that. I can't help but worry that I'm going to screw up the most important part of my life." Another point in Joe MacDonald's favor—devotion to family proved to be his first priority. Though they might butt heads over Kate, Trent understood his motivation.

Resting her head on Joe's shoulder, Kate said, "Not happening. When she looks back on today, she'll remember happiness and love. She'll have priceless memories of eating her daddy's barbeque, homemade ice cream and the love of her family. That's what she needs most."

The entire group of kids came running and screaming across the large yard and up to the back deck. Only Kylie and a little boy stayed behind, squaring off against each other.

"Shit. What do you want to bet she's found another lizard? My hands are full. I don't have time for another rescue." He opened the grill's lid and smoke wafted out. "I'll never hear the end of it if I burn her hot dogs."

Trent looked to Kate, busy mixing ice cream and ginger ale into a punch bowl. Her smile lit when she focused on him.

"Can you check on them? She's been known to collect reptiles and the occasional wounded bird. There's no telling what they're fighting over now."

A little girl with red hair stopped at the edge of the deck, calling out. "Uncle Joe? There's a snake in the yard!"

"What color is it?" Joe's responded immediately.

"Black."

"I'll go." Trent might not have the first clue about little girl birthday parties, but he could handle a little black snake. He made his way across the yard to see Kylie guarding something. If the boy went right, so did she, blocking his path without a care that he was nearly twice her size.

Her eyes pinpointed him. "Twent. I need your help. Wook." She cast a suspicious eye toward the boy then turned to point at the ground beneath the slide where a small black snake lay. "Derrick wants to smash it, but I want to wet it go. Can we take it to the cweek?"

"My mom hates snakes. I think we should kill it." The little boy stated his case.

"My daddy says black snakes are good. They kill wats and bad snakes. But I'm not allowed to pick snakes up anymore. I don't want to smash it. Don't kill it, Twent. Pwease." Enormous green eyes looked up to him, pleading.

"I won't. Why don't you point me to the creek?" A smile the size of Texas lit her little face. How could someone so small contain so much life and energy? He picked up the snake that was no longer than his forearm and held it carefully. With Kylie's focus on him, somehow the common, harmless reptile suddenly took on as much importance as the rarest of endangered species.

With adoration in her eyes, she took his free hand in hers and led him across the yard. The little boy followed with wide eyes. Trent looked down to peek at the snake as excited chattering met his ears as the entire gang of children caught up and followed them.

When had he become the damn pied piper?

In a few short minutes, they'd reached a shallow creek with a steeply sloped bank at the backyard's end.

"Can I go down, Twent? Sometimes Daddy wets me put my feet in but only if he's watching me. Will you watch me?" Big, green, puppy dog eyes looked up to him. He looked at the other kids and they all had puppy dog eyes. He nearly heard their pants of excitement.

"Not today, munchkin. It's your party day. How about you stay here and watch me cross to the other side. I'll put the snake over—"

"Fwank!" she interrupted.

"Huh?"

She giggled before she answered. "I named him Fwank the snake."

"Okay. I'll put Frank on the other side of the creek where he'll be safe then we can all go back to your party. I'm not sure your dad or Kate would want you get muddy today." That was a good enough excuse wasn't it? He prayed so. He could rescue a snake, but he wasn't sure he was up to wrangling a herd of kids in a muddy creek bed.

"Okay." Several voices rang out with different levels of excitement and disappointment.

He looked for the best place to climb down and jump over.

Kate watched as Trent stopped at the creek's edge with all nine kids looking up at him in varying degrees of hero worship. Front and center stood little Kylie. The poor man had no idea he'd made a friend for life in Kylie by rescuing a scaly animal.

Long, denim-clad legs stretched as he stepped down the bank and climbed up the far side. He bent and set the snake down beside a large rock and then looked up in shock when all the kids put their arms up in the air and cheered.

A silly grin split his face, and he retraced his steps across the creek. When Kylie took his large hand in hers, and he accepted it without blinking, she melted. A man who rescued something as small as a baby snake just to make a little girl happy and held hands with her even though they'd just met was a rare thing. He was the kind of man who wouldn't kick a dog. He'd take care of an animal without blinking and would be someone she could trust to care for her children. That was a man who was born to protect and love.

And Trent was the kind of man she could easily fall in love with.

He returned with his motley posse of little people.

"Daddy! Where's my soccer ball? Trent said he'd pway wiff me, but we have to teach him fiwst. He doesn't know how."

"It's in the garage." Joe answered from the grill where he piled hamburgers on a platter. "You've got about fifteen minutes to play while I cook your hot dogs, okay, pickle?"

"Okay! I'll get it!" In a blur of dark pigtails, Kylie was off.

There was something different in the way Joe looked at Trent. Maybe a grudging acceptance? She could only hope. She hated that two of the most important men in her life barely tolerated each other.

Kylie returned in a rapid-fire clatter of boot steps. She grabbed Trent's hand and pulled him in to the yard then proceeded to show him how to play soccer. At least the way she played soccer. Somewhere along the way, she'd added a few extra rules Kate had never heard of.

Joe pulled the pork from the smoker, and she took it inside to prep for sandwiches. She set the pan on the counter in front of the window so she could see the kids.

And Trent.

When Trent stumbled to avoid bumping into Derrick, the kids decided it was a fine time to knock him to the ground and wrestle with him. All nine of them pounced and he disappeared beneath a wriggling pile of little arms and legs.

Pain seared her hand as something burned her, and she looked down to see that she'd grabbed a corner of the pan without a pot holder. She set it down, shook her hand, and turned from the window. She needed to pay attention before she really hurt herself. She ran cool water over her fingers. Silly. She had work to do. There were at least twelve adults and a mess of kids to feed and she was mooning over Trent.

"Are you okay?"

She jumped.

She'd been so lost in her thoughts that she hadn't heard the door open or Trent come in. The heat of him wrapped around her as he moved in close and tucked her back against his chest.

"I didn't hear the door when you came in."

"You left it open."

"Oh." She probably had since she'd been carrying the hot pan. It was shameful what a man built like Trent in snug denim could do to a woman's concentration.

Or, more accurately, what Trent did to her concentration.

"Let me see." He pulled her hand from the water and looked it over. He took his time. "I don't think it's too awful bad." Low and husky, the sound of his voice melted her.

"It's not. I'll be fine." She couldn't get more than a whisper out as he turned her, capturing her with his stormy gray gaze. He took the finger that bore the biggest brunt of the burn and sucked it into his mouth. He drew on the digit with a slow, languid suction that she felt all the way to her toes and everywhere in between.

She released a shaky breath and gripped his shoulder with her other hand. He stepped back only to ask a question, but his eyes never left hers. "How much longer?"

She blinked and gathered her thoughts. How much longer? Forever. He could do that to her forever and then some.

He smiled a deliciously wicked half-grin that said he knew exactly where he'd taken her thoughts.

"Kate. How much longer?" He spoke slowly, making fun of her. She tried to shake off the haze of lust he'd conjured.

"Until the party's over?"

His wicked grin promised he had more in store for her at the first opportunity. "Yeah. How long do I have to wait?"

"A while yet, we still have to do presents and cake. Are the kids getting to you?" She tucked her hair behind her ear and took a deep breath to settle her racing heart.

"Not at all. I just want to know how long I have to wait until I can strip you bare and sink back into that sexy little body of yours. I want you, sweet Katie Marie." His volume was low, dark and all the more erotic for it as he whispered into her ear and then nipped the soft lobe.

"Pwesents! Huwwy, Katie. Daddy says we have to eat befwoe I open my pwesents." She looked around the wall of Trent's shoulders to see Kylie and the kids standing at the open doorway. They were all but shaking with excitement. "I want a hot dog and a bawbeque and fries. Did you make fwench fwies the way I like them?"

"I did. Exactly the way you like them."

"Yay!" Kylie split the crowd of kids behind her and ran back to her father. "Daddy! Katie made my fwies! Let's eat!"

"Dear God. Will she actually eat all that? She's so little." Trent's amazement made her smile. Clearly he hadn't been around growing, ravenous children very often.

"Yes. She probably will, plus some cake and ice cream. Where do you think she gets all that energy?" He watched the crowd of kids chase after her and shook his head. "Will you carry this out and put it with the burgers and hot dogs? I'll grab the fries and ketchup. Everything else is out there and ready."

He held out his hands and walked away shaking his head.

"I wanna sit wiff Twent!"

"Kylie, we're going to put the kids at one table that way you can all eat together." Joe handed his daughter a plate but carried her drink to a space near the end of the kids' table.

"But he's my new fwiend, and it's my birthday."

"Honey, I don't think there's enough room. Maybe next time." Kate tried to placate Kylie.

"But he's my fwiend." The child's tone turned plaintive.

"How about I move the tables closer together? I'll sit at the end of this table and you sit at the end of yours then we'll be close. Will that work?" Trent offered the most reasonable solution. Kylie made puppy dog eyes at him and nodded her agreement.

Everyone sat to eat. Just as Joe put his second bite to his mouth, a phone rang at his waist. She watched him close his eyes in frustration and put his food down with a frown. His expression only got worse when he looked at the caller ID.

"Daddy, you're not going to work on my pawty day awe you?" For once, sadly, Kylie's little voice wasn't filled with bright energy and spunk.

"No. I'm not going anywhere. It's your special day. I'll be right back. You eat like a good girl, so I can watch you open presents." He pushed away from the table and walked into the middle of the yard.

She assumed Joe's call was work related, as they usually were. The county was short staffed, and they always called on him to fill in. Of course, he usually went when they called. When his face turned thunderously dark and snapped to focus on Trent, she stopped breathing.

He said a few terse words into his phone and stalked over. At the edge of the deck, he paused as if getting his anger under control and closed his eyes tightly. Then he focused on Kylie. "Are you ready for presents?"

"Yes." She smiled up at him, but her usual exuberance dimmed at her father's dark mood.

"Let's go, pickle. Everyone can eat while they watch."

"Okay." She took his hand, and he led her to the gift table and chair.

He picked a random present and handed it over. She tore into it and squealed. "Wace car Wegos! Who's it fwom?"

"The card says they're from Kate and …they're from Kate." The gift was from her, but she'd also added Trent's name to the card. Ominous dread set in, killing her appetite.

"Tank you, Katie! I want Twent to hep me build it."

"No." Joe's response was deadly sharp. Then he softened. "Not today, pickle. It's party day. I'll help you later." What had the phone call been about? No, they hadn't become best friends, but she'd seen Joe soften toward Trent after he'd helped Kylie with the snake.

Kylie plowed through the mountain of gifts, thanking everyone with her bright happiness. Kate couldn't help but love the way every gift was her favorite. Soon enough, she was telling guests goodbye as Kate cleaned.

"Tank you for my cowboy hat!" Kate turned to see Kylie and Mr. Peterman, her great uncle, at the front door. He stooped down for their customary goodbye hug.

"You're welcome. Every pretty girl needs a cowboy hat. Thank you for inviting me to your party, sweetheart. I had a lot of fun." Kate could see by the brightness in his eyes that he meant every word. After Kylie's mother's death, he didn't have a lot of family left, which made the remaining members all the more important.

"It was the best fun ever." Kylie's smile was bright, but her spunk dimmed as after-party exhaustion crept in. Mr. Peterman patted her on the head and nodded to Kate in farewell.

"Hi, Twent."

Kate turned to see he'd come inside from cleanup duty on the back patio.

"Munchkin," he answered, placing one hand on the child's head.

"That your truck with the Bourbon County plate out there, Dawson?" Mr. Peterman looked out the open front door to the driveway.

"It is."

"Hm. What are the odds of that?" He continued to stare at Trent's truck as if he was working a puzzle. "How long you had that dent in the back fender?"

"A year or so. The truck wasn't six months old when one of the stable-hand's sons came out to bring his dad lunch and backed into it."

"You never made'm fix it?"

"Nah. The poor kid was terrified I'd fire his dad. I sent him on and never told Carl. He came to me the next day and apologized. Said his kid told him everything. It wasn't a big deal." Trent's tone remained easy, but when he met Mr. Peterman's eye, something serious lurked in the undercurrent. "Can I ask why you're asking?"

"You remember that day you were at the market with Miss Kate and you helped me and Bobby with that old TV?"

"Yeah, I do." From Trent's tone, he'd picked up on the weight of the question, too.

"Well, right before Bobby and I came inside, there was a guy diggin' around in a truck that looked exactly like yours. It even had Bourbon County plates and a dent in the same spot. You didn't have anyone with you other than Katie Marie, did you? A brother, or someone?"

"No. No, I didn't."

"Hewe! Katie made you a plate to take home so you don't have to cook tonight." Kylie held a foil covered plate up to the old man.

"That's great. Thanks, sweet pea. I should be going." He tipped his head and left, leaving Kate wondering if what he said could be true.

Trent's eyes met hers and then looked down to Kylie, who was nearly swaying on her feet. She got his message. They'd talk later.

"Tank you for my cake, Katie. Did you get a picture so I can keep it?" Her cousin leaned into her hip as if she needed the extra help to stay upright.

"I did. I took a lot of pictures. So did Gramma. Maybe we can make you a memory book." She ran a hand over her cousin's soft hair.

"Okay." Her little face drooped and she yawned. "Can I have another piece? Daddy went to his office and shut the door. He's got his work face on."

"Sure, but how about I fix you a hot dog first? It can be your dinner since your daddy's busy."

"Okay."

Kate fixed Kylie a plate and set her a place at the kitchen bar. She looked up when Joe walked through to the front door without looking at either of them. Had she seen a hint of guilt on his face?

He opened the door as if he expected someone, but she hadn't heard anyone knock. Most family just came right on in, simply announcing their presence as they came through the door. Curious and maybe even a little scared, she went to the living room and peeked out the curtain. In the early evening light, two police cruisers sat at the yard's edge. Both had Bourbon County painted on the side. Her belly cramped, twisting violently.

Trent lived in Bourbon County, but so had she and Preston.

"What's Daddy doing?"

"I don't know, honey. Eat so you can have your cake, okay?"

Only silence greeted her as Kylie came to the window and gripped her hand. Trent, who'd been in the backyard folding tables, came to her other side.

"Damn. Listen to me."

She heard him but couldn't break the haze of anxiety holding her immobile. Joe and three uniformed officers crossed the front yard, coming toward the front door. "Kate, look at me. We don't have much time." His callous-roughened palm cupped her cheek, and he gently turned her to face him. Grave eyes met hers.

"I need you to remember two things. It's important, no matter what. Number one, I need you to call Rick as soon as I'm gone. Call him and explain. He'll take care of everything. Promise me."

She shook herself and some of the haze faded, but it only left more anxiety and grief in its place. Why, she didn't know. Maybe she'd drunk a huge glass of denial, but all the same, the grief tightened her throat.

Why did it feel like she was on borrowed time? Sand in their hourglass fell faster and faster until there were only a few grains left.

"Kate? What's the first thing you're going to do after I'm gone?"

"I...I'm going to call Rick."

"Good. His number is in your phone. I made sure of it a couple of days ago when the detectives showed and asked me about my weapons. Remember?"

"Yes." She blinked fast, fighting inexplicable tears.

"Good girl. Here's the second thing I need you to do for me. I know you didn't want to bring this around..." He looked down to Kylie, whose gaze was transfixed by the cars out front. "No matter what happens here or what your feelings are, you do not leave this house until Rick comes to get you, okay? You make that call, and you stay here with Joe until you see Rick. You stay glued to Rick and do everything he says until I get out, okay?" He tangled his hand in the hair at her nape and tugged her close. He laid his mouth to hers and set the world on fire. Hard, hot and filled with ten years' worth of emotion, he burned her with his intensity.

"Kate. You, your safety? They're all that matter to me. You do what I say and, I promise you, I'll get out and get to the bottom of this." He pressed one more kiss, this one softly tender, on her mouth as the front door opened. He touched his forehead to hers and closed his eyes.

"Kylie. Come here, baby. Now." Joe, firm but kind, tried to get his daughter away from what was sure to be a scene. Kate knew what was happening but half of her brain refused to accept it. It had chosen to remain numb instead of facing the knowledge that the man she'd come to love was going to leave her.

"Trent Dawson, step away please. We need to—"

"I know. I'll cooperate. There's no need to make a scene. Give me one moment, and I'll go quietly, Joe." She watched him pin her cousin with the steel in his eyes. "Make sure she calls Rick Evans. Do. Not. Give her any trouble over it. Do. Not let her out of your sight until he gets here. Open your eyes and you'll see what this is. He wants her, and the best way to get her is to remove me from the picture. When Rick gets here, you let her go with him. That's what's best for her safety and everyone else's." He pointedly looked down at Kylie who hugged Joe's leg and watched with confusion in her eyes. Then his eyes looked into hers.

"Stay safe and do what I said." He kissed her cheek one last time and walked out the door. Then from behind the window she watched as they read him his rights, handcuffed and loaded him into a cruiser. He never resisted. Within moments the cars pulled out and she watched until the dark shadow of the man she loved disappeared around the curve.

They'd arrested her...Trent.

They'd arrested Trent for murder of her ex-husband.

Fire, angry and blistering hot, burned through her. Where was her fucking phone? She was ready to wage war against the mother fucker who'd done this.

"Honey, I'm s—"

"Shut it. Joe, don't you dare apologize to me. You knew this was going to happen and you just...let it happen? How could you? No, don't answer. I have a call to make." She found Rick's number and called. Later, she'd remember his curses, his voice and his reassurance that he'd be there and he'd take care of everything. But she had no clue what she said to him and if their conversation lasted thirty seconds or thirty minutes.

She set her phone down carefully when she would have rather thrown it at her cousin's head.

"Kate, I had to. It's my job and I asked them to wait until after, you know." He looked down at his daughter. The same reason Trent had gone outside and not offered one ounce of resistance. He hadn't wanted to upset Kylie in what was sure to be an ugly situation.

"Katie? Hewe." She looked down to see the little waif holding a wad of tissues up to her, her big eyes solemn.

"What are these for, sweetheart?"

"Cause you're cwying."

She wiped her hands over her face and found that her cheeks were damp. What the hell did she say to a six year old who'd just watched her newest friend get handcuffed and loaded into a police car?

And Trent hadn't even blinked.

Open your eyes and you'll see what this is. He wants her, and the best way to get her is to remove me from the picture.

Bailey had somehow framed him and killed her lousy ex-husband all in one move.

They needed to get a lawyer and then she needed to call Sandy and Harlan. They'd be so upset and…

Number one, I need you to call Rick as soon as I'm gone. Call him and tell him what's happened. He'll take care of everything. Promise me.

Trent had taken care of everything. He'd seen it coming and had put her and her little cousin above everything. He would likely spend the night in a cold jail cell while she was safe.

"Are you going to tell me what's going on? I can't tell you what they have on him, but it doesn't look good."

"Why should I? You already know what's best for me, right?" The dim, distant, reasonable part of herself understood that Joe was a police officer. There were rules he had to follow and following the rules was part of what made him a good man.

But the biggest part of her, her heart, didn't give a shit.

"Kate. My hands are tied. I hate this. I do." Regret filled Joe's words as he picked up a stuffed alligator on the floor.

"Come on, munchkin. How about we watch a movie for a few minutes?" Kate held her hand out to her niece.

Kylie smiled with calculation in her eyes. "Can I pick?"

"Of course. It's your special day." One that Kate prayed wouldn't be forever marred by the memory of police cars and handcuffs.

She helped her niece clean up, tucked her in and started the movie. Thanks to a busy day, within fifteen minutes she was sound asleep, surrounded by an army of smiling furry faces.

Joe met her in the kitchen where he'd gotten out two bottles of beer. He handed her one and waited patiently, torment in his eyes. "Talk."

So she told him everything and ended by telling him that there was no way that Trent had committed the murder because he'd spent nearly all the day prior to and the night of Preston's murder with her. They'd slept in the same bed and the way she'd been wrapped around him, there was no way he'd snuck out and not woken her.

"Kate, you can't tell anyone you know this. I'm breaking every rule in the book here, but how did a knife with his fingerprints and prints from boots that match the style and size he often wears both end up at the crime scene?"

"I have no idea. But even if I hadn't slept with him, Joe, I know deep in my heart he didn't do it."

"Until Bowie called and asked if he was here and told me what they found. I wouldn't have believed that a man who'd help a little girl rescue a snake would do this either, but I've seen some damn scary things over the years. I've been lured in by faces far prettier than his too." There was something in his tone that made her start. He'd cut himself off as if he'd said too much. What was he hiding?

"What? Who?"

"Nothing. This is about your mess." Did that mean he had a mess of his own? He seemed so tired and…beat down. "Kate, this scares me. I understand why you don't want to stay here around Kylie, but I think you should. We don't know this Rick very well."

"No. Absolutely not. She's been upset enough by tonight's drama. I won't let this touch her. I know I can trust Rick. I'll be fine."

"How do you know you can trust him? You barely know him."

"Because Trent does. That's enough for me." She took a long swallow of the beer, but it churned in her belly. Needing something to do, she finished cleaning his kitchen.

"Damn it, Kate. As much as I hate dishes, you've got to quit cleaning every time you come over." That was more like the Joe she loved.

"I need to stay busy. Leave me alone."

Not knowing what else to do, he actually listened to her. He stayed away, simply staring out the front window with his beer until Rick came about thirty long minutes later.

Without a word she kissed Joe on the cheek and met Rick before he'd had time to make it to the door.

She slid into the passenger seat and buckled in. "So, tell me what you've done and what we're doing to get him out."

"I called my attorney first and put him on it. As much as I hated to do it, I called Harlan next. He knows everyone who's anybody in Bourbon County. Trent's smart. He won't say anything until he has a lawyer present. Harlan is likely making calls as we speak. We should be able to at least get him out on bail by late tomorrow. It's not ideal, but it will have to do until we figure out who is behind this madness." He rattled off everything and ran a hand through his hair as he hugged a long winding curve on the way out of Riley Creek.

"What year is this, a '68? It's lovely." Any other time, she would have wanted to run her hand over the dash and touch every old button. Tonight, she couldn't muster up the energy to care.

"It's a '69. She's as close to perfect as you can get for a car that's over forty years old." Rick's somber voice lacked the enthusiasm she would've expected from a classic car buff.

"Did you restore her yourself or buy her?" Eager for a distraction, she pried as she watched the dark night race by.

"I stole her. She actually belongs to Trent." Rick's quiet words undid her.

She closed her eyes, leaned back against the seat and let the tears fall.

Chapter Eleven

He couldn't believe he'd been paraded in front of a judge. After his shitty start in life, he'd finally managed to find something good. He avoided trouble all his life, yet he wore an orange jumpsuit and fucking plastic shower shoes. His hands were cuffed in front of him, and he hadn't shaved. Hell, he probably looked the part of a crazed murderer.

He heard the door to the courtroom open behind him as people filed in. He didn't dare turn around to see if Kate and Rick were there. He felt their presence. At least, he thought he did. It was also possible that he was imagining it after having been awake for thirty hours. He hadn't been able to sleep. He'd spent the night worrying whether Kate had done as he'd asked and if she was safe. He'd even crossed a line he'd told himself not to repeatedly.

He'd wondered if Kate believed he'd killed Preston.

He hoped not. He wanted to think she trusted him. Plus, she knew that they'd been together the night Preston had been killed, so, surely she knew he didn't do it.

Knowing that didn't make the thought of her seeing him cuffed and wearing orange any more bearable.

What if they didn't let him out? He'd have to rely on Rick to keep her safe. While he trusted Rick with his life, he wouldn't be able to rest easy until he felt the softness of her body against his again.

Finally, after what felt like ages, the judge entered the room. Everyone stood as Judge Lawrence Miller entered.

Thank fuck.

He was an old friend of Harlan's and owned a horse Trent trained specifically for his only daughter who had special needs. Maybe there was hope.

A deep male voice cleared its throat from somewhere behind him, and he recognized the sound. *Rick.* He'd spoken to Rick's attorney and knew that Rick was on top of things. He also knew to the depths of his soul that he had no reason to be ashamed. He hadn't committed a crime.

But he couldn't make himself turn and face his friend. Or see if Kate stood beside him.

He stared at the carpet and thought through all the things he should be doing at the stables that day. His crew should be able to handle everything in his absence, and Harlan wouldn't hesitate to step in and lend a hand, if need be. Somehow, the knowledge didn't ease his mind. He reminded himself he'd been in far worse situations.

Above all else? Kate would be safe with Rick.

The bailiff told everyone to be seated and the room was filled with awkward shuffling.

But Bailey was after her. Of that, there was no question in his mind. He'd find out how the bastard pinned the crime on him if it was the last thing he did. Yes, Phillip Bailey was a senator, but Trent didn't see him having the smarts to construct something like this. Who did and why would they work for him? Was it for money or for some other reason?

Then a thought knocked him into full blown alertness. If they'd wanted him out of the way this badly, then surely they'd want to know what the results of today were. Somehow, someway, they'd be watching.

He fought the urge to turn and look at everyone behind him. He couldn't make trouble. He had to do whatever it took to get out on bail. He shifted, turned and found Rick waiting to meet his gaze. Trent swept his eyes over the room and prayed that Rick got the hint. When his friend's eyes widened and he gave a nod so slight it was nearly nonexistent, Trent tried to make one more sweep of the room, but his gaze locked onto Kate.

There was no fear, no revulsion visible in her lovely eyes. He only saw what looked like hope and concern for him. The judge spoke, and he tore his gaze from hers and tried to focus on what was being said between Judge Miller and his attorney.

Damn, but she was exhausted. She couldn't imagine how Trent must feel. Bail had been set at a ridiculously high amount but neither of the men had blinked at the fortune they'd signed over. It took ages to get the paperwork taken care of, but eventually the three of them had come back to his home and he'd gone straight for the shower. He hadn't even let her do more than give him a light hug when they'd finally gotten all the paperwork sorted and he'd been released. She understood. She would have felt dirty, too, but that hadn't made it any less painful. Logic had been her only saving grace.

She answered a light knock at the front door and found Rick had returned with bags of takeout.

"Kate! Don't. I'll be—" Trent walked out of his room with nothing but a towel hanging low on his hips.

She waved him back. "It's Rick. I'm fine. Just do your thing."

"I'll be right out."

"We've got things to discuss when you're ready." There was no mistaking Rick's dark tone as he sat on the couch.

"Damn. All I need is two minutes." Trent left the room with hurried steps.

Ignoring the voice in her head that sounded very much like a disapproving Aunt Jeannie, she grabbed a roll of paper towels, a couple of beers and bottled water and set everything on the coffee table.

She was unloading the bags when Trent walked in, pulling a shirt over his head.

"How are you, really?" Rick got straight to business as Trent sat beside her.

Trent raised his middle finger as he took a long swallow of beer.

Unaffected by the gesture, Rick continued. "Fine. We'll move on. I caught your clue about watching the room. What led you to think someone might be watching?"

"It didn't hit me until about five seconds before I turned to look at you. Whoever framed me has to be damn smart and skilled. They had to be able to break into my truck and get something with my prints without my knowledge. And the boots? I don't see Bailey having the knowhow. So someone has to be working with or for him." Trent grabbed a potato chip, then shook his head.

"Mr. Peterman saw someone in that truck he said looked like yours. Remember what he said about the Bourbon County license plate at Kylie's party? That can't be a coincidence." She placed her hand on his thigh.

"Yeah. That only cemented what I suspected was happening when the deputies showed up. It was no coincidence. I hadn't realized it was missing, but I'm guessing the knife I keep in my truck is gone." Trent's lips were set in grim lines.

"I watched the room as you indicated. There was only one person who seemed out of place. Here." He showed Trent a picture he'd taken with his phone. "It's not a good one, but what do you think?"

In the picture, a man hunched down in the corner with long dark hair and glasses. The hair was all wrong, almost fake, but there was something about the set of his jaw that seemed familiar.

"Son of bitch. That's not Campbell, is it?" Trent sat back and then looked a second time before handing the phone back.

"I can't be certain, but I think it is. I've got my guy digging into him and the picture. The last any of us heard, he was still hiding, like a cockroach, in Afghanistan."

"Who is he?" She couldn't shake the feeling that she should recognize him, but the knowledge wouldn't come.

"If it's who we think it is, we have a big problem. Boyd Campbell was one of us. We were in Sharanna, Afghanistan together. He'd split off from Justin, Rick and I. We heard what sounded like a struggle and a cry of pain in an alley behind a pile of rubble. He had Cara, a private, pinned against the wall by her throat. Her face was turning red and her shirt was torn open. She was putting up one hell of a fight, but Boyd had forty pounds of muscle on her and short fuse on his temper. She didn't stand a chance. We broke it up but while we made sure Cara was okay, he disappeared into the town." Trent grabbed a sandwich from the table then unwrapped it.

"You mean he disappeared and someone found him later? Please tell me he didn't get away with that?" *Poor Cara*. She wouldn't know the woman if she saw her on the street, but she felt for the woman who'd not only been so far from home in a strange land, then brutalized as well.

Rick swallowed a bite, then took over the story. "No. He split. Vanished into BFE Afghanistan. He'd gotten awfully friendly with a few members of the Afghan National Army, making it likely that someone there hid him or got him out of the city. No one has seen him since he had his hands on Cara's throat."

"How was she? I mean, was she okay? Or okay now?" Kate set down her untouched sandwich.

"She's tough, and she refused medical treatment. She went back to work with us the next day, bruises and all. You'd like her, I think." Trent draped an arm over her shoulders and pulled her into his warmth. She snuggled in without hesitation.

"The question is, how did the asshole get back undetected and how did he hook up with Bailey? If he is working with him, then the money transfers would fit." Rick wadded up his trash, took it into the kitchen and then paced between the two rooms.

"Money to get a new identity, get home and payment." Trent toyed with a lock of her hair.

"Do they have any prior connection or does the good senator have any ties to Afghanistan?" Rick rubbed both hands over his face. "Time to call in another favor."

"Maybe you should quit doing this favor-for-a-friend bullshit and make it official. Put him on your payroll," Trent suggested.

"Payroll? I don't even have a business." Rick appeared genuinely baffled.

"For someone so smart, you can be awfully dense at times." Trent pointed his beer in his friend's direction. "What do you think you're doing now?"

"I'm helping family, and now my best friend has been dragged into the mess. I sure as hell can't walk away now."

"You know, most people would charge for the type of work you're doing. It's called having a job, rich boy. And you wouldn't have walked away from Todd or Kate any more than you have me."

It was Rick's turn to give Trent the middle finger.

Kate shut the front door after walking Rick out. His friend had stayed the prior night on his couch while Trent had been in his frigid jail cell. Now that Trent was out and able to keep watch over Kate himself, Rick would be headed back to his hotel suite, leaving him and Kate alone.

He checked to make sure she locked up and set the security system the way he'd shown her. She followed his directions exactly and turned to face him. Fire burned in her expression, pinning him in place.

For a split second, he thought she might be angry with him, her look was so intense. But no, there was no anger. Her expression spoke of pure, heated desire.

She pointed her business finger at him. "You. You're sure you're okay?"

"I'm fine, I swear. It wasn't the most comfortable place I've ever rested, but it wasn't the worst either." If he could sleep on the unforgiving, desert ground of Afghanistan, then he could make it through a few hours in a cold jail cell.

Her eyes softened, weakening him.

"I'm not only concerned with you physically. What about up here?" She cupped his cheek in her soft palm and met his gaze. Warm, milk chocolate irises looked back at him with an emotion so deep he didn't dare put a name to it.

"I'm fine. Very relieved to be out where I can keep an eye on you. Rick didn't annoy you too badly while I was gone?" Things were getting deep fast, and he wasn't sure he could handle it. Jail cells? *Check.* Sifting through the sands of hell, searching for landmines? *Check.* Handling a wild, bucking stallion or a panicked mare? *Check.*

The sweet concern of a woman who was too loving for her own good? It scared the living shit out of him but, apparently, he didn't have much say in the matter.

"I missed you. Worried about you last night." She stood on tiptoe and feathered a kiss against the corner of his mouth. Her warm breath washed over him.

Light fingertips trailed down his face, over his shoulders and down his abdomen. They snuck under his shirt and scraped lightly, sending chills through him. But the heat of desire followed behind, scorching him in the best way possible.

"Off." Her perfect little nails trailed over him again and she gripped the hem of his shirt in her hands.

"Off?" He croaked the question.

"Yes. This has to go. I feel the sudden need to inspect you myself."

He raised his arms so she could lift his shirt. She lifted it as high as she could and raised an imperious brow. "Yes, ma'am." He was no dummy. He ripped the thing the rest of the way off and threw it to the couch.

When she put the moist heat of her mouth to the center of his chest, his gut clenched. She made a show of walking around his body, trailing those dangerous, wicked little fingers all along the way.

She inspected him as if he were a prized stallion at auction. He didn't mind one little bit. Neither did his cock. It swelled, hardening, eager for some attention of its own.

When she returned to face him, rasping a light touch over one nipple, continuing to the next and stopping with a fingertip posed over it, he met her gaze. "Does everything check out?"

"So far, but I'm not finished. Next, the pants have to go." Wordlessly, he obeyed and unfastened the denim. He slipped them off, thankful he'd gone commando in his haste to discuss business. He tossed them to the couch, too.

Frozen in place, he feared breaking the spell she'd woven. When she whispered into his ear, he would have moved mountains for her. "Thank you. I can't believe you went to jail for me, because of my mess. You are one of the best men I've ever known." Her mouth blazed a trail of warmth along his jawline, and he couldn't have moved if his life depended on it. Her words had more impact than her physical actions, but the combination slayed him—a man who'd come from nothing and, by all rights, should be nothing. Yet she worshipped him like some sort of damned hero.

He had to say something. He couldn't just stand there like an idiot, soaking up all of her sweetness. Damn, how he craved it. *Craved her.*

"Not your fault." His words weren't much more than a whisper as she knelt before him. "Kate, sweetheart, you don't owe me a damn thing. Please tell me this isn't a gratitude—" *A gratitude what?* Hell, he didn't know. He lost his words, every single one, as she wrapped a hand around his cock and took the head into the sweet heat of her mouth.

He tangled his fingers into the long silk of her hair. Glittering brown eyes looked up as she hummed and took him deeper. Gentle suction gripped him, held him tight, but those eyes of hers turned him to stone. Enthralled, he watched, breathless as her wet lips slid over his length. His sac tightened, strained but he didn't want to finish this way. He needed to be inside of her. Even more, he needed to give something back to the woman who gave him so much.

He eased her back until she had no choice but to release his length on a sucking pop. He put his hands under her arms and lifted her against him, wrapping her legs around his waist. Certain she wasn't going anywhere, he pulled her shirt over her head and whipped it away. At the sight of her lace covered breasts heaving in arousal, every intention he'd had of going slow went up in flames.

He needed to be skin to skin more than he needed his next breath.

Of a like mind, her hands flew to unhook her bra. She had it half undone by the time he'd tossed the shirt. It followed and landed somewhere behind them as he carried her to his bed.

He sat her at the foot where she looked up at him with a sassy grin that said she was with him all the way. She laid back on the bed and her hands went to unfasten her jeans, her breasts bobbing as she wriggled her hips. The denim inched down over her curves, making his cock ache with the need to sink into her. But, as much as he enjoyed the show, he needed to experience the feel of her even more.

He grabbed her pants, eager to finish the job she'd started. He'd managed to get them off one ankle when she quirked a grin and turned to climb up the bed, to run from him. On all fours, with her bare ass in the air, she looked over her shoulder as if to see if he'd chase.

Did she have any idea that she'd waved a red cape at a raging bull? There was no stopping him now.

Before she could turn, he leapt after her, grasped those hips and pulled her tight against his lower belly. The tip of his cock brushed the damp heat of her, freeing the last few vapors of his control. He tested her readiness and felt nothing but slick, tight heaven waiting for him. She moaned, low and hungry, arching back into his touch.

Damn, she was gorgeous.

He fumbled in the nightstand for a condom and slipped it on before he forgot and took her like a raging animal. He returned, used a hand on her pelvis to tilt her just so and eased into her on an agonizingly slow glide. The tight friction rasped over him in a delicious torture.

He pushed his cock into her and was rewarded with the toss of her head, her hair trailing over her shoulder and to the bed. The sleek line of her spine curved as she pushed back onto him, pressing the softness of her cheeks against his pelvis. He reared back until only the head of his cock remained inside and then plunged back in.

A pleasured whimper escaped from deep in her throat. Taking his cue, he repeated the motion and took up an unrelenting rhythm. He grasped her hips, swearing as their flesh came together again and again in a frenzied pace.

Draping his body over hers, he reached underneath her body to cup a breast in hand, the sweet, soft flesh a perfect handful. Her spine straightened, then bowed as her muscles tightened. With a low, throaty purr he felt all the way to his toes, she climaxed. Her body squeezed him with breath stealing intensity.

His sac drew up even tighter. Pleasure boiled and erupted through him. Helpless, he followed over the edge of madness and came. Holding her still, he let the strength of her orgasm milk him dry.

Damn, but the woman was dangerous on so many levels.

With a mountain of regret, he eased out of her body and helped her to lie down. He took care of business, returned and pulled her into his arms.

He was beginning to think that he just might have to keep her there forever.

"You're certain this is the way you want this done? I really think patience is your friend here. They have physical evidence on Trent. There's little doubt that they won't lock him away for ages when this goes to trial. I planted more than enough to hang Preston's murder on his head. When you add that to his current relationship with

Kate, it will be a slam dunk." He tried to get his uncle to listen to reason.

Bailey looked up from his desk, an odd, dead, glint in his dark eyes.

Despite never having children, his uncle was known as a family man first and a shrewd businessman second, two traits that screamed politician. Beneath that, there'd always been something odd in the way he'd viewed himself. He'd been smart enough to keep it hidden until recently. Whatever poison that lived inside his uncle had spread, gaining a firmer grip.

The evidence went beyond his recent odd obsession and had manifested in his fascination with plastic surgery. There was no telling how much money he'd invested in having his face reconstructed to resemble his idol.

As long as uncle-dearest wrote his paychecks, he'd pretend not to notice.

"That could take a year or longer. I don't have that kind of time and the courts fail people all the time. Somehow he got the best lawyer in the state, and they could paint him as some sort of damn war hero. He could get off on a technicality. It's too unpredictable and this is too important. I can't trust the system not to fail me."

He chose not to respond to Bailey's comment. It wouldn't help to point out the fact that the courts were there for the victim and the accused, not a spoiled, half-loony politician.

"I want him gone as soon as possible. Yesterday would suit me better. The election is coming up in a few months and I need everything in place before then. I don't care what you have to do, just get him out of the picture. Permanently." A loud smack rang out as Bailey slammed his palm against his desk.

"Even if he's gone, you know she might not cooperate. Women can be stubborn creatures." He should know. One woman in particular was the cause of all his troubles, but he'd see to her soon enough.

"If you do things correctly, she'll need a shoulder to cry on. I'll be the strong man she needs to lean on in her time of need. I don't pay you to think. I pay you to act. Nothing more. You have a plan, correct?" The senator rubbed his chin in thought.

"I do. I believe I've found a way to draw her out. Trent will follow. I can easily get him out of the way, but I may not be able to make it look like an accident. He may have to simply disappear." Eager to escape the weight of Bailey's madness, he stretched his legs out in front of him.

"Disappear? That might work just as well." The senator cocked his head, considering.

"Hopefully. If luck is with us, everyone will think the perfect Trent Dawson jumped bail and ran like a guilty coward. Those closest to him will have doubts and suspicions and may make some noise." He shifted in his seat, then crossed his ankles, impatient to leave.

"That can't be helped. Just see it through."

"Are you going to be able to keep her quiet and contained? She won't thank you for getting rid of Trent. She may very well hate you for it." He hated the tiptoe bullshit. He had to watch his every step and word. It was exhausting, but he couldn't get rid of his uncle until he had enough money saved to set himself up. A measly half million wouldn't last him long. "Her family in Riley Creek may not have any money or social pull, but they will make a stink. They're a close unit. How will you keep her from reaching out to them? How will you ensure her cooperation?"

"Why wouldn't she cooperate? She'll be the wife of a noble senator and future First Lady. Any woman would want that. She'll be honored."

He bit his tongue before he pointed out that his aunt hadn't felt honored. When she had begun to suggest that her husband should seek psychiatric help, she'd met a suspicious end. Now his uncle expected Kate MacDonald to be grateful they killed her new love interest? That she would simply accept being kidnapped and be happy about it? Maybe Bailey was far deeper into his madness than he'd originally thought.

He couldn't waste any more energy trying to reason with a madman. He needed to tie up his own loose ends and insure that there wasn't a single thread tying him to this ridiculous mess. As much as he'd like to milk a few more payments from his uncle, it would be smarter to cut his ties and ghost out of this nightmare.

He had his own agenda and business was business. "I'll have expenses that—"

"Fine. I'll make sure you're paid. Now quit acting like a cricket on my shoulder and get to work."

He nodded and turned on his heel, relieved to leave the oppressive weight of his uncle's madness.

Chapter Twelve

They'd just arrived at the small office on the outskirts of the next town over. The building looked as though a strong breeze could blow it over. Bright morning sunshine made Kate thankful she'd worn her sunglasses as she took in the rural setting. Trees and more trees surrounded them and shin-high grass bordered the cracked sidewalk. "Trent. Really, it should be fine. I called Doc Jones and he verified that the owner of Angels and Paws Animal Hospital passed away about six months ago. It makes perfect sense that his son would donate some of their things to animal rescues."

"I don't like it. How did they get your name? You're still in the plotting and planning stages. You haven't even decided on a name for your rescue yet. Only a handful of people know about your plans. You don't need handouts from a stranger. When you figure it all out, I'll help you buy whatever you need." Trent's jaw set in sheer stubbornness and she reminded herself he wasn't an asshole.

He worried about her safety. At any other time, he wouldn't be so hardheaded. She placed her hand on his cheek and leaned up to kiss the scowl from his mouth.

He took her kiss in a hungry tangle of desire. Their mouths dined on each other until they broke away, gasping for air. She stood on tiptoe and touched her nose and forehead to his.

"Everything will be fine. You're taking this protector thing a little too seriously."

"Never." He took her hand in his then, as if thinking better of it, let it go and settled for tucking her close behind him to keep his hands free as they walked across the deserted parking lot. Only buckled blacktop and a faded blue sedan parked near the front entrance greeted them.

Nudging him with her shoulder, she said, "I can't see anything beyond the moving brick wall in front of me. Do you mind?"

"Yes. I mind. If you can't see around me, chances are no one can see you. I don't like this. Are you forgetting that someone took a shot at you the night of the fire? Then someone set fire to your home, with you in it. A few days later, your ex-husband was found murdered and the blame placed on me."

"No. I haven't." She'd never forget the sight of Trent in handcuffs. Logically, she knew she wasn't to blame, but it didn't make her feel any less guilty.

"We should have waited for Rick." How he managed to sound part pouting toddler and part alert soldier, she'd never know, but he managed it.

"He'll be here soon with the other truck. I think he made another secret trip to Riley Creek. He said he'd catch up with us here. The vet's son only had a couple of hours to spare this morning, and I don't want to try his patience. His offer of supplies is too good to pass up. I want as many of the kennels as we can haul. What do you think Rick's doing to the old Caudill place today? Leigh told me that an anonymous donor paid to have the electric turned on and prepaid three months service. She stopped by to drop off another small care package and found a notice from the electric company on the door." She smoothed her palm over the small of his back.

"Idiot's already taken care of the water, so he's probably having the AC unit replaced. He was mumbling something about asshole-copper-wire-thieves a few days ago. His words, not mine. So, it looks like she's been returning?" Tension rolled off Trent in waves as they crossed the small lot.

"Yes. Leigh said that someone has definitely been taking advantage of the food and water they've left. The clothes and personal items have been used too. According to Leigh, she's a stealthy little thing. She and Rick have each separately made a couple of trips out there, but they've never caught a single glimpse of her. Poor kid. I can't imagine. Dad and I might not have had much but he was always, always there for me. He would have worked three jobs to feed me if need be." Even after all this time, she missed her father so much.

"You'd be surprised how resilient children can be. It's unfortunate as hell, but kids in bad situations learn how to take care of themselves so much younger than they should have to." The soft regret in his voice reminded her that he'd been born to a situation only slightly better than Leigh's little ragamuffin.

"I'm sorry. I'm always dredging up bad memories for you. Just call me Mary Sunshine." She touched his shoulder in apology.

"It was a really long time ago. You had nothing to do with the fact that there are skeletons in my closet. Don't guard your words because there've been a few rough patches in my life."

Rough patches? Skeletons? Damn stubborn man. She wanted to argue that a murder rap was an awfully big skeleton and, if it hadn't been for her, his closet would be significantly less crowded. He'd just wave it off as no big deal.

She grazed her fingers down the long line of his spine, putting her hand at his waist. The muscle there bunched tight with tension.

She barely resisted telling him that she'd like to stay on the donor's good side and if he stomped in like some pissed off bodyguard, her possible donations might end up going to another home. As generous as Trent was, she couldn't keep taking from him.

No donation was too small when she had to make every penny count. The better she managed her resources, the farther she could spread them.

Or so she hoped.

"Trent?" It might not be the time or place for it, but she couldn't help herself.

"Huh?" He didn't offer much more than a grunted acknowledgement as he stopped a few feet from the front door.

She wrapped her arms around his waist and pressed herself tight against his back. "Thank you for everything."

The air heaved out of his chest in a heavy sigh.

"Let's get this over with so we can go home and relax." *All business, her Trent.*

She kissed his shoulder. "I want to check on Bonnie."

He stopped before the door and turned. "Okay. We'll relax after we check on Bonnie."

"You know I can handle her by myself. I know she's getting big but I don't need your help. You can take a break this evening. The stables are locked up tighter than Fort Knox."

"That's because my horses are more valuable." He said it as though he was boasting, but she knew, to him, they were priceless. Although they were expensive animals, the value went well beyond monetary.

It reminded her of the day when her father brought Jack and Miss Priss home. Greatest horses in all of equine history, simply because they'd been theirs. She smiled at the memory, filled with warm light.

Trent paused and she bumped into his back. "Sorry."

He just shook his head and she caught a glimpse of his mouth quirked in amusement. "Hello?" he called out and got no response as he opened the door.

They stepped into a barren room where murky light filtered through dusty windows. "Honey, this place looks like it's been out of business a lot longer than six months. More like six years. Hello?" He called into the room, the sound a hollow emptiness. "I don't like it."

"Maybe he's not here yet?" An ugly, heavy sense of dread filled her.

"Maybe, maybe not, but we're not staying any longer."

A sudden scurrying sound ticked across the floor and she looked down just in time to see a Godzilla-sized rat trample over her feet. In a flash, it vanished as fast as it had appeared.

Startled, she jumped and plastered herself to Trent's back, wrapping one leg around his waist and half-climbing him like a monkey. "Shit! Shit, shit, shit."

"Kate, what the fuck?" His words were garbled with her arm around his throat. He stumbled under her panicked attack and bowed back under her unexpected weight.

A deafening report echoed through the small space and Trent dropped to the floor, half on top of her. Silent and still.

Oh God, no.

Blood poured from a wound above his right eye. He'd been shot. She stared, frozen, disbelieving. Not her Trent. No way. He was so strong and big and warm.

Invincible.

She'd believed that as long as she was with him, she was safe. And now he'd been shot.

She tried to gather her wits. He needed her to take care of him. It was no time to panic. She untangled herself.

But, what if?

She couldn't give into the panic digging its dull, painful claws in between her ribs and squeezing her lungs. She had to keep her wits together. She placed her hand on the side of his neck.

"Let's go. He's dead." An unfamiliar male voice broke through the silence.

She startled as man in a dark knit mask stormed into the room. Sand colored, military style boots crunched over the dirty floor. Tan cargos met an olive shirt and it was all so average except for the mask and the glittering dark brown eyes lancing terror into her heart.

He'd shot her Trent. Damn him. No!

Trent's flesh felt warm beneath her fingers, but the masked man grabbed her arm and yanked her to her feet and shook her before she could find a pulse.

The sound of a large vehicle pulling in could be heard through the partway open front door.

She opened her mouth to scream a warning for Rick a millisecond before white hot lightning zapped through her and the world went black.

The sheet of paper lying on the passenger seat called Rick to look at it again but he resisted. Barely. He needed to focus on the curvy country roads and meet with Trent and Kate. Trent would be chomping at the bit to get Kate her gear and then stashed safely back at his place.

Rick knew everyone thought him crazy for everything he'd done out at Mary's house but he didn't give a shit. He'd actually thought about walking away. He'd done a good deed. He could call it finished, and his conscience could take a long walk off a short pier.

Except that he couldn't. He simply could not make himself turn his back. He didn't think he'd ever get the sight of that filthy little face or that pitiful pile of belongings out of his head. He'd tried and tried again, but there was no shaking her.

Without moving his focus from the road ahead, he reached over to the empty passenger seat and turned the sheet of paper over so it was face down. He turned up the radio in a vain attempt at drowning out the thoughts in his head.

No such luck.

Resigned to another day of worry, he found the little shack that was supposed to have been a veterinarian office and pulled into the parking lot. He parked one space over from Trent's truck and turned off the ignition. Unable to control himself, he picked up the paper turned it over.

Yet again, he was dumbfounded by the jaw-dropping, dark beauty that practically jumped off the page. With his heart cracked in two he placed it on the dash and climbed out. He walked inside fully expecting to get a glare from Trent.

And what could he say? He deserved it. He was supposed to be there fifteen minutes ago.

Instead of an irritated glare, he found a bleeding Trent, crumpled on the dirty floor.

His throat tightened and his stomach dropped. He fell to his knees, brushed the blood from Trent's forehead and felt for his pulse.

When the steady thump pulsed he released a heavy sigh, then sucked in a harsh breath. The wound on his head, a laceration, had creased a deep furrow over his left eye. Other than that and his unconsciousness, he appeared to be okay.

But, shit, what had happened and where was Kate? Had she gone for help or had something worse happened than a blow to Trent's head?

"Trent? Hey, man, are you all right? Trent? What the fuck, man? Kate!"

No answer other than a low groan from his friend.

Another groan, which included several curse words, as Trent rolled to his back and looked up at the ceiling. He squeezed his eyes tighter and then opened them. He rubbed a hand over his forehead and surprise filled his face when he saw the blood smeared on his palm.

Then he truly woke up.

"Kate? Where the fuck is Kate?" He sat up in a drunken totter, looking around as if the room spun around him.

"I don't know. I hoped like hell you knew. What happened? I don't see her taking off and leaving your side, especially when you're wounded."

"No. She wouldn't." He struggled to stand, and Rick gave him his hand, pulling him the rest of the way up. "Kate!"

The only answer to Trent's shout was a cold, flat echo.

"He has her. I don't know what the fuck happened, but he has her." Tense, tightly leashed fury turned his friend into a stone-cold statue.

Fearing the slightest thing might push Trent's anger into a full blown rage he gave his friend a moment. Rick looked in the backrooms and the surveyed the area behind the building. As expected, he found nothing but more cracked blacktop. He returned and found Trent staring out the murky front window, waiting. "Anything?" His friend asked without turning.

"Not really. Only what is likely a bullet hole on that wall over there. You think that could be a graze on your forehead? They're probably long gone now."

"Fuck. Me."

"Yeah." He couldn't imagine the frustration and pain his friend felt. Rick's was immeasurable and Trent's could only be worse.

It always was when a heart was involved. "Are you calling the police, or am I? We need to think this through."

"Shit. I'll call." Trent did. The wait for the Potter County deputies was the longest of Rick's life. *Eight fucking minutes. How could they sit and do nothing while Kate was only God knew where?*

He wasn't one bit surprised when the first cruiser to pull into the lot, sirens blaring, tires squealing, belonged to Joe MacDonald.

Fuck.

In a single blink, Kate's cousin was up in Trent's face, hands tangled in his shirt. "What the fuck, Dawson?"

"He got her." The pain on Trent's face had nothing to do with his injury.

"Talk." Joe spat the order at Trent.

Rick silently stood by while Trent told Joe everything. A couple of deputies looked around inside. Two more stood with Joe. One watched with disbelief and the other horror as his gaze ping-ponged between Trent and Joe.

"This shit is all true? This and everything that happened out at her house?" Joe ran a hand through his hair.

"Every single word. I thought I could protect her. I fucked up." Rick disagreed with Trent's words, but that battle would have to wait for later.

Joe said nothing, turned his back and walked away.

Trent turned and faced Rick, every muscle clenched in anger. "I want Bailey's head. Both of their heads."

"I do too. We won't rest until we find her. I'll drive. You ride and we'll send someone back for your truck. Are you sure you don't want to get checked out? A hospital might not be a bad idea. I understand why, but I'm not sure you should have sent the ambulance away."

"No."

He'd expected the response, but had to try. They pulled out and Rick put his foot to the floor. Why? He wasn't sure because they had next to nothing to go on and no plan. He guessed it was the only thing he had control of.

They rode in silence until they pulled into the farm on a quick stop and the paper on the dash fell into Trent's lap. He grabbed it, marring one corner with sticky, half dried blood.

"What's this?" He handed it over with a puzzled look. Rick took it from his hand, noting the brick red thumbprint in the corner.

Everything snapped into place.

"A gift. A very dear gift." Rick took the paper and looked down at the image. Artwork, priceless in more ways than one, drawn on cheap paper.

"I'm sorry about the blood. I must be a mess." His face, his shirt and his hands were covered in streaks of blood.

"The blood's not big deal. Let's go. I've got some phone calls to make." A man with a mission, Rick hopped out of the truck and hurried into the house.

Trent went into the restroom at his place to wash his face. The dried blood on his eyelid made blinking awkward, and he hoped the ice cold water would rid the last of the fog from his head.

Had he really been shot? From all appearances, it looked as though he had. He looked like a horror film extra. A bullet was the only way he could see anyone getting the jump on him. The thought of what might have happened to Kate made him want to simultaneously vomit and put his fist through the mirror.

Neither action would be of any help, so he crammed everything back inside and dried his face. The wound continued to ooze but that couldn't be helped.

He found Rick on the phone in the kitchen as he paced the floor.

"Great. As soon as you can. I appreciate it, Ramsey. We'll talk money when you get here. Later." He disconnected and dialed another number before Trent could ask what was up.

In no time, Rick spoke and everything made a little more sense. "Hey, James, how are you doing? That sucks. Yeah, I've been spinning my wheels, wasting time and not doing anything productive. But that's over now. Trent and I have a situation and we could use your help. Is there any way you could lend us a few more days? I'll pay you for your time and it may lead into more work when we're finished. We're holed up at Trent's for now. This evening would be awesome. Thanks, man."

Rick hung up and repeated the process once more.

Why hadn't he thought of that? James Holloway and Noah Ramsey? They couldn't ask for better help. Yeah, he would have gotten around to the idea eventually but clearly his head was a mess. But Rick? Whenever things went to shit, he became absolute, cold precision. His icy intelligence had saved them on more than one occasion. Damn, it was a relief to know he had Rick in his corner. With his team behind him, there wasn't a damn thing they couldn't accomplish.

Then Rick's words registered on yet another call. "Hey, Pete. How are the ladies? Yeah? Listen. It's go time. I want you here as soon as possible. Things just got nasty." And Rick continued and, by the sounds of it, pulled another man into in group.

But really?

Rick disconnected and turned to him.

"Pete Taylor? Really? You called in that pup?" Trent didn't bother to hide his disbelief.

"I did. He's the best tech guy I know. Can you deny that?" Rick quirked a brow.

"No. You're right. I can't. It'll be good to see the guys again. I'm glad you called them in. Do you have a plan yet?"

"I'm thinking on it. Did I miss anyone?" Rick's absentminded question seemed directed at himself.

"No. What is all this?" He watched as Rick walked over to the counter where he'd laid the bloodied sheet of paper.

"Dark Horse Inc. You and Kate are my first clients. When I toyed with the idea of starting a business I'd thought it would be more of a personal protection business, but apparently hostage recovery is also going to be part of the deal."

Dark Horse. Rick stared at the sketch he'd seen in the truck. It was a stunning work of art—fine, sweeping pencil lines on plain paper. A huge, proud stallion came to life surrounded by ominous storm clouds. Steam puffed from the horse's nostrils and the eyes seemed to contain a living soul.

"Where'd that come from? It's amazing."

"Mary. I found it inside that pitiful little house, laying on the floor in the corner where Leigh and I have been placing supplies. There were two drawings. This one had another sheet of paper on top of it that said *Mr.* Beneath it was this drawing. Beside it lay another with a sheet over it that said *Lady.* I couldn't help myself and peeked at Leigh's gift. It was equally beautiful, but where this is wild and dark, hers was light and peaceful. Serene. The kid needs to be in art school, not hiding in some dump in BFE." Rick clenched his fists at his side, then raised his head to face Trent.

He nodded his agreement and pushed memories of his own shitty start in life aside. "She does. Hopefully, with a little more time, she'll reach out to you or Leigh."

"Anyway, I figure our best bet to get Kate back to you in one piece is bringing in help. We'll put our heads together and get her back." His friend turned his back on the drawing to stare out the front window.

"You're sure she's...okay?" He couldn't bring himself to say the word alive aloud. He refused to believe that she could be otherwise.

"I am. Bailey wants her for some reason and, as difficult as it is to think about, I don't think it's for something as simple as killing her. It sucks, but we have some time. Park your ass on that stool and let's see if we can get the bleeding stopped. You won't be up to a recovery mission if you continue to leak. Where's your first aid kit?" Rick came closer to peer at his wound.

"In the closet beside the hall bathroom. Since when do you know how to suture?" Doubt crept into his voice as he watched Rick walk down the hallway.

His friend called out over his shoulder. "I'll figure it out. Chicks dig scars, right? Sit and I'll get it."

Trent stewed while Rick played nurse. It killed him to sit on his ass and do nothing but watch the time creep by. Kate. His Kate. He'd never met anyone like her. Yes, she was the most beautiful woman he'd ever seen, but she was so much more than that.

She was love and life and light and family.

Shit. He had a call to make of his own.

The moment Rick closed the first aid kit, Trent dialed his cell.

"Dawson." Joe MacDonald answered before the first ring ended.

Now was not the time for bullshit. Trent got straight to the point. "We're going after her tonight."

Joe interrupted before Trent could finish his thoughts. "You're not leaving me out of this."

"I don't have a problem letting you in, but you gotta understand we're doing this our way. I don't have the time to wait around on warrants and bullshit politicking. We have no proof and no judge in his right mind will get us a warrant without hard proof, but we know he has her. This could get us in trouble. If you don't want to risk your badge, you might want to rethink this." He met Rick's gaze as he spoke as his friend nodded in agreement.

"My badge won't mean shit to me if something happens to her. I'll be there in thirty." Kate's cousin disconnected without another word, no doubt already on his way.

The world came alive in a screaming ball of aches and pains. Every muscle in her body felt as if it had been beaten by a baseball bat. She checked her arms, expecting to see black and blue, but no. They looked just fine.

She turned her head from side to side and tried to throw off the haze that lured her back to sleep. In the realm of black, there was no pain. Yet, something wasn't right.

She looked around and found herself in a bedroom fit for royalty. She lay on a plush, high four-poster bed that probably cost more than her barn. A soft, thick bedspread lay beneath her and cream, silk papered walls surrounded her.

She was in Hell.

Everything came back to her in a rush as she remembered the sound of a gunshot and the feel of Trent falling under her weight.

Someone in a mask had come barreling into the room and then she'd been...electrocuted?

Tased? Had the asshole used a taser on her? It was the only possible explanation.

Oh God. Trent. Was he okay or not? He had to be okay. Head wounds bled a lot, right? She knew she might be grasping at straws, but so be it. She refused to believe that her strong, rock solid Trent could be taken down so easily.

"Ah. There she is. My pet is finally awake. Such nasty business, but you proved to be so stubborn." Chills invaded her, smothered her, and nausea curled in her belly at the sound of an all-too-familiar voice. "That's all right. In the end, you're finally where you're meant to be, and we'll need your stiff backbone where we're going."

She looked to the door and found her nightmare had come to life. Phillip Bailey wore a serene smile as if greeting her after he'd come home from a day at the spa. His voice was satin smooth, but his words chilled her to the bone.

"A man couldn't have asked for a sweeter woman than my first wife, but she didn't have the spine a woman needs to stand tall in political circles. She had enough grace for three women, but she was full of troubling ideas. A man in my position can't be seen going to a psychiatrist. Can you imagine?" He opened his palms and his expression said he thought she'd understand.

Oh. Dear. God.

Trent had been right. The donation offer had been a plan to get her away from the protection of Trent's farm. She'd been taken and Trent...she prayed he was okay. She couldn't bear the thought of him being hurt or worse because of her stubborn insistence. A few animal crates and free supplies had in no way been worth the risk.

Damn it.

Rick. Someone, most likely Rick, arrived just before she'd been tased. He would have gotten help for Trent and then started a search for her. They'd both worked so hard to keep her safe. It was possible they had leads already. All she had to do was bide her time. She'd cooperate, play nice and wait for either a chance to escape or until help arrived. She had no doubt that it would come.

"Up and at 'em, my dear. We have much to address today. You don't have time to lie abed like a pampered princess. A true queen works hard for her kingdom." He smiled at her like a doting husband and she wanted to vomit as fear and revulsion twisted in her belly.

"I'm sorry, Mr. Bailey, but I really need to get home. I have family that will worry when I don't get back on time." Well aware she was talking to a madman, she figured it was worth a try. She needed to stall.

"Ah. Yes. Your family. I had hoped to give you a little time to acclimate before we discussed the...more unpleasant topic, but you insisted. Follow me, my dear."

Unsure of what she should do or what was to come, she followed. They wound their way out of the bedroom, down a long hallway and a flight of stairs before they entered his study. He pointed to a leather wingback chair and sat at his desk. "Sit," he ordered

Lost, she did as told and looked at the grandfather clock in the corner to mark the time. Why? She had no idea. She had no idea how long it would take Rick and hopefully Trent to come and get her. She had no reason to count down the minutes.

"First, as an obedient wife should address her loving husband, you'll address me as dearest or Phillip. You're honored to have that privilege and will behave accordingly."

"Wife?" She nearly choked on the word. She'd never again be the wife of someone who cared more about what the public thought than what she wanted. She'd die first. He thought she'd simply stand beside him and smile? She couldn't fathom the depths of his madness.

"Yes. You'll be my wife. I have two friends coming tomorrow. One will officiate our quiet, simple ceremony and my attorney will act as our witness. Now, before you waste any energy thinking up ways to escape our home or send for help, you need to open that." He pointed to a plain, cream-colored folder lying on the desk before her.

As if it were a snake coiled, ready to strike, she cautiously picked it up.

He waited silently with his fingers pressed together and pointed toward his chin. His seemingly confident silence worried her more than if he'd continued his chatter.

She braced herself with a deep breath and opened the folder. The breath she'd taken left her lungs in one painful exhale. Her mouth dried and felt as though it had been filled with dust. A stack of photos lay neatly inside the folder.

"I have a reliable source who claims that your cousin is very important to you. Is this correct?"

She couldn't form a single sound, let alone a full word.

"No answer, my pet? I'll assume by the paleness of your face, that my information is accurate." She stared at the photo in her lap. The picture caught a smiling Kylie halfway down a slide with her arms up in the air. She recognized the slide as one from the elementary school Kylie attended. "There are plenty more pictures where those came from. Go on, you can look through them while I explain how things are going to work from now on."

With shaking fingers, she flipped to the next picture. Kylie and Joe's mother held hands as they walked into the grocery store.

Kylie wore a matching red and black shorts outfit with her favorite mismatched boots.

Something cold and slimy slithered in her belly.

"Tomorrow we will marry. You will tell everyone in your family that you are happy and you want to live here as Mrs. Phillip Bailey. You will stand by my side and act as the perfect First Lady when the time comes." He nodded to something on her left. She woodenly turned her head and saw a painting of Jacqueline and John F. Kennedy.

She suddenly understood why he looked familiar but not quite like himself. The plastic surgery had been to make him look more like the former president.

Terror for herself and sympathy for Marilyn Bailey flooded her.

Noah Ramsey showed up first and, Trent had to admit, he wasn't surprised. He'd always been the rule follower. He'd been the first to roll call at basic and the last to call it quits on the firing range. He'd lived and breathed every job until it ended, whether it had been assigned or if he'd taken it on by choice. Quiet, stalwart and all business, they'd teased him mercilessly and the brick wall took it in stride—a damn good thing, considering the amount of ribbing he received.

"Trent." The single word and a nod of his head said it all.

"Thanks, man." What else did a person say when a friend they hadn't seen in over five years showed to take part in a dangerous and deadly, off-the-books rescue mission? He didn't have adequate words to cover his feelings. He gestured for his old friend to come inside and get comfortable.

Much the same as he'd always done, he came in and took a place near the corner and waited.

"The rest of the crew should arrive soon. You want something to drink?" Damn, how Trent hated the situation. They'd taken Kate and anything could be happening while they stood around twiddling their thumbs.

"I'm good. How's your head, man?" Noah peered at him as if looking for cracks in his skull. "Are you sure—"

"I'm sure I don't need a visit to the ER." Trent looked up to the ceiling in exasperation.

"That looks vicious. Son of a bitch. I believed Rick, but it all sounds unreal. I'm glad you called me in on this. That bastard really did shoot at you and steal your woman." His old friend shook his head.

"Yeah, or someone working for him did. We think we know who it might be. I won't rest until she's home." He met his friend's gaze and let him see his determination.

"Here's a picture of Kate from a charity event a little over a year ago. Her hair is a little longer and darker now." Rick turned his laptop around to display an image from a newspaper article and Noah moved in.

Trent couldn't bring himself to look at the image. Turning to the window, he found an old, beat-up Jeep tearing up his driveway. A monstrous blue pickup he recognized as Joe MacDonald's personal ride followed close behind.

Good. It was best to get the chest-thumping and fist-swinging out of the way so they could get to what was most important—bringing Kate home. He itched for a fight, but as much as he hated to have a go at her cousin, he wouldn't hesitate if it meant he could get to business sooner.

He barely spared Pete's rust-bucket Jeep a glance as he headed straight for Joe. The man stepped down and looked Trent over as he did the same in return. He'd come in dark jeans, boots and tee. "What, no uniform? You're wearing the wrong color."

"I left my uniform, my badge, and everything else county issued at home. We need to talk. Damn, you look a little pale. Are you sure—"

Good God. Not again. "No, damn it. I'm on my feet, aren't I? Nothing matters except bringing Kate home."

Joe appraised him once again. Unless it was his head wound talking, there might have been a dash of grudging respect in Joe's gaze.

"Trent? What's going on? We got trouble?" Pete stood beside them, watching as if ready to jump into the fray. Standing tall at his full five-foot-six, Pete Taylor weighed all of a hundred and thirty pounds. Every single ounce of it was loyal and brave to the point of near stupidity.

"Nah man. It's all good. We're heading inside to get down to the real business." He turned to his friend and forced a weak smile. "When are you going to get rid of that deathtrap set of wheels?"

"It's the only ride I've got that doesn't have a baby seat in the back. Crystal won't let me take the girls anywhere in it. I can't even drive them to the mailbox. It may be the only chance I get to drive it for another six months." Pete ran his hand over the Jeep's dented hood.

Trent smiled in amusement "How old are the girls now?"

"Six and three. They get prettier and smarter every day." It never failed to amaze Trent how proud Pete was to be a father. He'd married his high school sweetheart the week before basic and never once looked back.

"You're going to have your work cut out for you if that's true."

"No shit. But I wouldn't have it any other way. Best and most important job I'll ever have. Let's go figure out how to get your girl back so you can put a baby in her belly."

Joe, who'd been silently walking beside them, stopped dead in his tracks as disbelief washed over his features. He blinked and then anger filled his gaze.

Trent barely resisted pulling out a chunk of hair and thanked the heavens when a dark gray SUV pulled in behind the Jeep. He'd never been so thankful to see James Holloway.

Tall and lean, he stepped out and considered their gathering. He seemed to gauge each man's mood before he stopped and looked to Pete, shaking his head. "Runt, are you making trouble again?"

"Yes—" Pete always made trouble.

"No. What did I say?" Pete genuinely looked confused as he looked from Trent to James.

"Would you girls quit with the gossip and get in here? We've got work to do." Rick called from Trent's open door. Beyond eager to get to work, Trent jogged up to the wide porch and released a sigh of relief as the sound of booted feet followed.

"How are we going to do this? I mean, I'm itching to go in, guns blazing, but we can't bust in blindly. That'll do more harm than good." Noah looked up from where he'd pushed Trent's couch back and shoved his dining room table into the middle of the living room. Piercing green eyes flashed in anger. He ran a hand through his russet hair and shook his head as if in frustration. "A living target and not only a living target, but one who essentially belongs to one of ours? That's like leaving a girlfriend or wife behind enemy lines. It could be our most important mission ever. We can't make a single mistake. Holloway, take this for a second." Noah lifted Trent's TV from the entertainment stand and handed it to James to hold while he disconnected the satellite cable. Trent ignored the throbbing pain in his head and watched as Noah finished removing the cable and took the TV back. He sat it on the table and connected Rick's laptop to it.

"Agreed. There's no question, Kate's rescue is the most important mission we've ever taken on. Getting in and getting her out safely is the number one goal." Trent knew they'd understand the seriousness of the situation, but hearing it straight from James's mouth reinforced his confidence that they'd done the right thing by calling them.

"I have just the thing we need to gain an edge." Rick's words blindsided him as he held the front door open. Pete came in the door carrying a backpack and slid out his laptop and placed in on the table. He returned with a chair and sat, almost gleefully, in front of the computer.

"Runt, where'd you get a beast like that? That is a high-dollar machine, not something the local electronics store would carry. Did you rob a bank?" James asked and, like a kid who'd been caught with his hand in the cookie jar, Pete flushed.

"Uhm. Well." The room went silent as everyone stopped and shifted their focus to Pete.

"It's mine, but it belongs to Pete as long as he works for me. I've had him digging for dirt on Bailey and a few other projects. He's come through for me several times now. It's a damn good thing he did, too. Joe, this is your last chance to back out before the line between black and white gets blurred."

"Hell, Rick, blurred? Try broken into bits." The importance of Pete's words hadn't seemed to dim his enthusiasm as he ran a hand lovingly over the laptop.

Trent looked to Joe. "As a member of Kate's family, you're welcome on our team as long as you remember that's exactly who and what you are. A team member. You follow orders and there will be no lone wolf action. If you're willing to be a team player and are able to forget your badge and skirt the law for the day, you're welcome to join us. Otherwise, you need to turn around, head out that door, and trust that we know what we're doing. Kate is coming home tonight. It's up to you whether you want to participate or wait patiently."

"I'm in. All the way. I said I left my badge at home and I meant it." Joe's eyes met his and Trent saw anger and determination that equaled his own.

"Okay, cop. Welcome to the dark side." Rick gestured to him to join the group and find a spot in the makeshift planning room.

"Damn. I forgot the cookies."

Four male voices groaned in unison over Pete's lame joke.

Rick shook his head at the group and began a rundown of everything they'd dug up on the senator, Boyd Campbell and Preston Hayes.

"How the hell did Campbell get from Afghanistan to the States without getting caught?" Noah asked as he brought a chair in, turned it backward and sat with his arms crossed on the back.

"Bailey has ties with a couple of civilian contractors who are based in Bagram. It's my best guess that he may have been able to come home on a private flight or with cargo of some sort."

"This is the most recent image we have of Boyd. I snapped this on the sly in the courtroom. We suspect he's the one who took a shot at Trent and took Kate." The slightly blurry cell phone picture appeared next.

"You're certain she's alive?" Trent's gut clenched when the soft question came from James who stood behind the seated group.

"We are—" He began his answer to the hated question without anger. As much as he refused to believe that she could be anything other than alive and well, waiting for his rescue, he understood where

James's question came from. The bad guys didn't keep their captives in pampered comfort… if they kept them alive at all.

Rick interrupted, his voice pure steel and one-hundred percent business. He was in his element. "We are and I have proof that, as of ninety minutes ago, she was taken to Senator's Phillip Bailey's home."

Trent's head snapped to his friend. "Proof?"

"Pete?" Rick gave an order and they seemed to be miles ahead of the game while Trent played catch up.

"On it." Pete left his laptop and moved to Rick's and the TV it had been connected to. Video came to life and displayed a street or long driveway leading up to a Colonial style mansion. Then the image split into two images. It flickered and then there were three video feeds displayed on his TV. "Live feed is up."

He didn't know whether to flatten Rick because he clearly hadn't shared everything he'd been doing or kiss him for being a devious bastard and providing a minor miracle.

"How long have you had Bailey under surveillance?" Joe leaned in to take a closer look, his words were directed to Rick, but his gaze never wavered from the TV. Trent wondered if Joe was trying to look into the windows just as he was, even though the mansion would have been built for privacy as much as it had been elegance.

"Four days. Once it became clear that they wanted Trent out of the way badly enough to frame him for murder, I put a few things into place. Trent may be pissed at me now, but his focus needed to be on Kate. I had the time and the ability, so I…played around a bit. I brought in Pete and James the day Trent was released on bail. It took a little time to get things set, but it may have been worth it. They installed the cameras before daylight as soon as I received the equipment. We've been taking shifts watching and reviewing the feed since." Rick gave him a pointed look that said he needed to chill.

"And? What have you seen?" With his impatience getting the better of him, Trent returned the look but tried to check his anger. The suspense was killing him. He knew, logically, Rick would have let him know if anything vital happened. He knew from experience that his friends basically were on a homebound stakeout and likely been bored out of their skulls. Yet, impatience reared its ugly head and demanded to be heard. Only years of friendship and trust kept it at bay.

"Three times in the last few days we've seen this SUV arrive late in the evening. It usually parks in front and here's the driver." The TV split into two halves. On the left, a live feed while the right showed footage dated three days ago with a time stamp of 7:47pm. They watched in silence as a tall, rangy male stepped out and walked right on in as if he were a member of the household.

Even though the driver never faced the camera, he'd bet his truck it was Boyd Campbell. The man's size and build looked familiar, and he'd always walked like he owned the ground he walked on, even when he didn't.

"Campbell." Disgust laced Noah's voice.

"Yeah. We haven't been able to get a clear look at the driver's face, but we're certain it's him. Now, this is what happened ninety-three minutes ago." Heavy, oppressive silence filled the room as the same SUV drove up the driveway at a much faster speed than previously. A second person, with dark hair just barely visible, slumped in the passenger side, as if sleeping with their head lolled back on the seat. "Every time he's come by, he's followed the same pattern and parked in front, just like on the prior video." The SUV pulled around back and disappeared from view. The video sped by in fast-forward then it returned to its normal speed just in time for them to watch the SUV leave as quickly as it had come. He stayed less than two minutes.

But now the "sleeping" passenger was no longer present.

Son of bitch.

"Damn it." James punched the table.

"Mother fucker." The quiet, always calm Noah's voice grated with tightly leashed anger.

"When the fuck can we go in? If we don't move soon, I'll go alone," Joe said.

"As far as we can tell, Bailey's help leaves at seven each night." Rick tapped his fingertips on the table, still watching the video.

"That's why Campbell always shows late in the evening." Trent wanted to throw something at the wall. Like pieces of a sick puzzle, things fell into place.

"We think so, yes. Now, we don't have any cameras on the south or west sides of the house. We only have a small portion of the east, but typically after seven the place goes quiet."

"So we go in at 7:30?" Joe asked the question they all wanted answered. He gripped the chair arms tight, poised as if ready to charge in at that very moment.

"I know this is going to piss you off, but I think we wait until 0200 to go in."

"Fuck. Okay. It shits me to wait, but yeah. Okay." Joe fisted his hands on the table before him and blew out a breath.

Trent stayed silent, half afraid he'd lose his temper and do something stupid. Dread twisted and then coiled into a nauseating ball of worry.

"Kate is strong and she's damn smart. She knows we'll come for her, no matter what." Rick was right. Every word he said was true.

"That's over nine hours from now. Why wait so long?" Joe leaned back and crossed his arms over his chest as if he fought the same battle as Trent.

And he realized that was likely true. Joe's love for Kate was an altogether different type, but that didn't make it any less powerful.

"Because we're going to plan this op down to the very second and we're doing more than bringing Kate home. We're going to clear Trent's name while we're at it. We're not going to bring her home only to leave her watching over her shoulder every moment of every day. While I think she's happy here on Trent's farm, I'm sure she'd like to be able to come and go freely without worry or fear."

"Bailey and Campbell aren't getting away with this." Trent would die before he'd let that happen.

"Fuck no." Joe grated out and it was good to see that they were on the same page for at least one thing.

Chapter Thirteen

The sun had made its nightly disappearance hours ago. Shortly afterward, Rick finished going over his plan. Again. Simple in theory, everything depended on their timing.

All Trent had to do was wait. The one thing he hated doing more than any other.

Bonnie twitched her ears and nuzzled his hand. The little filly had grown so much since the first time he'd seen her. There was no question Kate had a way with animals. He'd scoffed at the idea that a beauty queen wouldn't mind getting her hands dirty. In no time, she'd shown him wrong. Not only did she not mind getting them dirty, she seemed to find pleasure in the act of helping something beautiful come to life from nearly nothing.

Her loving nature amazed him.

He'd be lost if anything happened to her.

"She looks a little lost without her momma. My sister took one look at that pitiful, scrawny little foal and knew that she was meant for Kate. Now look at her." Joe stepped farther into the stable and took a place at the door to Bonnie's stall. "My cousin has always loved horses. It's horrible how relieved I was when Leigh called demanding to borrow my truck so she could pack Kate up and bring her home. I should feel bad for being happy that her first marriage failed, but none of us ever cared for Preston. Now, I'm hoping that she'll finally find her happiness. No one I know deserves it more." Joe turned his gaze from Bonnie to meet Trent's head on.

"If she's happy with you, and you give her the freedom to be the woman she wants to be, then you have my blessing. I won't stand in your way after she's home. The only thing I want is for my family to be safe and happy."

"What about yourself?"

"I don't need anything as long as mine have everything they need." Something in Joe's tone belied his words, but every man was entitled to his secrets.

"How's Kylie? I hope she wasn't too upset after I left." He absolutely hated that her birthday party ended with him being put into handcuffs and stuffed into a patrol car while she watched.

Joe's smile became sincere. "She bounced back the next day. When I told her you were out of jail, she released a big sigh of relief. She wants to come out and see your horses. She likes my cattle okay, but I think she'll be a horsewoman like our Kate."

"She's welcome anytime. I have a few mild-mannered mares that are excellent with children. I have no doubt Kate would love to teach her how to ride."

"No doubt." Joe quirked a partial smile, but it didn't quite make it past one corner of his mouth.

"Spit it out, MacDonald. What caused your about-face?" The man lived and breathed by his family and his badge. If he willingly left it behind, something was up.

Trent turned from Bonnie to meet him eye-to-eye. After a long pause punctuated by a heavy sigh, Joe let it out. "I didn't bring it up at the meeting because it's nothing concrete and it doesn't affect tonight's plans." Joe turned his gaze from Trent's and back to Bonnie.

"Go on."

"I went to the Sheriff with your suspicions about Bailey. I recounted each of the encounters Kate had with him. I expected that I'd get a vague and noncommittal response. You know, something along the lines of, 'we have to tread carefully and can't act without concrete evidence' kind of lecture. Instead, he gave me a cold and brutal reprimand and, basically, he told me to mind my own business or else it would cost me my job. I don't know if I caught him on a bad day, or if there is something going on, but my gut did not like the warning."

"Fuck me." Trent rubbed Bonnie's neck.

"Yeah, exactly. I don't think we'll be getting much help from Potter County Sherriff's Department. I love my job, but it means nothing if it doesn't have the power to protect my family." Joe shook his head then turned to walk out.

Kate lay awake in the dark of her room and stared up at the ceiling. She'd been forced to share an awkward dinner with Phillip Bailey while he calmly discussed measurements and wardrobe fittings. It had been like a dark and twisted caricature of her past.

After he'd eaten, he showed her back to her room—at gunpoint, no less—told her a pleasant good night then locked her in. She'd resisted the urge to immediately rip apart the room. Someway, somehow she had to get free. She needed to know what happened to Trent and let Joe know that Bailey had someone watching Kylie.

Rage and nausea flooded through her each time she remembered the pictures she'd seen. It was bad enough, sick and twisted enough, that Bailey thought he could kidnap her, hide her away and mold her into some sort of model Stepford wife. Using a child as leverage was ten times worse.

She'd concentrated on cooling her rage when she would have rather thrown something through the window. Minutes later, once she got herself under control, she'd tried lifting the chair in the corner of the room. She'd prefer to play it smart, but if push came to shove, she'd throw it through the fucking window and then run like the devil was on her heels. No doubt the windows were alarmed, but she couldn't make a single assumption. The damn thing wouldn't budge. It had been attached to the floor somehow. She tried the same with the accompanying table and got the same result.

She'd thoroughly investigated the room and found nothing good and everything bad. *Were there books with instructions on how to keep prisoners locked away in comfort?* The windows, as beautiful and fragile as they appeared, were sealed shut. The bathroom had no window or way out. Everything was attached, stuck in place. Even the damn clothes hangers were attached in the closet, similar to what one would find in a hotel.

How long had he planned this?

Defeated and frustrated, she'd lain back on the bed and let her mind whir. Her brave, stubborn Trent. Her little, spitfire cousin. Joe would be beside himself with worry when he found out she'd been taken. What about the masked man who zapped and taken her? Would he back? She figured he was probably the bastard who'd killed Preston and framed Trent. Was he done with them, or did they have some other madness planned?

Tears slid down her face as she closed her eyes and hoped with all her heart that Trent was okay.

Startled, awake, she gasped when a large, rough hand covered her mouth. A dark shadow moved in close and whispered into her ear. "Shhh." It was a quiet, low familiar purr that she knew well. Her body went lax with relief. "It's me. We've come to get you out of here."

She reached up, wrapped her arms around his neck and breathed in his scent. Dark fabric covered his face, and she wanted to rip it away to inspect him for injury. She'd hoped beyond hope that he hadn't been wounded as badly as it had appeared, had nearly convinced herself of it, but the little demon of doubt had never released its hold.

"I'm going to carry you. We want to make a silent exit and have everything mapped out. Just trust me. I've got you, no matter what comes. I'll always have you."

"I know." And she did.

Their words were barely audible whispers, more breathed into one another than spoke aloud.

"Up. Let's go." At his words, she stood and he hefted her into a fireman's carry. It was awkward but she knew it was easiest on him and left him with one arm free if he needed to grab his gun.

She sensed, rather than heard, another presence at the door. Trent exited it. She caught glimpses of shadowy men both in front and behind them as they fled the mansion like thieves in the night.

In no time, they were outside and Trent was running across the yard. He stopped and she was practically thrown over the fence. She landed in another set of familiar arms. She looked up into a masked face, but she knew the voice that greeted her better than she knew her own.

"Causing trouble again? Good to see you, brat."

She wrapped her arms around Joe. Of course, he'd be there.

A soft thud sounded beside her and she turned see Trent had followed her over. Another masked man landed beside him and then a third. He touched something at his ear then nodded to everyone.

Trent grabbed her hand and they ran through the night. At the property's edge, they stopped just as a dark SUV pulled to the curb.

Doors flew open and Trent shielded her as he all but shoved her inside. Doors shut and then they were off.

"Joe!" She turned to her cousin. "He has someone watching Kylie. He showed me pictures of her playing at school." Her words tumbled out in a fearful rush.

If she hadn't known him her entire life, loved him with all her heart, she would have run from him and the raw, primal fury that marked his features. His mouth formed a tight, grim line as he remained a silent deadly bomb, ready to explode at the barest upset. She ached to hold him, but feared tipping him over the edge.

Scenery flew by, but she barely noticed as she turned to Trent. He pulled the black mask over his head just as she reached for it. Fabric rustled from every seat in the vehicle, but she only had eyes for him. She examined him as best she could in the dark. The light of a streetlamp passed over them with its pale glow. He pushed his sweat damp hair back from his face inadvertently making his wound visible. Almost three inches wide, it split the skin halfway between his hairline and his eyebrow. It'd looked as though it had been stitched haphazardly, but somehow it only seemed to add to his strength.

"Not fair." She whispered to him in the darkness.

"What?" He looked utterly baffled.

"Why is it when men get battle wounds it's sexy, but for women, they're just ugly scars? That's not fair."

Giving her a cocky, one-sided grin, he tucked her into his side and looked her over. Solid. Caring. Gruff. Loving. He belonged to her.

"Are you okay? Do you have any injuries we can't attend to at home?"

"No. I'm fine. Now. What about your head? He shot you. Are you sure—"

"No hospital!" Three male voices said at the same time with a ferocity that startled her. Then Trent smiled as if that was somehow amusing and, when he wrapped his arms around her shoulders, pulling her close, everything was okay.

"Kate? Baby?" She stood at the porch rail, watching the sunrise.

Trent woke to find the sheets beside him empty and cold. Startled, he threw on jeans and all but ran out of the house. His heart had yet to settle, even after finding her safe on his front porch. He had no idea how long he stood in the doorway, watching her as she stared at the skyline. She wore nothing besides one of his tees, which came nearly to her knees. All that glorious hair, draped over her like a witch's cloak. She'd wrapped her arms tight around herself.

Irrationally, he'd feared that, like a beautiful apparition, she'd vanish if he broke the spell of dawn's silence.

"Hmmm." It wasn't much more than a low murmur as she kept her back to him. He scanned the fields for anything that might trap her attention so raptly, but there was nothing. Just acres of green fields and white fencing shrouded in a thick fog.

"How long have you been out here?"

"A while. I couldn't sleep."

"Dreams?" It killed him that after the terror of being kidnapped victims were left to carry the ugly cross of nightmares and ever present memories that refused to let them live in peace.

"No. No nightmares. Just no sleep." Her quiet words made him want to wrap his hands around Bailey's throat. He couldn't stand her distance any longer. He went to her and pulled her back to his chest. He tucked the top of her head beneath his chin and savored the sensation of having her in his arms.

"How much sleep have you had in the past two days?" There was no possible way she'd had much rest the night they rescued her and they'd been wakened only a few hours later by the guys' return. The night before, she'd stayed up late while he and the guys were occupied with plans on how to trap Bailey and Campbell. The only thing they'd all agreed on was that the two bastards had to go down and go down quickly and permanently. Finally, after everyone left, he'd gone to bed and tucked her into him. He'd held her close, but her body had never lost its tension.

"Not much." He'd failed again in his care of her. He'd been so concerned with catching Bailey and Campbell that he'd neglected her. It wouldn't do. She deserved so much more.

"Let's go." There was only one way he could think of to get her to sleep. And it was no hardship on his part. There was no denying he'd desire her until the day he died. Maybe it was time he showed her exactly what she meant to him and see if he could chase the shadows from her eyes.

He turned her to face him and saw her confusion. He lifted her, cradling her against his chest. Her weight was a soft, warm burden that he'd never again take for granted. Her hair, a curtain of silk, fell over his arm as one slender, toned arm reached up. Her hand found his neck, a thumb grazing over the pulse in his throat.

The minutes she'd been gone felt like months and the hours turned into years of fear. He didn't want one day to go by without her knowing how important she'd become to him. He...he loved her and she deserved to have that knowledge. He'd give her the words, though they'd never be enough.

He carried her through the dark of his house to his bedroom. *Their bedroom.* She didn't know it yet, but she was never again sleeping in another bed without him. He laid her out on the bed and cracked the curtain to let the morning light in, washing her in a silver glow.

"Trent." She reached for him.

"No. Lie still. It's my turn to take care of you." He found the bottom of the shirt she wore and slid it up and off. A work of art, made of satin and gold curves, she looked up at him, with a curious expression on her face. What did she see when she looked at him?

He ditched his jeans.

"I'm fine. You don't have—" He stole her words with his mouth as he parted her legs and got close. The sweet heat of her called to him now, urging him to sink inside and lose himself but he told himself no.

Kate first. Always.

Her thigh brushed his cock, teasing. She sighed softly into his kiss and his head spun in a drugged dance. He forced himself from her mouth and nipped her chin with his teeth, a punishment for her wicked lure. Licking a path down the line of her throat, he savored her taste.

He took one breast in hand and the other into his mouth. Full and tipped with hardened brown nipples, he'd never seen a sexier sight. The buds tightened for him, pouting for equal attention.

The hitch in her breath assured him she was right there with him. Her fingers tangled in the hair at his nape, a delicious tug. Her flesh warmed beneath him as she arched and wrapped her legs around his waist. The damp heat pressed against his lower belly, making him see stars.

He ran a finger over her. Silken dampness and fire. Her limbs tightened signaling him that she neared climax. He bit down on the tight nub and grazed a light touch over her clit. When she arched harder and gasped he smiled. Her body bucked and her low cry sounded in his ear.

One down.

He released her breast and looked into her dark glittering eyes. Spreading her legs wider, he pinned her in place, demanding her sole focus. "Kate, you're mine. From here on out, you belong to me every bit as much as I belong to you. I love you. I'm keeping you now, when this is finished, and for the rest of my days."

"Trent." His name wasn't much more than a sigh on her kiss-swollen lips, and he'd never heard a more beautiful sound. "I'm not going anywhere. I love you more than I can ever say."

"Good. I'm glad we're on the same page, because you've already been kidnapped once. I'd hate to have to kidnap you myself." He moved down her body and took her into his mouth. Luscious and musky, she was pure perfection as he licked over and into her. He entered her tight little body with one finger and was rewarded with her cry of pleasure. Taking the hard button of her clit into his mouth, he hummed and began a ruthless siege.

With his hands and mouth, he worked her until she panted and writhed under his care. Sweat dampened and glorious in the pinkening light of a new day, she humbled him even as his swollen cock and heavy sac throbbed, impatiently waiting its own release.

He pulled a condom from the nightstand, slipped it on and met her eyes. Trusting, flushed with desire and filled with love, he'd never forget the sight of her glittering eyes locked with his. He touched the tip of his cock to her sex and slammed home in one straight push. Encased in her taught grip, he lost his breath. His chest heaved, fighting to regain air and control.

When those small hands tangled once again in the long ends of his hair and her mouth met his, he lost the battle. He reared back and entered her again with a powerful thrust. Her wide, blissed-out eyes gave him the only sign he needed. He pumped into her, a steady, ruthless pace, shaking them both on the physical and mental planes.

He wrapped an arm tight around her, pulling them ever tighter together and tilted her hips into his. Mere breaths separated them as they raced, getting closer and closer to the final ledge.

Lost, knowing he couldn't hold back much longer, he brushed his thumb over her clit and held it in a light touch. She whimpered into his kiss as he felt where their bodies connected. Losing control, he increased his rhythm, pounding into her. She tightened around him on a cry. Her hips bucked and she pulled his hair, urging him onward until she shook with the force of her release.

Lost to her beauty and touch, he followed her over. His body tightened as his sac squeezed, emptying into her. He pumped with each pulse, holding her close and thanking the stars she was his.

Cursing the loss of her tight hold, he pulled out and tended to business. He pulled her into his arms and held her as the sun broke over the horizon. "Sleep, beauty." He'd keep the demons away if it was the last thing he ever did.

Boyd looked down at the caller ID on his burner phone and swore. There was no way his batshit crazy uncle's call could be good news.

He continued to pack his bag as he answered. It was past time he left this shithole hotel. Just outside of Riley Creek, it had become way too close for comfort. Even though he'd changed locations several times, he had the itch at the base of his neck that meant someone had him under their sights.

"Campbell." He shoved the last of his clothes into his bag and headed to the bathroom.

"She's been gone two days and time is wasting. I need her at home where she belongs." How could the man sound both petulant and commanding at the same time? It defied logic

"You do realize what we did and what you're asking me to do again is called kidnapping? It's a crime. Dawson may dress like a dumb country boy, but I promise you he's not. You're buying trouble."

"I know what I'm doing. I give the orders and you'll follow them."

Not exactly. Yes, Bailey wrote the paychecks, but he wasn't in control.

He would never allow anyone that kind of power over his life, even if they had more money than God. But he wasn't dumb, and he wasn't above taking advantage of any situation presented to him.

"Fine. Make the transfer and I'll do this one last job. If you're not careful, you'll get caught. Not even your position or friends in the right places will be enough to keep you from prison."

Jesus, his uncle was sliding down the slippery slope of sanity even faster than he'd thought.

"Don't talk down to me, boy. I know what I'm doing. Just get me what I want." There was a near desperate edge to Bailey's words. A sickening twist in his gut warned it was past time to get out. He would have to bail before reaching his goal. It shit him to cut and run, but he battled his disappointment with logic. He'd have to make adjustments to his plan, but he'd rather be free than locked up, any day.

"Just make the transfer. Once I confirm the money is there, I'll put something in motion. You'll hear from me then and not a minute before." He disconnected and threw the phone on the bed. He scrubbed his face with his palms.

He couldn't let greed get the best of him. *Freedom before money.* He repeated those three words again and again.

How did he finish the job and keep his own ass out of the line of fire?

Freedom before money.

Chapter Fourteen

Lightning flashed and thunder shook the house, but she knew better than to be fooled by the threat. This pitiful excuse for a storm did nothing aside from making noise and pushing the humidity through the roof.

Kate removed another of jelly jar from the boiling water, set it on the towel beside the already sanitized lids and wiped her brow. The last of her strawberries had been turned into jam. It was a bittersweet feeling to know she'd taken something so simple and turned it into something she could use to help start her shelter. She could see it in her mind, and her heart swelled with the potential that lay before her.

Riley Creek Animal Rescue would take a ton of sweat and work, but that only made obtaining a dream that much sweeter. No, the four-legged critters wouldn't care where the money came from, but it meant something to her to know that she'd done it. Realistically, the money from her sales wouldn't do much more than buy food for the first few months, but she'd also begun making a list of contacts and people willing to donate funds or time.

I am doing this.

The knowledge brought tears of satisfaction to her eyes. She'd received a call from the attorney who'd taken care of her father's affairs for her years ago. He'd agreed to help Riley Creek Animal Rescue with both paperwork and a donation for startup costs. He'd filed the application for 501c3 status that morning. And the bonus? She'd received a call from Preston's attorney. Preston had never changed the beneficiary on his life insurance policy or his will. When they cleared up his murder investigation, she'd receive that and the majority of their prior belongings.

She was one enormous step closer to making her dream a reality.

The door busted open and, thinking it was the wind pushing it from Trent's grasp, she smiled and carefully set another jar on the towel. She wanted to launch herself in his arms, knowing he'd catch her, but she'd have to get the last of her jars out first.

"Hey, handsome. I have news. Listen, Dad's—"

He reached around her to turn off the stove.

"Grab your shoes. Lets' go." He'd never used such a harsh tone with her, even when he'd been his maddest.

"What's wrong?" Her stomach knotted.

"Fucking stable's on fire. You're going to stay up at the big house with Sandy and Harlan."

Oh dear God. No. No, no, no.

Gripping his shirt, she rushed her words. "I can help with the horses. Bonnie. I need to get Bonnie out. Oh. God. Trent."

"No, baby. All the stable hands are there now. I don't like this. The sprinkler system failed, and it was just inspected on the first. My gut is screaming at me, but damn it." He ran a shaking hand over his face.

Her heart sank to her toes. The horses were his everything.

He grabbed her hand as they ran out to his truck where he all but pushed her inside.

"Are you sure you don't want me to help? You know I can." Her heart raced, beating against her sternum.

"I do, Kate. You have as gentle a hand with them as anyone I've ever met, but I can't have both you and my horses in the same danger. I just can't do it. If you're at the big house with Harlan, I'll know you're safe and then I can focus on the horses. Fuck, me, they'll be half-wild with fear. Just promise me you'll stay inside. I need to know you're okay."

His truck tore down the driveway and across the seemingly endless acres.

"Okay. I promise. Just call me as soon as everyone is safe."

"I will." He pulled up directly to the house and ran her to the door where Harlan and Sandy waited with worry in their eyes.

"Son, I'll go help. They'll be mad with fear," Harlan offered.

"I know. Just stay here with Kate and Sandy. You, these two women and the horses are all I have. Keep them safe. I don't like this."

Her belly twisted with nausea. Tears tracked down her face.

"Come on, sweetheart. Trent knows what he's doing. All we can do is let him have this so he can concentrate." Sandy wrapped her arms around Kate and hugged her close. She met the woman's gaze and saw fear and worry to match her own in tear-filled green eyes.

"I know. It doesn't make it hurt any less, does it?"

"No it doesn't, but it's what a farmer does, sweetheart." Deep and low, Harlan's quiet words boomed through her all the same.

"True enough." They pulled her into the house as smoke began to rise in the distance.

"Trent tells me you've been working hard on your charity. Have you chosen a name yet?" Always so very sweet, Sandy was one of those people who should have been gifted with a houseful of children.

"I think so." Suddenly even her favorite topic had lost its sparkle.

His tires squealed to a stop and he threw the truck into park so abruptly it was a wonder he didn't break the shifter. He jumped out just as Shannon led a skittish Tallahassee out and into the open.

"We're taking them down to the south paddock, okay, boss?"

"Good. Little Bonnie?"

"Dick's already gotten her out. He took her and Scarlet to the foaling barn."

"How many are left?"

"Four." Shannon passed the visibly nervous Tallahassee off to another hand who murmured and jogged with her in the direction of the paddock.

Trent went inside and headed straight for Willow, a two-year-old filly who was full of sass on a calm day. Today? She'd likely put the devil to shame.

She and Sandy sat at the bar in her kitchen with Sandy's cell phone between them. The kind woman had opened the notepad app and they were making a list of supplies she'd need before she could open the rescue. For the third time, she wondered why. It was a poor attempt at distraction. She'd already made a half dozen lists and she would probably make ten more before she opened her doors.

What was the point of listing bridles, leads, cat litter, newspaper, leashes, collars and soap when the only thing she could think of was Trent?

She pushed back from the bar and paced. Wrapping her arms around her middle, she stopped at the window but it did her no good. The beautiful view faced east and the stable was on the house's west side. Even still, on a farm this big, the gently rolling distance made watching impossible, which was just as well. There was nothing she could do from here.

Sirens wailed in the distance.

Damn, how she prayed this was some sort of false alarm even when she knew it couldn't be.

"Katherine? Let's go. Your visit with the Walkers is over. We have work to do." *That voice.* As long as she lived, she'd never forget it. Nausea bubbled and chills raced through her. Dreading what she'd find, she turned to see Phillip Bailey standing in the kitchen's large doorway with a nasty looking pistol aimed her way.

"Bailey, what's wrong with you? You're not welcome here." Harlan stepped in front of Sandy.

"Harlan, good to see you again, but Katherine and I must take our leave. Let's go, dear."

She was so over being told what to do. *No. More.*

"My name is Kate. My friends and family sometimes call me Katie or Katie Marie, but never Katherine. Get lost, Bailey, before the police find you. Your time is limited. Trent will have the horses out and safe in no time then he'll come for me. If you have a single brain cell left, you'll realize you do not want to be here when he comes back."

"He'll be occupied for some time. I've made sure of it."

Of course. She should have known he was behind the fire. Trent's horses were his everything. He ran a topnotch operation. Sabotage was the only way something as serious as a fire and the sprinkler system failing could happen on the same day.

Her sweet Bonnie.

All of Trent's horses. His world. It was all in danger because of this selfish bastard.

Enough was enough.

She stepped forward, ready to end things on her own. He wanted her to be his perfect polished First Lady. He wouldn't hurt her.

The gun's shifted from her to Harlan's chest.

"That's the last one, boss. They're nervous as can be, but they're safe now. They probably won't settle until the smell of the smoke is gone and the thunder quits rumbling but other than a couple a minor scrapes they're all accounted for and good." He heard Shannon's words come from behind him and the meaning registered but he focused straight ahead. The sight made his blood boil.

"Count again." It didn't matter that he'd already counted them twice himself.

"Will do."

He looked over the mess they'd found. Someone was fired. He didn't have proof yet, but every one of his staff showed to help except one, Ray. He never would have expected trouble from the old farrier, but things weren't looking good.

He looked up at the sprinklers and the security cameras in the stable. His anger morphed into something else altogether. Suspicion. It looked as though they'd been outright disconnected. What the fuck?

His phone buzzed again in his back pocket. It had vibrated several times, but hadn't bothered to check it. Everyone knew he was busy.

Everyone but Rick, who'd gone out to Riley Creek. What if he'd found something on Bailey?

He pulled it out and opened the messages. He had one from Sandy.

Bailey's in the house. Has a gun. We're all in kitchen. HURRY. Come in quiet.

Fuck. Fuck. Fuck.

How could he have been so fucking stupid? It was so obvious! What better way to get him away from Kate than to use his horses as a distraction.

He tore out of the barn and called out to Shannon. "Call the police! Trouble at the house."

The sixty seconds it took to make the drive crept by until finally the Walker home came into view.

The kitchen. Sandy's text said they were in the kitchen. That had been a full five minutes ago. Were they still there? A town car sat parked at the front steps, waiting and empty. There was no way he was waiting. What did he do?

He grabbed his pistol from the fingerprint coded lockbox beneath his seat and removed it from the holster. He ran for the porch and paused. Panicked, his heart screamed at him to hurry. Light speed couldn't get him to Kate fast enough. Twice so far, he'd failed her when nothing could have been more important than her life. If anything happened to her, he'd never, ever forgive himself.

He came to the wraparound porch, ready to blast through the door. At the first step, he stopped on a dime. His gut yanked him to a hard stop. He heard Sandy in a long ago memory chiding them for thundering across her porch. She'd said she'd never understand how two small boys sounded like a heard of buffalo when they ran.

He grasped a stranglehold on his impatience and stepped on the outer edge of the steps. Standing to the side of the wide front window he quickly peered in, thankful Sandy loved summer storms and always opened the curtains to watch them roll through. Both the large entryway and front room were empty. But the front door was the obvious entrance and Bailey had only one thing on his mind, Kate. If he watched anything at all, it'd be the obvious route. He continued around the house, peering in each window until he heard voices. They were in the kitchen. He ducked under the wide window and moved around the corner of the house to the mudroom door. He eased it open and his blood chilled when he heard Kate. The voice he loved so much was all wrong, tight and strained.

Then he heard her words he understood and was both proud and furious with her.

Kate saw Sandy's fingers quietly tapping away on her phone while Harlan blocked her from view. How did she get them out of this? She had to stall for time and get Bailey to aim the gun somewhere other than Harlan. Stubborn and all-male, she'd bet that everything Trent learned about being a man had come from Harlan Walker. She owed him so much for taking in and raising the boy who'd become the man she loved with all her heart.

The world needed more people like the Walkers.

She wanted to spend the next fifty years of her life with Trent. The love that she'd seen shining so brightly between the Walkers at the auction was hers for the taking. There was no way she'd let one creep bastard take that dream from her.

What had he said she was allowed to call him? Dearest? She'd do him one better and knock him for a loop.

"All right, my love. I apologize for my tardiness. We were discussing…wedding dresses. Even if you and I do have a short, private ceremony, I think we still need to have pictures, don't you? You never know when they'll come in handy." She poured pure, southern sweetness into her words.

The perfect southern belle. The woman her aunt had raised her to be. She wanted to vomit. No, there was nothing wrong with it for the right woman, but it wasn't her anymore. It had never been. She wanted her callous-handed, gruff man—muddy boots and all.

She knew the moment her words registered. He blinked his eyes in disbelief then a smile lit his face. He looked every bit the proud, demented husband. Bile climbed her throat and bubbled.

But he turned to follow her as she both stepped closer to him and further from Harlan and Sandy. The gun shifted away as his focus trained on her. She acted as if she were slowly moving to leave with him.

"Did you have a nice visit, Katherine?"

She controlled her wince, reminding herself to play along.

"I did. I—" A shadow moved behind Bailey as his brow furrowed in confusion at her pause. "I found something I really think you'll like, but it needs to be a surprise. You know, to keep with tradition. It's bad luck for the groom to see the bride's dress before the wedding." She drew his attention until he turned yet again, ensuring his side faced the shadow she'd seen.

He beamed just as Trent silently stepped forward, pistol in hand. Stone hard, his face looked honed by thunder. Steady, solid, his stance never wavered and his gun appeared to be a part of him, one deadly weapon, made of man and steel.

Trent's gun boomed and blood spattered from Phillip Bailey's hand.

His gun hit the ground.

She flinched and Sandy cried out in shock.

"Harlan!" Trent called.

"I'm on it." He was already moving.

Trent stood still, rock steady with his gun pointed at a confused Bailey. Sandy picked up her phone to call 911, and Kate sagged with relief as the woman's shaky voice spoke to the dispatcher.

She watched, silent and still, as Harlan left and quickly returned with a length of rope. She wanted nothing more than to run to Trent's arms, but that would have to wait until they'd cleared out the trash.

The moment Harlan restrained Bailey, Trent's gaze met hers. "Are you okay?"

She nodded and took a deep breath. She'd always be okay as long has she had him by her side.

"Faster Twent, faster!" Kylie rocked her body atop the old mare who plodded along as if completely unaware she carried a rambunctious child on her back.

"Not yet. You need to settle down so you don't scare old Scarlet." Kate watched with a smile. She loved the way he used the same patience he held for his horses on Kylie. Scarlet was older than dirt, and nothing short of a nuclear blast could nudge her into a run, but Trent was right. Kylie needed to learn to slow down around the horses. She was used to Joe's lazy cattle and it was possible that her daddy might let her run a little wild.

What good was childhood if you couldn't enjoy it to the fullest?

"I sowwy, Twent." Immediately, she stopped rocking then Trent continued to lead them around the paddock.

"Daddy! Wait. Does that mean I have weave now?" She turned to Kate and asked the question with all the seriousness of a heart attack as Joe's truck came up the driveway.

"I don't know, honey. He's a little bit early, but even if you have to leave, you can come back soon. Okay?" Although it might be Kylie's first visit to Walker Farms, everyone doted on her. Harlan and Sandy happened by and fell in love with her on the spot.

"Okay." With her enthusiasm dimmed, she greeted her father with a wave.

Joe met her at the fence and they watched the riding lesson in content silence. Trent and Scarlet finished their meandering lap and returned. He helped Kylie down.

"All right, Kylie. Why don't you go up to the big house and wash your hands? Sandy's waiting to drive you up. She's been known to have cookies and milk for good girls."

"Yay!" She threw her arms up in the air. Catching herself, she lowered her voice. "Tank you, Twent." She'd slowed her pace and walked to a smiling Sandy who sat waiting in her SUV.

Trent smiled after her cousin and then turned to Joe. "If you're in a hurry, I'll follow in a few minutes and Kylie can take her cookies to go, if that's okay."

"No, it's fine. I need to talk to you and Kate for a few minutes. It's a conversation not fit for little ears. Trent climbed over the rail in an easy two-stepped swing that made her want to swoon.

What was it about men with long muscled thighs in snug faded jeans? She'd never tire of watching him work around the farm.

"They searched Bailey's house and offices today. It took a little time to get the warrant in order. They wanted to make sure every *T* was crossed and every *I* dotted. Long story short, they found a pair of blood-spattered boots in his garage. Size fourteen. They'd had tissue paper crammed into the toes as if someone with smaller feet had worn them. It'll take some time before the tests come back, but everyone is sure the DNA will match Preston's. The good news is, there's plenty of evidence to put Bailey away. The bad news? There is nothing anywhere that points to Boyd Campbell. He's a ghost."

"Fuck."

"What are the chances that he'll come after Kylie or me?" She hated to voice the thought, but it was there, a monster lurking in the dark.

"Slim." Trent didn't look happy about there being even the slightest chance.

"None." Joe answered at the same time.

"Chances are he was a hired gun, so now that the money is gone, he'll be gone too." Trent tucked her into his side, her new favorite place to be. He pressed a kiss to the top of her head.

"I agree, and so does Bowie. He thinks that by placing the boots in Bailey's garage that was his way of tying up loose ends before he left town. He'll want to be as far away from Bailey's trouble as possible."

"So Trent's really in the clear?" She knew it in her heart, but she wanted the world to know it as well. She wouldn't rest easy until it was official.

"Yeah, cuz, as soon as the DNA comes back, he's golden."

She smiled.

"Let's go get pickle before we have to roll her out of the house. Sandy has never met a skinny kid she could resist feeding." Each time Trent used her little cousin's silly nickname, her breath caught. Knowing that hitch would stay with her for the rest of her days settled something in deep inside her. She'd never been happier.

About the author

As a teen Amy read horror and fantasy as fast as she could get her hands on it. She'd never met a Dean Koontz book she didn't like.

Until one day at the bookstore she stumbled across a pretty blue cover complete with a bare-chested, sword-wielding Highlander. That Highlander and his heroine showed her the magic of a happily-ever-after and she's never looked back.

She's read and written her way from Kentucky to Arizona and California then back to Kentucky which she and her family now call home.

Who says characters with a dark side can't find love?

If you have a moment to go to your preferred retailer's site and leave a review, well, that would be absolutely wonderful! For more information on Amy's other books go to amyjhawthorn.com